KU-059-511

Rockets Galore

The establishment of a guided missile range in the Outer Hebrides caused a great deal of concern. An age-old way of life was being threatened, and the islanders had the audacity to protest, if they could do nothing else.
But when the Ministry of Protection took on the combined forces of Great and Little Todday, scheduled for part of their rocket site, the issue was never in doubt. The people of the two Toddays had not forgotten their routing of authority over the S.S. *Cabinet Minister*'s cargo, nor their days of glory as the best trained company of the Home Guard in the Highlands and Islands. How could Whitehall hope to win a battle of nerves against such stalwarts as the Biffer, Roderick MacRurie, Duncan Bàn, and the irrepressible Mrs Odd?

KEEP THE HOME GUARD TURNING and THE RIVAL MONSTER, two more of Compton Mackenzie's famous Island comedies, are also available in Tandem editions.

Map of the Islands

Rockets Galore

Compton Mackenzie

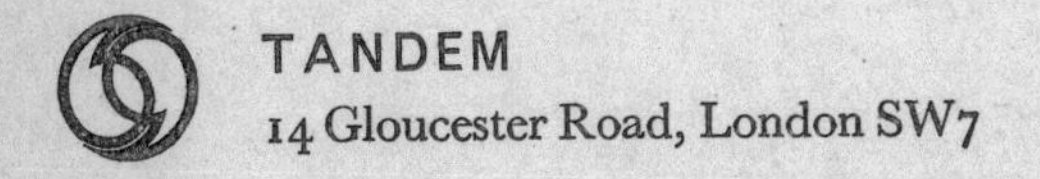

TANDEM
14 Gloucester Road, London SW7

Originally published in Great Britain by
Chatto & Windus, 1957
Three impressions

First published by Universal-Tandem
Publishing Co. Ltd, 1972

© Compton Mackenzie 1957

Made and printed in Great Britain by
C. Nicholls & Company Ltd

To
JOHN LORNE
and
MARGARET SHAW CAMPBELL
of Canna
with affectionate regard

This book is sold subject to the condition
that it shall not, by way of trade, be lent,
re-sold, hired out or otherwise disposed
of without the publisher's consent, in
any form of binding or cover other than
that in which it is published.

CONTENTS

Chapter 1

THE FIRST THEY HEARD OF IT

"I DO wish these confounded fellows at the Ministry of Protection would know their own minds," said Mr Andrew Wishart, the Conservative member for North Lennox and one of the Under-Secretaries of State for Scotland.

Mr Wishart was speaking to Hugh MacInnes, his Private Secretary, who shook his head in a gesture of sympathetic despair.

"We managed to get the rockets on West Uist accepted as vital to the security of the Free World, and as you know, Hugh, it wasn't all that easy."

"It certainly wasn't," said Hugh MacInnes, a tall good-looking young man whose skill at taking a hard low pass at fly-half from a greasy ball had marked him down as one likely to be useful in any crisis of the Scottish Office.

"I've made young Hugh MacInnes my Private Secretary," Mr Wishart had announced. "Of course, they tried to push one of their young men at St Andrew's House on to me, but I said, 'No, I do not want a Civil Servant. If I'm landed with a Civil Servant as my Private Secretary I might as well put myself in Duncan Forbes's pocket and stay there.'"

Sir Duncan Forbes was the extremely able Permanent Under-Secretary of State, and it is the quiet ambition of every Under-Secretary of State and of every Parliamentary Under-Secretary to be able to feel that he has left his mark on whatever Ministry to which he has been attached at what he considers an inadequate salary without all the credit for that mark he made being taken by the permanent officials.

"What were we told, Hugh?" Mr Andrew Wishart went on. "We were told the Protection Research Policy Committee had decided that an experimental and training station for guided missiles must be formed as quickly as possible, and that after most careful consideration the only suitable site in the British Isles was on the west coast of West Uist. The Scottish Office didn't like the idea. The Secretary of State foresaw that as usual he would be blamed for it. Walter Douglass doesn't mind that. He doesn't mind anything except perhaps when the Scottish *Daily Excess* write leaderettes accusing him of affectation for spelling his name with two s's. And I don't think he minds that very much. Oh yes, we were prepared to be unpopular. We knew that *The Caledonian* would print columns of idiotic letters from long-winded Nationalist cranks and Jacobite sentimentalists and one-track-mind ornithologists and Edinburgh old maids. We expected questions in Parliament, and of course we knew that we could answer them with satisfactory ambiguity because a clear answer would not be in the national interest for security reasons. We promised that before the undertaking was launched a public enquiry should be held to ascertain if West Uist had any objection to being turned into a rocket base and if Mid Uist resented the notion of a mixed population of trainees in guided missile warfare being landed on them. You must have brought hundreds of sedative letters for me to sign, Hugh. What is our reward? We are told now that owing to the need for preserving Anglo-American relations we must establish a base for guided missiles rather larger than was originally contemplated, and we are asked what would be the reaction in Scotland if the people of the two Toddays were evacuated to the mainland so that the rocket experts could get on with the top-secret stuff in absolute security."

"I should think the reaction would be pretty fierce," said Hugh MacInnes.

"That's what I told the two Protection fellows who asked the question, and what do you think one of them said? He actually asked me not to talk so loud because the project was top secret at present."

"They're rather like kids playing at Indians, aren't they, sir?" Hugh MacInnes laughed, "What did Mr Douglass say?"

"He said one reaction might be that the next Nationalist candidate at a bye-election would save his deposit. He thought he might even win the seat, now that the Scottish Socialists had declared against a Scottish Parliament in order to have more money to spend on nationalizing house property."

"And what did Sir Duncan say?"

"He said that St Andrew's House was not prepared to take on the job of settling some two thousand Islanders on the mainland. He'd been through it before years ago when he was sent to make arrangements for the evacuation of the people on St Kilda. He had been storm-bound on the island for a week with the Liberal member for the North Hebrides, who grumbled all the time because his hat had blown over a cliff. And they had nothing to eat except salted-down puffins, and on top of that Sir Duncan had to buy twelve pairs of prickly unwearable socks knitted from the local wool."

"And were these chaps from the Ministry of Protection impressed?"

"They saw that Sir Duncan had no intention of making things easy for them."

"So what was finally decided?"

"The possibility of evacuating the Todday people is to be sent back to the Research Policy Committee for further consideration. But we were left to understand that the Ministry of Protection was not prepared to abandon *sine die* the project of establishing a base for guided missiles on one or other or both of the Toddays . . . but look here, Hugh, this is an absolute secret. Only the Secretary of State, Sir Duncan and myself know about it. It's so secret that even the other two Under-Secretaries haven't been told. The

Minister of State hasn't been told. They thought it wiser to keep him in ignorance in case of a question in the Lords. One can deal easily enough with questions in the Commons, but these old boys who've been pushed up into the House of Lords after years in the House of Commons are terrors, and we thought it would be politic for Lord Glenbucket to be able to reply quite sincerely that he had never heard of any project to establish a guided missile base either on Great or Little Todday. So you see what a deadly secret the whole business is."

"I shan't forget that, sir."

"No, I'm sure you won't, Hugh. What do you think our chances are in the match against England next month? It's bad luck that this leg of yours will prevent your playing."

"I think we have just a chance of winning," said last year's fly-half.

"You know, when they send up people from London to try and swing something like this Todday business on us I long for us to win the Rugger match. It may sound rather high-falutin', but you know, I can almost imagine at Murrayfield that I'm at Bannockburn. I do hope we shall win next month."

"What puzzles me, sir, is why they want to put these guided missiles in the west. I should have thought the obvious place for them was in the east. I mean to say, the Yanks were rather bloody-minded over Suez, but nobody ever imagined for a moment that they would start buzzing rockets at us. The only rocket was the one Eisenhower let off at Eden."

"Yes, but we have to consider the North Sea Convention, Hugh. If we started letting off guided missiles all over the North Sea we should be up against the trawling people. Not only at Hull and Grimsby and Aberdeen but also in Norway and Iceland and Denmark, and for that matter Russia. We've come to an arrangement with the Russians over the White Sea."

"I didn't know that."

"Oh, it's not a secret, but we don't want it publicized," Mr Wishart went on. "When these Protection people decided on West, Mid and East Uist, they made a great point that they were the only part of Great Britain where at the cost of a little interference with the life of three islands there would be a minimum risk for shipping. I think that's why we hoisted the flag over Rockall."

"Oh, I thought that was done to show the world after we ratted from Suez and made such a mess of Cyprus as a substitute that we were still an Imperial race," said Hugh MacInnes with a wry grin.

"I say, I hope you don't talk like that, Hugh, outside this room," Mr Wishart observed gravely. "And I'd rather you didn't talk like that even between these four walls."

"Don't worry, sir. I won't get offside again. Meanwhile, what do we do about this scheme for the Toddays?"

"We do nothing, Hugh," said Mr Wishart firmly. "The next Minister for Protection may change the policy. Ministers of Protection only last about three months usually, because every time a new one is appointed the Government hopes that the taxpayer will believe it is part of the drive for economies in Government services. No, I don't think we need worry too much. It was a bit of a shock, of course, when Dr Hamburger and Air Chief Marshal Sir William Windermere suddenly put this question about evacuating the Todday people, but we made it absolutely clear that the Scottish Office couldn't accept any responsibility for the consequences of such a precipitate step."

"Who's Dr Hamburger?" Hugh MacInnes asked.

"I gather he's the big noise in developing something or other to do with this guided missile business. Apparently the Russians have invented something about a hundred times as powerful as the V2 which flies five hundred miles up into the air at five thousand miles an hour with a nuclear nose or something, and this has made a good deal of what they're doing on West Uist obsolete already and they want to do something else on the Toddays. I really don't know exactly what they do want. I get out of my depth when I listen to people like Dr Hamburger, who I thought had a German accent. In fact, I said as much to the Air Chief Marshal, but all he did was to stroke his enormous moustache."

"Telling it to lie down, I suppose," said Hugh MacInnes.

"Oh well, let's forget about the Toddays," said Andrew Wishart. "We've got to soothe the Provost of Drambuie . . ."

"Drumbooey, sir," his Private Secretary put in. "I must say I think they might have found a better place for this atomic reactor affair than the middle of the Drumbooey golf-course."

"Yes, I know," Andrew Wishart sighed. "But wherever they propose to build these atomic affairs it always seems to upset the neighbourhood."

"The trouble is that these fellows always think first about their own convenience," said Hugh MacInnes. "Apparently by putting this reactor place or whatever it's called in the middle of the golf-course they will be a mile nearer to the railway station."

"Well, we must appeal to the Provost's patriotism. Thank goodness, Drambuie . . ."

"Drumbooey, sir."

"Thank goodness, Drumbooey isn't in my constituency. That's the sort of thing which costs a fellow his seat sometimes. By the way, Hugh, are you a good sailor?"

"Reasonably good, sir."

"The reason I asked was that the Secretary of State wants me to go to Nobost in Mid Uist and address a meeting there next week, and I thought you might like to come along. It may be pretty rough at this time of year."

"We could fly to East Uist," Hugh MacInnes suggested.

"Yes, but I don't like flying if I can help it, and I thought we might have a look at the two Toddays on our way. The boat calls at Snorvig before it goes on to Nobost. My own impression was that these Protection people might come back to this scheme of theirs for evacuating the two islands, and I'd like to see for myself what we are likely to be up against on the spot."

So it fell that in the dusk of a wild morning in the front of March Mr Andrew Wishart and his Private Secretary pressed forward from the railway station against the wind that swept the Obaig quay by which the *Island Queen* was lying.

Luckily Mr Wishart was a short stocky man with not so much as a toothbrush moustache to catch the wind, added to which he had taken the precaution of carrying his own suitcase to act at once as anchor and ballast; otherwise he might have been blown into the harbour. Hugh MacInnes, who had gone down on the ball in front of too many Scottish club packs in full cry to be beaten by a mere wind, lowered his head and plunged forward, occasionally gripping the arm of the Under-Secretary and thereby perhaps preventing a bye-election at a moment when the Government was in no mood for one in North Lennox.

"It looks as if we shall have rather a rough passage, Hugh," said Mr Wishart when they found themselves aboard and able to speak again. "Ah, steward, I think you have a cabin reserved for me."

"What is the name?" asked the steward, a large man with a face whose cheeks had suppressed every other feature.

"Mr Andrew Wishart," said his Private Secretary. The steward looked blank.

"The Under-Secretary of State," Hugh MacInnes added severely.

The steward still looked blank.

"Both berths in all four cabins are occupied," he said.

"But instructions were sent from the Scottish Office to reserve two cabins for Mr Wishart," Hugh MacInnes protested.

"Every cabin in the *Island Queen* has been reserved for the Ministry of Protection until further notice," the steward announced. "But there's plenty room in the saloon."

There was in fact very little room in the saloon, which

was thronged with earnest men in black coats and pin-striped trousers, all nursing brief-cases on their knees.

"It's like the rush hour in the tube," Hugh MacInnes exclaimed in disgust. "You'd better take this seat in the corner, sir."

"But you haven't got anywhere to sit, Hugh."

"Oh, I'll get a place somewhere. I'm going to have a shot at getting hold of the Captain."

Captain Donald MacKechnie was not in the best of moods. He had not been able to make the crossing to the Outer Isles two days before on account of the weather, and he was thinking that he might not manage it again this morning. This was Captain MacKechnie's last year of service, and he resented bitterly every voyage out of which he was cheated by the weather. For more than forty years, first with the old *Ptarmigan* and then with the *Island Queen*, he had been sailing three times a week from Obaig to Nobost and three times a week from Nobost to Obaig, calling always at Snorvig both ways.

"Who are you at all?" he turned round from the glass to squeak angrily when Hugh MacInnes found him in the wheelhouse.

"I apologize for intruding like this," said Hugh. "I'm the Private Secretary of Mr Andrew Wishart, one of the Under-Secretaries of State. The Scottish Office asked for a cabin to be reserved for Mr Wishart, but the steward says that every cabin has been reserved indefinitely for the Ministry of Protection. It looks as if we should have a lively crossing. . . ."

"A lifely crossing. We will have a hell of a lifely crossing. What is your name?"

"Hugh MacInnes."

"Is that so? My wife was a MacInnes."

"I'm proud to hear it," said Hugh.

"Have you the Gaelic?"

"I'm ashamed to say I haven't."

"That is a great pity, because if you had the Gaelic I

would be able to tell you what I think about these plutty plack peetles from London."

"You've expressed your feelings about them very clearly in English."

"Chust running about my ship like a lot of cockroaches. *A Thighearna*, and their foices! Chust a lot of pepples curgling away in the throats of them. And these Teddy-poys."

"Teddy-boys?" Hugh exclaimed. "Surely not Teddy-boys in the Islands?"

"Yes, inteed and inteed. Walking about like train-pipes and the hair on the top of their heads like a tuck's arse. I don't know at all how the Scottish Office allowed such things to happen as this tam shame of a rocket range."

"We couldn't help ourselves," said Hugh. "The Ministry of Protection insisted."

"Ay, I suppose they had to do what Mr Tulles told them. I saw a picture of him last week and he looked very like my old schoolmaster in Skye. *A bhalaich*, and we had to do what he told us right enough. Well, I'm glad to have met you, Mr MacInnes; we'll be sailing in a few minutes now."

"And you can't suggest any place of refuge from the black beetles for Mr Wishart?"

"He can sit in my cappin. I'll not be there myself at all with this tirty weather."

Of that voyage the less said the better. Almost every passenger was either being sick continuously or about to be sick continuously. Oh yes, Mr Wishart was sick, and when Hugh MacInnes told him he'd heard Guinness was good for one in such circumstances, his only acknowledgment of the information was to be sick again. As for Hugh MacInnes, when he tested the validity of the Guinness theory he was sick too.

"I wish Dr Hamburger and Sir William Windermere were on this blasted ship," Mr Wishart muttered.

"Would an Air Chief Marshal be sick?" Hugh asked.

"An archangel would be sick on a crossing like this," Mr Wishart declared. "I think we'd better fly back."

But when the *Island Queen* drew alongside the pier at Snorvig the Under-Secretary changed his mind.

"I'm beginning to get my sea-legs," he announced hopefully.

"We've still got twenty miles or so before we reach Nobost," Hugh reminded him.

The plan to go ashore and have a look at Great Todday's metropolis fell through because Captain MacKechnie, after the mails were delivered, was determined to push on at once to Nobost and unload the cargo when the *Island Queen* returned to Snorvig that night.

"We're two hours late, Mr Wishard."

"Well, it was thanks to you and Almighty God that we got here at all."

"Ay, ay," Captain MacKechnie squeaked reflectively. "Two good men."

It was dark when the *Island Queen* reached Snorvig, but as Hugh MacInnes paced up and down the pier, letting the wind blow away the memory of that stormy voyage, he was filled with a desire to come back to Great Todday and explore the island at leisure.

"Extraordinary thing, sir," he told Mr Wishart when in the lee of the island they were proceeding northward to Mid Uist in a comparatively calm sea, "but that place fascinated me."

They were tramping round and round the deck.

"All I saw of it were half a dozen muffled-up people on the pier with lanterns," said Mr Wishart. "They didn't look much like mermaids to me."

Hugh laughed.

"That's all I saw. But I had a sudden feeling that if this scheme to evacuate Great and Little Todday goes through it will be a crime."

"Be careful, Hugh," Mr Wishart protested, with a nervous backward look. "That scheme is absolutely hush-hush."

"All those leatherbottoms are still fugging in the saloon."

"But one of the cabin doors may be open."

"Sorry, sir. It's a good job the meeting is fixed for to-morrow night. Hullo, it's beginning to rain. The wind may drop."

Anything that might have been lacking in Mr Wishart's reception by the steward of the *Island Queen* was atoned for by the warmth of the welcome he received from the land-lord of the Nobost Hotel. Filled though it was by technicians, engineers and officials, with a sprinkling of khaki and airforce blue, Mr Wishart was given as comfort-able a bedroom as he had ever known. It was in fact the bedroom of Mr and Mrs Farquharson, the host and hostess, who found a resting-place for themselves in one of the attics. Hugh MacInnes was asked apologetically to put up with a shakedown in the billiards-room, where another shakedown had been made up for a Mr Meeching, a gaunt young man with horn-rimmed spectacles, an exceptionally large and active Adam's apple and a collection of instruments.

"When do you expect to let off your first rocket?" Hugh MacInnes asked as they were preparing to undress.

The Adam's apple of Mr Meeching bobbed about in his throat for a moment or two like a cork. The question had obviously agitated him. He gulped deeply, and the Adam's apple recovered its poise.

"That is hardly a question I am in a position to answer," he said in a tone of prim and reproachful modesty.

"Sorry. Aren't you a boffin?"

"I am a surveyor."

"What do you survey?"

"I am at present engaged in surveying and measuring the additional ground required by the Ministry of Protection. This is being done for the valuation of the extra crofting land required with a view to estimating the exact compensation the crofter at present in possession is entitled to claim."

"And I suppose the Ministry of Protection will try to squeeze that out of us at the Scottish Office?" said Hugh.

"I have not the slightest idea," Mr Meeching replied. "My own job is quite enough to keep me preoccupied."

"Yes, it must be an unpleasant business, surveying and measuring a chap out of his croft."

"It is indeed. The natives here are a very tricky lot. In fact, we've had to ask for guards from the 1st Ballistic Regiment to prevent all the markers we put up being moved about every night. Indeed, sometimes they disappear altogether. There's one old man of nearly ninety who's an absolute terror. Would you believe it? He actually hid my theodolite in his byre—as they call a cowshed here."

"How did you find out?"

"Luckily one of the native lorry-drivers who are making a packet every week and are naturally jolly grateful for what we're doing for them told me where old Michael Macdonald had put it."

"And so you were able to rescue your theodolite."

"After a good deal of difficulty, because old Macdonald's byre was full of those long-horned Highland cattle and the old man himself pretends he can't understand English. Laughable, isn't it, in the second half of the twentieth century? Oh, we've had no end of a time in these godforsaken islands. And not only from the natives. When we marked out suitable ground for huts to house six hundred of the Electronic Corps with their wives and families, a lot of these bird-watchers arrived and complained we were upsetting the swans on one of these locks. One of our fellows made rather a good remark. He said the swans would enjoy being fed by the kids. And no sooner had we choked off these bird-watchers than a bunch of old fossils arrived and said we were proposing to cement over some prehistoric remains. And the same fellow who made that remark about the swans asked how long it was since these old fossils had lived in these remains themselves. And your Scottish Office hasn't been too helpful, especially those Department of Agriculture fellows in plus-fours you can smell fifty yards away. Peat fires? They only burn peat because they can't get anything better. You'll soon see how much peat they'll burn when we've electrified the three islands properly."

"Aren't you going to use nuclear energy?" Hugh MacInnes asked.

Mr Meeching's Adam's apple began to bob about again.

"I am not in a position to answer that question," he said. "And if you don't mind I'll turn over and try to sleep. I've got a heavy day before me, and this shakedown isn't very comfortable."

"No, there's not much down about it," Hugh MacInnes agreed. "Are you often left without a bedroom?"

"I gave up my room to Dr Hamburger, who arrived unexpectedly this morning."

"Oh, he's here, is he?" Hugh MacInnes murmured to himself as he walked across to switch off the light.

Chapter 2

THE NOBOST MEETING

"DID you have a good night, sir?" Hugh asked when he and the Under-Secretary sat down to eggs and bacon next morning.

"I slept marvellously," Mr Wishart assured him. "How did you get on in the billiards-room?"

"Not too bad. I had a curious dream. I dreamt I was in a scrum which never broke up all through the game. I must say I'm glad I never played forward. But I'm afraid I've got some rather unpleasant news for you."

Mr Wishart looked apprehensive.

"This Dr Hamburger is here."

"Oh lord, I don't want to be nobbled by him," Mr Wishart exclaimed.

"I didn't think you would, sir. We'd better get Mr Farquharson to let us have one of the hotel cars and drive across to West Uist so that you can look round for yourself. You don't want to be shown round by these Protection people."

"I certainly do not."

"The bridge over to East Uist won't be finished before autumn, they say."

"I wish now we hadn't agreed to build the bridge over the West Ford," said Mr Wishart. "The Protection people would have had to build that as well."

"And then we can have a look at the road they're making between Loch Stew below Nobost and Loch Stuffie. That's useless from the point of view of the islanders, because it runs all the way through a peat bog without a croft near it."

"What are they making it for, then?"

"Apparently they're going to build a port in Loch Stuffie at the north-east corner of Mid Uist which will be reserved for unloading secret material with a prohibited area round it. Why I mention this, sir, is because in your speech to-night you won't want to allude to this road as one of the benefits which the rocket range is going to bring to Mid Uist. The road will run for nearly twenty miles through absolutely desolate country."

"Yes, but when this road reaches Loch Stew this secret material will have to travel along the present road from Nobost to the West Uist bridge. Why couldn't they take the road from Loch Stuffie to the bridge direct?"

"Apparently the hills would make that too long and too complicated an engineering business."

As Mr Wishart and his Private Secretary were leaving the hotel to get into the car, a lean grizzled man with a weather-beaten face, wearing tweeds and a deer-stalker cap in which were stuck half a dozen artificial flies, came up and spoke to them.

"Forgive my intrusion, sir, but I believe you are Mr Andrew Wishart, Under-Secretary of State for Scotland. My name is Hotblack. Lieutenant-Colonel Henry Hotblack, 16th Hussars. Retired. I believe you will be addressing a meeting in Nobost Hall this evening, sir?"

"I shall be addressing a meeting, sir, yes," said Mr Wishart.

"I do not know if you are a fisher, sir?"

"Oh, I occasionally indulge, but nowadays it's hard to find the time," Mr Wishart replied with a sad little stock smile.

"You have never fished for sea-trout in Mid Uist?"

"Never."

"Then you are not aware that the finest sea-trout fishing in all Scotland is in danger of being destroyed by this disgraceful rocket project?"

"Surely, Colonel, that is rather strong language for a military man to use," Mr Wishart protested.

"Iniquitous! Abominable! *And* fatuous!" Colonel Hotblack spluttered. "In fact, sir, I do not hesitate to call it sacrilege."

"But why should the fishing be destroyed?"

"Do you think you can set loose a mob of undisciplined . . . the 1st Ballistic Regiment . . . the Electronic Corps . . . good gad, sir, do you think that they are recognizable as military?"

The Colonel put up a hand to loosen his shirt collar: a blue pulse above his temple was throbbing.

"For the last twenty-five years, sir, interrupted of course by the war, I have been coming to the Nobost Hotel to enjoy the magnificent fishing, and soon I may as well go and sit beside the towing-path with a bit of bread at the end of a hook trying to catch roach in some miserable suburb of London. I simply cannot understand how the Scottish Office allowed itself to be bluffed into this nonsensical experiment by this new-fangled Ministry of Protection which is messing up the three Services, and won't be happy till they've turned the R.A.F. into a toyshop and the Gunners into a firework display. I apologize for bursting in like this, but you must forgive an old soldier for speaking his mind."

Colonel Hotblack bowed stiffly and drew back to let Mr Wishart and Hugh MacInnes pass on to their car.

The wind had dropped under the weight of rain that was teeming down as they drove westward. To right of them the hills of Mid Uist rose in a melancholy monotone of rusty grey to lose themselves in the low cloud. To left of them, beyond the expanse of level grassland discoloured by winter, was the Sound of Todday and ahead of them was the Atlantic scarcely distinguishable from the mournful sky above it.

"I think the roof of the car is leaking," said Mr Wishart presently.

"Change places with me, sir," Hugh urged.

"No, no, it's only a drop that gets the back of my neck at intervals. You know, Hugh, I rather sympathize with Colonel Hotblack. My father commanded the Lothian Fusiliers in World War One and he used to lay off like that.

It was a great blow to him when I went into politics. He said he would almost have felt it less if I'd gone on the stage. I wonder if Colonel Hotblack will be at the meeting to-night. I might say something about the regret we should feel if the splendid fishing here should suffer."

"Well, sir, if I may suggest it, I think you had better leave fishing out of it. You don't want the critics of this rocket business to say that you are more concerned for the future of fish than of people."

"Yes, I see what you mean, Hugh. Yes, perhaps you're right. Isn't that the bridge over to West Uist ahead of us?"

Soon they were crossing the bridge, about half a mile long. Below them, the tide being out, stretched an expanse of sand and pearl-grey pools of sea-water blurred by the drench of rain. On the other side the road went round a line of low hills to reach a crofting township the houses of which were clustered round the Roman Catholic chapel.

"This is Balmuir we're coming to," the driver pushed back the glass screen to tell them. "Will you be going to see Father Macdonald at the chapel house?"

"I think we'd better go and have a look at the site for the rocket range first," said Mr Wishart.

"They won't let you in," the driver warned him.

"Oh, I think they'll let *me* in," said the Under-Secretary.

The driver shook his head doubtfully but drove on beyond Balmuir across a stretch of the grassland by the sea that is called machair.

"Good pasturage here," Hugh MacInnes observed.

"Bound to be," said Mr Wishart. "Whenever the Army or the R.A.F. choose a site, they always choose it on the best pasturage or arable land they can find. Yes, there you are."

Sprawling about on the machair ahead of them were huts of every size, all facing in different directions, and presently the car stopped at a gate on either side of which barbed wire stretched seaward and landward. Beside the gate was a sentry-box, out of which stepped a soldier with a rifle.

"Can I see your passes, please?" he asked.

"This is the Under-Secretary of State for Scotland," Hugh MacInnes told the sentry.

"Nobody can proceed beyond here without a pass," he said. "This is Government property."

"And I happen to be a member of the Government," said Mr Wishart.

The sentry winked amiably.

"Yes, sir, I'm sure you are. But without a pass signed by Air Commodore Watchorn I'm afraid I can't let you through."

"Have you no way of communicating with the Air Commodore?" Hugh asked.

"He's up at Port Stuffie this morning with Dr Hamburger, and Colonel Bullingham's over in East Uist. I'm sorry, sir, but I'm afraid there's nothing I can do."

"Och, I knew you wouldn't get in," said Johnnie Galbraith the driver when the car was going back the way it had come. "The English are very peculiar people right enough. They're after thinking the sun rises in their backsides. Och, we get plenty sensible and decent English among the fishers and the shooters," he added, quickly. "Colonel Hotblack is a very fine gentleman. He's usually away by now after the snipe-shooting, but I believe he's staying on just to keep one of these rocketeers out of a bedroom at the hotel. Rocketeers, that's what the Colonel calls them. It's really a beautiful word. We haven't got that word in the Gaelic. Will I be taking you now to the chapel house?"

Father Macdonald was a jolly little man, anxious to stand up for the rights of his parishoners, but uncertain how far they would support him in case they should be throwing away a chance of prosperity.

"And I really think, Mr Wishart, that the opposition in the three Uists has died down. It mostly came from the older people. Of course, you'll understand that it is hard for a crofter to see the house he has built and the land he has cultivated taken away from him. And the interference with the common grazing caused a good deal of grumbling at first. But I think they are resigned now. The younger people were taken with the notion right away from the start. They believe they will be getting good money."

"Do you think the people really are resigned, Father Macdonald?" Hugh MacInnes asked. "Or do you think they feel that resistance is useless and they've just decided to make the best of a bad job?"

Perhaps if Mr Wishart had been allowed through that gate by the sentry he would have rebuked his Private Secretary for that interjection. As it was, he waited in silence for the parish priest's reply.

"That's a very difficult question for me to answer," he said. "But I do not think you need be afraid of any unpleasantness to-night, Mr Wishart. The meeting is announced for eight o'clock. So I think we'll be able to start by nine at the latest, or even by half-past eight. You won't be rushed at all for your dinner."

In spite of the rain, the Nobost hall was packed out that night by half-past eight, and Mr Wishart, who was devoted to his own punctuality, was able to avoid wounding it too deeply by appearing on the platform a minute later, where he was received with polite applause. In the front row of chairs were Father Macdonald and the two parish priests of Mid Uist, the Church of Scotland minister of Mid Uist and the Wee Free minister of East Uist, the Reverend John MacCodrum, Mr and Mrs Farquharson, Colonel Bullingham, Colonel Hotblack, the local doctor and his wife, and several merchants without their wives. At the extreme end of the first row sat a man with a domed forehead and a flat back to his cropped head. This was Dr Hamburger.

The chair was taken by Jonathan Campbell, the convener of the Rural District Council, the most prosperous merchant in the three Uists whose reputation as a County Councillor was so great that in spite of being an elder of the Church of Scotland he was always returned by a Catholic majority at the head of the poll.

Jonathan Campbell opened the proceedings with a few words in Gaelic and turned to Mr Wishart.

"I now have the pleasure to call upon you, sir, to address this meeting, which in spite of the rain is very representative indeed of the three islands, and I am particularly pleased to see that the Reverend Mr MacCodrum has braved the weather to cross the East Ford. Mr Wishart, if you please."

The Under-Secretary of State for Scotland, dressed impeccably in black coat and pin-striped trousers, rose and stepped forward amid some more polite applause.

"*A chairdean* . . ." he began, and paused. Mr Wishart had not told even his Private Secretary that he intended to prefix his speech by addressing the audience as 'my dear friends' in Gaelic. That was a pity, because if he had, Hugh MacInnes would have led some appreciative applause. As it was, the audience didn't realize that Mr Wishart was calling them 'my dear friends' in Gaelic: they thought he was coughing, and preserved a courteous silence in case he wanted to cough again.

"My friends," the orator continued, "my first duty is to tell you how much Mr Walter Douglass, the Secretary of State, regrets that owing to the calls of Parliament he is unable to be with you this evening. Mr Walter Douglass has been deeply—er—indeed—er—profoundly aware of the importance for West, Mid and East Uist alike of the rocket establishment which the Government under the imperative demands of protection for our beloved country against aggression have decided to instal in West Uist. Mr Douglass is profoundly aware that such an establishment may entail a few changes in the life of the islands, for though the actual rocket range—and I do not think I am violating the Official Secrets Act by revealing this. . . ."

Mr Wishart paused hopefully for a ripple of mirth, but in a silence even more profound than the Secretary of State's awareness he hastily resumed.

"The actual rocket range, as I say, will be established on West Uist, but the two sister islands of Mid and East Uist will both be affected by the scheme. You will all be aware by now of the reconstruction of the little harbour of Loch Stuffie. It will now become officially known as Port Stuffie. This will not entail any interference with the regular island service of MacPayne's. The good ships *Island Queen* and *Island Princess* will continue to call as usual at Nobost and Loch Luny. Port Stuffie will be used exclusively for the vast stores of material which will be called for by the rocket range and also by the plan to establish a training-camp for service-men whose job it will be to master this complicated business of guiding—I should say guided missiles. I may observe here that there have been wild estimates of the number. I can state authoritatively to-night that they will not at first exceed four thousand. I cannot claim to know anything of ballistics myself, and I do not suppose that many of you know much about ballistics, but it must be clear to all of us that if our national existence is to be imperilled by the ballistics of other nations it is the vital duty of any Government to leave no stone—er—I should say to do all in its power to protect ourselves. But let me come back to that later. You know how bad the present road is between Nobost and Loch Stuffie. And thanks to our chairman, Mr Jonathan Campbell, I venture to say that there is nobody in the Scottish Office who doesn't know how bad that road is."

From the body of the hall a powerful bass voice ejaculated.

"Good shooting, Jonathan, *a bhalaich.*"

The Uists' priests looked round. They had been unaware of the arrival of Father James Macalister, the parish priest of Little Todday, at dusk in a fishing-boat.

"Look out for squalls," Father Macdonald chuckled to Father MacIntyre.

"That road," Mr Wishart continued, "is now to become a four-way arterial road from Port Stuffie to Nobost. Furthermore, the bridge over the East Ford, the expense of which has hitherto rendered its construction impossible, is now being built by the Ministry of Protection. Furthermore still, the present aerodrome on East Uist is to be greatly enlarged, as a proportion of the trainees will be lodged on East Uist. These are only a few of the benefits that will accrue to the three islands. I know, ah, yes, I know well that inconvenience may be caused to crofters by taking over their crofts and enclosing some of the grazing land. I regret this. We all regret it. At the same time, twenty years in the House of Commons has taught me that the minority must give way to the majority. We shall do our best to provide other crofts as soon as possible for those who are dispossessed. The Department of Agriculture, working in closest accord with the Crofters Commission, the Highland Panel, and the Forestry Commission, will leave no stone—I mean, will do all that is humanly possible to ensure that the crofters dispossessed shall suffer the minimum of inconvenience. When the rocket scheme was first announced there was a certain amount of agitation. Oh, it wasn't very effective agitation. It came from a few sentimentalists living comfortably in cities who were used to don the kilt when the weather was warm enough and who would come back from their holiday to tell of the wonderful ceilidhs that they had been enjoying. They wrote letters to the papers, and I am glad to say that hard-headed men who knew what were the conditions of life out here wrote and put these sentimentalists in their place. Islesmen who were not so lucky as the people of the three Uists showed quite clearly how much they envied the opportunity that was being given to the Uist people to attain a standard of life far beyond anything that had ever been dreamt of in the Outer Isles. It was soon quite apparent that so far from resenting the Government proposal to establish a base for guided missiles on West Uist the Uistites themselves . . ."

"Ay, ay," boomed that sonorous bass from the body of the hall, "very tight indeed."

". . . the people of Uist themselves warmly welcomed the proposal. They saw the advantage of marching in step with modern times. They realized that they were the spearhead of the Free World, and they were proud. Once upon a time it was the privilege of the Macdonalds to fight on the right of the line."

Although half the audience consisted of Macdonalds, hardly one of them had heard of this old Macdonald privilege and therefore the response Mr Wishart had hoped from his martial reminiscence was not forthcoming.

"But why do I turn my eyes to the past?" he asked. "It is to the future that we gathered here to-night are looking. And I am speaking for the Government when I say that the Government is proud to think that it has been able to offer to such intelligent, far-sighted and patriotic communities a solution of so many problems that were coming to seem insoluble. For years we have been trying at the Scottish Office to fit the Hebridean way of life into the framework of the modern world. No stone—everything that could possibly be done has been done."

"Why didn't you put the Scottish Fisheries Act of 1895 into operation?" a lean man with purposeful eyes and a purposeful mouth rose from the middle of the audience to ask.

"I have to confess that I do not understand my friend's question."

"If you had put that Act into operation you could have saved the fishing industry in the Islands and West Highlands, but you let yourselves be frightened out of it by the trawler lobby in the House of Commons."

"I'm afraid that I am rather at sea myself at this moment," said Mr Wishart.

"You are an Under-Secretary of State for Scotland?" the lean heckler asked.

"I certainly am."

"And yet you have never heard of the Scottish Fisheries Act of 1895?"

"I must admit that I have not."

"Where ignorance is bliss 'tis folly to be wise," the heckler scoffed as he sat down contemptuously.

"I do not understand the point of my friend's interruption. He is probably a Scottish Nationalist," said Mr Wishart.

Usually at a Conservative meeting that observation could be counted on for a giggle from the audience. Somehow it fell flat to-night. Mr Wishart cleared his throat for his peroration:

"I speak for the Government to-night, my friends of West and Mid and East Uist, when I thank you for the patriotic devotion with which, in spite of a few interferences with your time-hallowed way of life, you have decided to accord your fullest co-operation with those who have after long and anxious consideration decided that Britain must take advantage of the generous way in which the Government of the United States has agreed to supply some of the guided missiles which Great Britain does not yet possess. We do not wish to use those guided missiles for aggression. They are a protection for ourselves; they are not a menace to any other nation on earth. In co-operating with the Government over this rocket establishment you are doing your part to secure peace for the world. I know that I do not have to tell you this. I know that any sacrifices of your immemorial way of life you may be called upon to make will be made with willing enthusiasm because you know that you and your three islands are privileged to be the spearhead of peace in this unhappily anxious world of to-day. Every rocket that goes roaring into the air will seem to you an olive branch carried by the dove of peace."

"Good shooting!" boomed that voice again from the body of the hall, and as Mr Wishart sat down to polite applause, Father James Macalister rose to his feet. He was over seventy by now, but save that his hair was snow-white there was nothing in the vigour of his bearing, the resonance of his voice or the ruddiness of his cheeks to suggest that he was any older than he was when the S.S. *Cabinet Minister* struck the Gobha rock off Little Todday and when the whisky she carried was drunk in its native land, except the cases that under orders from the Excise were presented to Davy Jones.

"Mr Wishart," said the burly priest, "I would like to ask you a question. Is it true that under the arrangement made with the Government of the United States to supply poor old Britain with rockets the island of West Uist will be handed over to our friends across the Atlantic to supervise the secrets?"

There was a murmur of apprehensive indignation from the audience.

Mr Wishart jumped quickly to his feet.

"I can assure my reverend friend . . ." he hesitated and Jonathan Campbell leaned over to whisper his name.

"I can assure Mr Macalister that I have not heard the faintest breath of any suggestion that American experts will have the slightest say in the future of the three Uists, and I have no hesitation in stigmatizing such a rumour as a typical piece of Communist propaganda."

"Ah, well, that's very satisfactory, but I hope Mr Wishart will take back this message from the Outer Isles to-night. 'One Cabinet Minister has already been wrecked here. Take care that all the rest of them are not wrecked here also!'" Then he turned and spoke in Gaelic to the audience amid continued outbursts of spontaneous applause.

"Can't you stop him?" the chairman was asked by the Under-Secretary.

"He's a pretty difficult man to stop," Jonathan Campbell murmured back.

"What's he saying?" Mr Wishart asked.

"He's being very sarcastic about the Government."

"Yes, I thought as much. Did he say something then about rock and roll?" Mr Wishart asked after a burst of laughter.

"He said the men of the West would rock the Government off their balance and roll right over them. I think I'd better call him to order."

"I certainly think you had."

Jonathan Campbell rapped on the table, and Father Macalister sat down amid shouts of '*glé mhath!*'

"What does 'clay var' mean?" Mr Wishart asked.

"It means 'very good'."

"Yes, I felt it meant something like that."

The Reverend John MacCodrum, the Wee Free minister of Gibberdale in East Uist, now rose. He was a small dark man and suggested a Cairn terrier with its bristles up.

"I have two questions to ask Mr Wishart. Will he give a solemn undertaking on behalf of the Government that not a rocket will ever violate the Lord's Day, and will he do all he can to prevent the Sabbath from being desecrated by aeroplanes landing on the aerodrome in East Uist?"

"I'm afraid I am not in a position to give anything in the nature of an undertaking that no rockets will ever be fired on Sunday, but I can assure my reverend friend that I will convey to the Minister of Protection the desirability of not offending the religious feelings of the good people of West, Mid and East Uist by any unnecessary ballistic activity on Sunday. But of course this will have to be left to the discretion of the experts. With regard to the movements of planes on Sunday, I am afraid I dare not venture to encourage my reverend friend to indulge in the hope that any exception will be made in favour of East Uist. It might create a precedent, and everybody is anxious not to do that."

When Mr Wishart and Hugh MacInnes were back in the hotel seated in their host's private sitting-room and sipping the two generous whiskies he had poured for them, Mr Wishart was annoyed to see Dr Hamburger and Colonel Bullingham at the door.

"Ah, come in, come in, gentlemen," said genial John Farquharson. "What can I offer you? I have a rather special bottle of malt here."

"Malt?" Colonel Bullingham, a button-headed man with pale-blue prominent eyes, echoed in surprise.

"Malt whisky."

"Thanks very much," said the Colonel. "I'll try anything once. Fill it up with soda, please."

The brow of genial John Farquharson was faintly clouded for a moment as he spurted the gas from the syphon into half a tumbler of mellow Glenbucket. "Dr Hamburger?" he turned to ask.

"No, thank you, I never drink," said Dr Hamburger firmly.

"I was sorry to be away when you came along this morning, Mr Wishart," Colonel Bullingham assured him with a slightly excessive heartiness of assurance. "And so was the Air Commodore. He said how sorry he was he couldn't manage to be at the meeting to-night. I think it went off pretty well. There's no doubt the people here are settling down. You feel that, don't you, Mr Farquharson?"

"I wouldn't be too sure of that, Colonel. I hope that *too* many will not be turned off their crofts. There *might* be trouble if too many were turned off."

"Trouble? Ha-ha," the Colonel laughed. "I don't think there'll be much trouble when there are four thousand troops on the three islands, as there will be presently. Ha-ha!"

"Over twenty-five thousand troops don't seem to be able to avoid trouble in Cyprus, sir," Hugh MacInnes said quietly.

"Were you in the war?" the Colonel barked.

"No, sir, I was too young."

"I thought so," the Colonel snapped. "You young fellahs mustn't try to teach your grandmothers to suck eggs. Done your National Service yet?"

"Yes, sir."

"What regiment?"

"The Clanranalds."

Colonel Bullingham snorted, but it may have been from excess of soda, not lack of manners.

"If you will allow me to make a small criticism, Mr Wishart," said Dr Hamburger, "I felt you were a little too indulgent with your audience. That priest, for instance. I was surprised when you and the chairman allowed him to gabble away in his own language like that. Who is he?"

"Father James Macalister is the parish priest of Little Todday," John Farquharson put in.

"Little Todday, eh?" Colonel Bullingham repeated sharply. The meaning glance he exchanged with Dr Hamburger gave the impression that for a moment he had pocketed his own pop-eyes in the deep sockets of Dr Hamburger's.

Hugh, who by this time had been seized with a fierce longing to scrag Colonel Bullingham, hoped that Mr Wishart had observed the exchange.

"It's a mistake to tolerate local languages," Dr Hamburger went on. "They encourage people to suppose they are more important than they really are. The Germans found that with the Poles."

"I thought the general feeling in the audience was distinctly friendly," Mr Wishart said. "I felt they appreciated the reasons for any self-sacrifice they may be called upon to make. Of course, I was rather at a disadvantage because I hadn't seen the site of the rocket establishment myself."

"Yes, as I told you, the Air Commodore and I were sorry about that, but the sentry was not in a position to judge for himself, as I'm sure you've realized." The Colonel smiled the tolerant smile of the man who knows the value of discipline for those who, like Mr Wishart, had never enjoyed the advantage of being under discipline. "But even soldiers don't always seem to understand," he went on. "This fellow Hotblack who stays with you, Mr Farquharson, talks too much. He's retired, of course, and there's not much we can do about it at present, but when things are tightened up I think Colonel Hotblack may find it not quite so easy to come to Nobost for his fishing."

"Tightened up?" John Farquharson repeated.

"I hope the Secretary for Scotland will be consulted

before the Ministry of Protection take any steps to interfere with the life here unless such steps are demanded by military necessity," said Mr Wishart anxiously. "People in Scotland are very sensitive nowadays to anything that savours of being overruled from London."

"Don't worry, Mr Wishart. The Ministry of Protection has no desire to set the parish pump creaking."

"I had a short talk with Colonel Hotblack this morning," said the Under-Secretary. "He was very amusing about the 1st Ballistic Regiment. I suppose these old cavalry men are naturally suspicious of anything so novel."

"I command the 1st Ballistic Regiment," Colonel Bullingham announced severely.

"Oh, I'm sorry. I didn't realize that."

And when Dr Hamburger and Colonel Bullingham had retired, Mr Wishart said to his Private Secretary, "You know, I couldn't resist that dig at Bullingham, Hugh."

"I don't blame you, sir. I was itching to scrag him."

"Did you notice the look that passed between Bullingham and Hamburger when Farquharson said that Father Macalister was the parish priest of Little Todday?"

"I certainly did."

"You know, Hugh, I'm worried. I feel there may be trouble ahead. I wasn't at all satisfied that the people here really are resolved to co-operate. I think Sir Duncan is too optimistic. One reason why I didn't go round asking the crofters a lot of questions was that I knew I should only get the answers they thought I wanted to hear. And that would have made *me* optimistic. Making allowances for the fact that I was addressing an audience most of which use Gaelic as their natural tongue, I didn't feel somehow that they really responded to these remarks I made about the defence of the Free World and arming ourselves for the sake of peace. What did you feel?"

"May I be perfectly frank, sir?"

"Of course, of course."

"I think they thought you were telling them something you didn't for a moment believe."

"Humbug, in fact?"

"Yes, sir. Humbug."

Mr Wishart sighed. "That's what my old father used to dislike about politics. He said all politicians had to be humbugs if they wanted to get to the top," he murmured sadly.

Chapter 3

JANE KINSELLA

HUGH MACINNES had been found a bedroom for that second night, and after a comfortable sleep he walked down before breakfast to the quayside on Loch Stew. Father Macalister was talking to a small swarthy man on the deck of a sizable fishing-boat called the *St Tod.*

"When do you want to be away, Dot?"

"By ten o'clock, and that means ten o'clock, Father," Donald Macroon, the skipper, told him.

"I'll be aboard by a quarter-to. I've one or two friends to see in Nobost."

"Not too many, Father James, or we'll miss the tide."

Father Macalister turned and wished Hugh good morning in Gaelic. "*Am bheil gàidhlig agaibh?*" he then asked.

"I expect you're asking me if I have the Gaelic," said Hugh with a smile. "And I'm afraid I'll have to reply 'not a word'. I wish I could have followed what you were saying last night in the hall. I'm Mr Andrew Wishart's Private Secretary."

"Are you indeed? Poor wee man! I felt really sorry for him last night." The priest sighed gustily. "Ay, ay, he was out of his depth, just out of his depth, and no land in sight except Colonel Bullingham."

"Father Macdonald at Balmuir seemed to think that the people were reconciled to the idea of the rockets and that the money the Ministry of Protection was going to spend on the island would compensate them."

"Och, the little man is not so sure about that now, at all. It's *Timeo Danaos et dona ferentes* with him now. He's afraid of these invaders and their gifts. They were pretty plausible at first. Just a few square yards for the rocket site, that was all they asked at first. And now they've already wired in more than two thousand acres."

"What would you say, Father Macalister, if there was ever a proposal to set up a rocket establishment on Great and Little Todday?"

"I'd say more than I've said in all the sermons I've preached since I was in the Scots College in Rome, and I'd do a good deal more than I said. But is there talk of rockets galore for the Toddays?" Father Macalister asked sharply.

"Oh, it has not been proposed yet," Hugh said. "But I think it could be. I'd awfully like to visit the Toddays."

"Come along, my boy. We'll give you a great welcome so long as your pockets aren't full of rockets."

"Would May be a good time to come?"

"May's a beautiful glorious month on Little Todday. Flowers all over the machair and the curlews calling. Come along, my boy, in May."

And that is how at six o'clock of an azure morning in May Hugh MacInnes walked from the St Ninian's Hotel in Obaig to go on board the *Island Queen*.

"Isn't your name MacInnes?" Captain MacKechnie asked. "Ay, I remember you fine that day you came along with us to Nobost. You and Mr Wishard. Ay, ay, poor old Nobost. Chust like one of these offices in Glaschu. Chock full of black coats and pale faces. Och, but the lasses like it fine, rocking and rolling around with these Teddy-poys. Well, we'll be away in a minute. Will you stay up here with me for a while?"

"I will come up later, Captain MacKechnie, when we're clear of the sound," said Hugh. "I don't want to be a nuisance."

But it wasn't entirely consideration for Captain MacKechnie that led Hugh to this decision. He had been intrigued by the sight of a tall slim girl up in the bows with her back to him who was gazing out into the west.

"Ay," said Captain MacKechnie, "you'd better go and

talk to her. She's from Ireland. They're very like ourselves, these Irish, but they're more sure of themselves than what we are. She wass singing to us last night and playing the *clàrsach* for herself. Ay, a bonny lassie, and a beautiful singer. It wass really a treat."

"What's a clarsach?"

"Och, it's a thing with strings on it. Ping, pang, pong with a big pung now and again."

"A harp?"

"Ay, what we'll all be playing one day, so they tell us, if we don't break the Sabbath. I remember when I wass a nipper I asked the Reverend Mr Mackenzie of Portree if I would be playing my harp on the Sabbath when I wass in Heaven, and Mr Mackenzie wass taken clean off his guard. 'You will be, Donald,' he said to me, and I said as quick as a piece of lightening, 'Then why cannot I be playing my whistle on the Sabbath, Mr Mackenzie?' And tash it, he had to steer right through the Fourth Commandment before he could give me an answer."

"And what was his answer?"

"'Because you cannot, Donald,' is what he said."

"It wasn't a very convincing answer," Hugh commented.

"No, no, it wassn't. It was really a todge of an answer. But I'd taken the poor man off his guard, you see."

The tall slim girl was still gazing away in the bows when Hugh walked forrard along the deck.

"It looks as if we're going to have a splendid passage."

She turned as he spoke, and that was that. It was only the combined influence of Fettes, Trinity College, Oxford, and training for National Service in the Clanranald Highlanders that prevented his ejaculating:

"My god, you have the loveliest eyes I've ever seen in all my life!"

Under the influence of those two stars he asked if she was going to Snorvig too.

"No, I'm going to Nobost."

And her voice . . . it was as lovely as her eyes. Hugh

could have kicked himself for putting in that 'too' after Snorvig. If he hadn't, he could have put it in after Nobost, where a shakedown in the coal-cellar would have left him undismayed. As it was, he had committed himself to Snorvig, and if he stayed in the boat and went on to Nobost she might think that he was much more sure of himself than any Irishman.

"Have you ever been there?" he asked.

"I was there this time two years ago, collecting Gaelic songs."

"I wish I had come on board last night. Captain MacKechnie said you sang and played for them on your clarsach?"

"Do you play the clarsach?"

"No, no. I only play Rugger."

"I have a cousin who plays football for Ireland," she told him.

"What's his name?"

"Sean Kinsella."

"Good lord, I've played against him. Centre three-quarter."

"It might be," she said vaguely. "I never know what anybody is at football. It's a terribly muddling game to be watching."

"You don't take much interest in it?"

"Och, I like to hear that Ireland has beaten England. That's why I told you about my cousin Sean. He kicked a try against England two years ago."

"Is your name Kinsella?"

"It is."

"My name's Hugh MacInnes."

"Hugh MacInnes," she echoed, and Hugh realized for the first time what a melodious name he owned. The knowledge emboldened him to ask her what her other names were.

"Ethne Jane. Well, as a matter of fact it's Jane Ethne. But if you call yourself Ethne Kinsella you sound more like a professional singer. All my friends and relations call me Jane."

"You're very young to be a professional," Hugh observed.

"I'm twenty," said Miss Kinsella indignantly. "Nearly twenty-one really. I'll be twenty-one next November. And Radio Eireann have promised to give me a quarter of an hour sometime in the autumn. That's why I'm going to West Uist. I want to take back with me some Gaelic songs which nobody in Ireland has heard. I'm hoping to stay with some lovely people at Balmuir."

"At Balmuir, eh? They've been serving notices on a lot of the people there to quit their crofts."

"Why?"

"To make room for rockets," said Hugh.

"Ah, yes, I was reading something about that in the papers. We don't have that kind of thing in Ireland, except in the Six Counties of course. But that's their own fault."

"Did you hear from these people you're staying with? Are they expecting you?"

"I'm sure they will be. I wrote and said I was coming."

"I hope it will be all right. What is their name?"

"Macdonald. Joseph Macdonald has the croft, and his wife is Catriona. She's a lovely singer and has lots of songs. Joseph's old father, Michael, lives with them. He's over eighty, and he has wonderful stories."

"But don't you find it hard to follow Scottish Gaelic?"

"Oh, it's terribly difficult, but Father Macdonald—that's the priest in Balmuir—was very kind and wrote out the words of Bean Iosaibh's songs, and I find it quite easy to read Scottish Gaelic. It's the pronunciation that's so different from ours. Of course, I never managed to follow old Michael Macdonald's tales properly, but I used to love just sitting and looking at him while he was telling his *sgeulachdan*. You'd think he was seeing it all with his own eyes. There were times when I would turn round and look behind me to see what he was looking at. Oh, Balmuir is a wonderful place. It's like a beautiful dream you don't wake up from."

While they had been talking, the *Island Queen* had glided on her way down the pale blue sound, and they were still talking when she came into the little harbour of Tobermory. Hugh told Miss Kinsella—he did not ask if he might call her Jane until they had left Ardnamurchan behind and reached the open sea—about the efforts to reach the Spanish galleon.

"What a pity it was," she sighed.

"Buried treasure never gets found except in books," Hugh laughed.

"I wasn't thinking about the treasure; I was thinking what a pity it was that the Spanish Armada was defeated."

"Oh, I say," Hugh protested.

"Ireland would not have had to suffer so much and so long," she murmured.

"Yes, I suppose it might have been better for Ireland," he admitted.

It was about five o'clock of a golden afternoon that the *Island Queen* swept round into the Coolish, as the narrow sound between the two Toddays is called.

"Doesn't Little Todday look perfect," Jane exclaimed. "It's very like the land round Balmuir. I hope they won't start putting rockets there."

The low green island with the two high basaltic isles of Poppay and Pillay guarding it to the north and to the south did look a most tempting playground for rocketeers. From their point of view Great Todday, with its three bens over 1200 feet high, its rugged moorland and forbidding coastline would seem less suitable. But of course they would want sites for camps. After all, Mid Uist was not going to serve as a rocket range, but that had not prevented its being overrun by the disagreeable accessories of a rocket range.

Hugh MacInnes looked at the little town of Snorvig—well, it wasn't more than a big village really—and recalled the way he had divined the fascination of these islands on a dark tempestuous night a little more than two months ago, and now as the *Island Queen* came alongside the crowded pier he felt a bit proud of his own perspicacity. A moment later the edge of his pleasure was blunted when he saw Jane Kinsella leaning over the rail and realized that he must bid her good-bye.

"I do hope you will find everything all right on West Uist," he told her. "But if you don't, do come back by way of Snorvig instead of going back by Mallan. I'll be here for three days, staying at the hotel. If you sent me a wire, I'd come up to Nobost and meet you and we could come back together. I can't tell you how much I've enjoyed this crossing. But look here, if you do find everything all right, I'll come back by way of Nobost. I expect Father Macdonald would be able to find me a room. And I do want to hear you sing. You will let me know your movements, Jane? You will, won't you?"

"Why, I believe I will, Hugh."

He shook her hand and floated down the gangway as in childhood he had floated downstairs in dreams.

A boy of about sixteen on the pier stepped forward to ask if he was Mr MacInnes who was staying at the hotel.

"I'll take your bag, please."

Hugh was about to turn and wave to Jane Kinsella before following young Roddy MacRurie, a grandson of the hotelkeeper, when he was accosted by a thin elderly man in his late sixties with a sharp slightly upturned nose. He was dressed in a tweed suit with plus-fours which once upon a time had looked like Putney on Boat Race day but which time had mellowed to resemble the blue mist over a twilit stream.

"I think I ought to warn you," he said, "that all the sporting rights in Great and Little Todday belong to me and that I cannot allow anybody to fish any of the locks without special permission, which I give very sparingly to visitors, very sparingly." The inflection of his voice as he repeated the last two words rose in a sort of dreamy admiration of his own cleverness.

"I've no intention of fishing," Hugh assured the thin man.

At that moment a large yellow dog nuzzled Hugh.

"Don't make a nuisance of yourself, Monty."

The large dog's tail swept from side to side in the gratification of being addressed by his master.

"He's getting almost too old for work now, but he still has a wonderful mouth. He's called after my favourite general in the war. Field-marshal Lord Montgomery to-day. Aren't you, Monty, old boy?"

The large dog's tail swept from side to side faster than ever.

"My name is Waggett," said the thin man, his pale-grey eyes alight with self-esteem. "I live at Snorvig House. It's beyond the hotel further up the hill."

"You live here all the year round?"

"Mrs Waggett and I go south to England every year to visit our married daughters. In fact, we are only just back. But we are here for most of the time. May I ask what your name is? Indeed? Any relation of the Hugh MacInnes who plays fly-half for Scotland? You are the same Hugh MacInnes? What a strange coincidence! I used to play right half—we used to have right and left half in those days—for my school more years ago than I care to remember. I was at Eppleigh. I always regretted leaving when I was eighteen to go into business. I should almost certainly have got a Blue."

At this moment the siren of the *Island Queen* sounded to indicate her speedy departure for Nobost.

Hugh and Jane waved to each other.

"You have a friend on board, I see."

"We only met at Obaig this morning for the first time."

"I always say that people make friends very quickly on board ship."

Paul Waggett's grey eyes glittered in appreciation of his own experience as an observer of human nature.

"Well, if you're walking up to the hotel," he went on, "we can go up the hill together. Mrs Waggett will be very glad if you care to have tea with us some afternoon."

"Thank you very much."

"We shall expect you to-morrow. You'll enjoy the view from our lounge of Little Todday across the Coolish."

"I was hoping to spend a day or two on Little Todday."

By now they had reached the half-dozen shops in a row at right angles to the pier that looked across the picturesque little harbour.

"You know, of course, that the Little Toddayites are all Roman Catholics?" Paul Waggett asked.

"I know that. I'm not a Roman Catholic myself," Hugh added quickly to anticipate the question.

"No, I didn't think you were. I can nearly always tell a Roman Catholic. Yes, there's a curious look in their eyes. I'm never wrong. However, I'm bound to say the Little Toddayites did their bit in the Hitler war. Were you in the war?"

"No, I was fourteen when it came to an end," Hugh said.

"Of course, I was in the Kaiser's war as well. One of Kitchener's Army. And in Hitler's war I commanded the Todday Home Guard. You may think it an extraordinary thing to say, but I was always just a little bit disappointed that the Germans didn't invade us in '40 or '41. We should have wiped them out if they'd landed here. The Zonal Commander told me he considered my company the best trained company anywhere in the Highlands or Islands. Well, of course they had the advantage of being commanded by one of the Old Contemptibles."

"I thought you were in Kitchener's Army, sir," Hugh said.

"Those *were* the Old Contemptibles," said Paul Waggett with a tolerant smile for a young man's ignorance. "What do you do? Are you in business?"

"At present I'm Private Secretary to Mr Andrew Wishart, the Under-Secretary for Scotland."

"Really? That's most interesting. Then I suppose you know about this rocket establishment in West Uist. I must say I've been rather disgusted by the ingratitude shown by some of the crofters there. We should have been only too glad if the Government had chosen the two Toddays. But ingratitude is rampant all over the Islands. I've had one or two examples of it myself, I'm sorry to say. One tries to help in one's humble way, but *they* know best."

"Do you really think Great and Little Todday would welcome the idea of being turned into a rocket establishment?" Hugh asked.

"Oh, we should have the usual agitators stirring up trouble, but all the Islander thinks about is his pocket. These writing fellows come here and write a lot of sentimental twaddle—and when I say twaddle I mean twaddle—about ceilidhs and folk-songs and the old Gaelic way of life, but in actual fact the Islanders think the Gaelic way of life means a hard struggle for their daily bread and the younger ones escape from it as soon as possible, when they can."

They had reached the gate of the sloping garden in front of the hotel, and Roddy MacRurie was carrying Hugh's bag up to the entrance. The owner of it paused to look across the Coolish to Little Todday washed with the gold of the westering sun.

"I don't think I could leave that very easily," Hugh said.

Paul Waggett smiled indulgently.

"Oh, Mrs Waggett and I are always quite glad to see the view from our lounge again when we come back from our annual trip south. One of my sons-in-law is a partner in my old firm of chartered accountants and the other is Reader of Palaeontology at Norwich University. I hear he may get the Chair fairly soon. You know what Palaeontology is, of course?"

"Yes, I do."

"A lot of people don't," said Paul Waggett. But he was not to be cheated of his instructiveness by the stranger's hasty affirmative. "A lot of people don't know that it means the study of extinct organized beings."

"Your son-in-law may have some scope one day for investigations in the Outer Islands," Hugh said.

He was regretting the indiscretion of such a remark by a Private Secretary in the Scottish Office when Paul Waggett relieved his conscience by saying, "No, no, my son-in-law William Brownworth says opportunities for research in that direction in the Outer Islands hardly exist. Well, good-evening, Mr MacInnes. That's Snorvig House further up the brae. Mrs Waggett and I will expect you to tea at half-past four to-morrow afternoon. I've taken to photography in my old age and I have some very good snapshots of my grandchildren which you'll enjoy looking at."

With relief Hugh saw his insistent entertainer pursue his way up the hill.

"Welcome to the country, Mr Maginnes," the resonant voice of Roderick MacRurie, was saying. Ruairidh Mór, as he was known from Barra Head to the Butt of Lewis, from Mallan or Obaig to Inverness, was a tall man whose bulk had swelled very steadily with every decade and he was now a snow-capped mountain of a man, exercising as much influence as ever. So long as he represented the island on the County Council, Great Todday knew that it would benefit, often in a minor degree to Ruairidh Mór himself it is true, but still that it *would* benefit from the road or jetty or new school or water-tank or additional bursary that its representative had extracted from the ratepayers of Inverness-shire.

"You'll take a tram before your tea, Mr Maginnes?"

They seated themselves on either side of the fireplace in the dining-room, and the hotel-keeper stirred the peats.

"It gets cold enough when the sun goes down," he said. "And what does Mr Wishard think about all this argumentification in West Uist? Stupit people, stupit people, who can't see their own noses in front of their own faces. The Government made a pick mistake. Ay, ay, they should have done petter to put the rockets on Todaidh Mor and Todaidh Beag."

"Mr Waggett thinks that."

"Mr Wackett thinks that?" Roderick MacRurie did not seem to relish such support for his opinion. "Ach, well, the man can think right sometimes. And maybe the Covernment will put a rocket range here."

"There's no question of putting a rocket range on the Toddays," said Hugh firmly.

"Is there not now?" Roderick asked with a piercing look at his visitor, a piercing look, however, that was veiled by the heavy lids of his eyes.

"If there is, we've heard nothing at the Scottish Office. So I hardly think it can be true."

"Maybe not," said Roderick doubtfully. "But we had a fellow here last week who wass all round the islands with a book, and wherever he went he wass scrippling in this book. He wassn't one of these bird-watchers. He wass too well tressed for that nonsense. He wassn't from the Excise, because there's nothing for the Excise to look for. It wass all trunk long ago. *Taing do Dhia*, for I would be out of my business if it wassn't. We had a lot of excitabilities looking for the Loch Ness Monaster, and this fellow wass none of that kind. And we had Ben Nevis here looking for a boot he said we'd stolen from his Home Carts. But that wass during the war. I wouldn't say this fellow wass looking for anything himself. I would say he wass chust looking for something other people were looking for. He took a tram or two with me of an evening, but not a word would he say. Chust 'hum' and 'hah' and then 'hum' again."

"Did he go over to Little Todday?"

"Ay, he wass over there quite a bit with that book of his. Iosaibh wass telling me."

"Who's Iosaibh?"

"Choseph Macroon. He's the postmaster and pickest merchant in Little Todday. He's the County Councillor too.

Ay, Iosaibh wass telling me this fellow wass asking if he could give him a room anytime."

"Does he keep an hotel, then?"

"Not at all," Ruairidh Mór replied indignantly. "Chust a room or two he lets for towrists in the summer. Kate Anne, his youngest daughter, looks after it all."

"I was wondering if he could put me up for a night or two," said Hugh.

"Ay, I'm sure he would. He'll be over to meet the boat on Friday. But you'll be a bit disappointed in Little Todday, Mr Maginnes. Nothing to see at all. Chust a lot of machair. Nothing at all like Great Todday."

When Hugh came back from tea at Snorvig House, where he had been shown every snapshot Paul Waggett had taken of his grandchildren and had been lectured by his host on the theory of photography, there was a telegram waiting for him at the hotel. His heart sank. It was probably to fetch him back.

But it was not. It was from Jane Kinsella to say she would be arriving with the boat from Nobost on Friday night. Hugh made up his mind at once that Jane as a Catholic would feel more at home on Little Todday and went down to the pier to see if there was any prospect of getting transport across the Coolish. He was lucky enough to find Archie MacRurie well pleased of an excuse to visit Little Todday. The Biffer, now not so far away from seventy, was still as apparently active as he had been in lightening the hold of the *Cabinet Minister* of whisky. The thinning of his hair had added to the impressiveness of that great beak of a nose. His little boat the *Kittiwake*, feared by all the lobsters in the neighbourhood, was moored below the steps of the pier.

"I'm anxious to call upon Father Macalister," Hugh explained.

"A grand man," the Biffer declared emphatically. "I'll take you over with pleasure."

Little Todday was beautiful on that late afternoon of May. The young grass had won back from the salty blasts of winter its vivid green and was spread with a bright veil of buttercups and daisies right across the surface of the island that undulated in knolls as gently as the lazy ocean from which it nowhere raised itself higher than a hundred feet.

Apart from a small cluster of houses round the diminutive haven of Kiltod, beyond which stood the towerless church of Our Lady Star of the Sea and St Tod, there was nothing like a village in over twenty square miles of machair. Isolated houses, all at different angles, were dotted everywhere, each one with its patchwork croft, and everywhere all at different angles the cattle and ponies of Little Todday were tranquilly grazing. There was one metalled road which ran from Kiltod to Tràigh Swish, the long white sandy beach that gleamed almost the length of the western boundary four miles away. From this road tracks far better suited to the local traffic of ponies wandered off in every direction.

"What do you think of this rocket business in West Uist, Mr MacRurie?" Hugh asked as they drew in to Kiltod.

"Poor souls, poor souls."

"What would you say if there was ever a suggestion to have a rocket establishment on the two Toddays?"

"Are you one of these Government snoopers?" the Biffer asked suspiciously.

"No, no, but I was at the meeting in Nobost last March and I couldn't make out exactly what the people there did feel about the prospect for their future."

The Biffer was not prepared to be communicative. It was obvious he felt by no means convinced that Hugh was not a snooper. He waited to see what kind of reception his passenger would receive from Father Macalister.

Chapter 4

BREAKERS AHEAD

"I MET you on the quay at Nobost, Father Macalister," Hugh reminded the priest when his housekeeper had shown him into the cosy sitting-room of the chapel house. "And you kindly told me to call on you if I ever came to Little Todday."

"No kindness at all. You'll take a wee sensation?"

The priest pointed to a chair beside the coal fire and busied himself at a cupboard, from which he extracted the sensation.

"And you'll be staying up at Big Roderick's hotel," Father Macalister said when each of them had drunk his dram and they were seated opposite to one another under the large oleograph of Pope Pius XII hanging above the fireplace.

"Yes, but I have planned to come to Little Todday to-morrow. MacRurie says that the postmaster here takes visitors, and if he can give me a room I thought I'd stay on here till I go back on Friday week."

"You'll stay with me, my boy."

"But, Father, I . . ."

"You'll stay with me," the priest repeated sonorously.

"But there's still another problem of accommodation."

Hugh told Father Macalister about Jane Kinsella.

"And it looks to me," he said, "as if these Macdonalds at Balmuir have either been turned out of their croft already or are going to be turned out immediately. I thought I'd go up to Nobost to-morrow afternoon by the boat and bring Miss Kinsella back. But where will she stay?"

"She'll stay with Mistress Odd, who has a cottage two or three miles from here. She's well into her eighties, but she's as lively as I am, and that's pretty lively, my boy. She's an

Englishwoman, the mother of Sergeant-Major Odd, who married one of Joseph Macroon's daughters. Peigi Ealasaid herself with the children will be coming along next month. And Odd himself will come up later when he can leave his shop in Nottingham for a while."

"But won't Mrs Odd mind having an Irish girl dumped on her all of a sudden?"

"I'll go over and see her to-morrow. You'll go to Nobost and bring back Miss Kinsella, and Joseph will send over the *Morning Star*. How did you come over this evening?"

"In a boat called the *Kittiwake*."

"With the Biffer! Ach, a real gem, one of the chosen few."

"He was a bit suspicious of me."

"Suspicious?"

"Yes, I think he suspects me of being a Government snooper. I didn't dare tell him I was Mr Wishart's Private Secretary. I don't believe he would have brought me over. Apparently there was somebody prowling around here only last week."

"There was. I believe there are breakers ahead. Ay, ay, breakers ahead," he rumbled to himself.

"You would absolutely oppose a rocket range here?" Hugh asked.

"Absolutely."

"And your people would back you?"

"I don't think one of them would encourage the enemy. Joseph Macroon might be a little wistful about the wealth he would think he was letting slip through his fingers. But he would be as staunch as any of them in resistance. Yes, yes, the machair would be practically the same as the maquis. And we have a splendid schoolmaster here in Kiltod—Norman Macleod. He used to be at Watasett in Great Todday and the Inverness Education Authority were a bit worried that he might be a Communist. Then in the war he was with the R.A.F.—on the ground of course—and down in Preston he married a Catholic girl and became a

Catholic himself. So we got him here, when Andrew Chisholm retired. Oh, he's a splendid fellow, and the children here think there's nobody like him."

"His experience with the R.A.F. wouldn't make him support a rocket project?"

"No, no, no. He and Duncan Bàn will stand one on either side of me."

"What about Great Todday?" Hugh asked. "I fancied that Roderick MacRurie would welcome the idea."

"Ruairidh Mór knows which side his bread is buttered, and, by Jingo, so he should, for the butter's thicker than the bread. But there are good men on Great Todday. There's George Campbell, who became headmaster of Snorvig School after Alec Mackinnon left us. He's married to Norman Macleod's sister, Catriona. And there's Airchie MacRurie, the Biffer, who brought you over. . . ."

At that moment the door opened and Father Macalister's housekeeper came in to say that Airchie MacRurie was wondering when the gentlemen would want to be getting back to Snorvig.

"Send him in, Kirstag. There you are, Airchie. Come right in. You'll take a snifter, my boy, and you'll have a *deoch an doruis*, Mr MacInnes."

The Biffer downed his dram with gusto.

"Och, well, Father James, that's good stuff right enough," he declared with reverence.

"I hear you've been taking Mr MacInnes for a Government snooper, Airchie."

"Och, I didn't say that at all, Father James."

"No, but you looked it, Airchie," the priest said. "Well, you needn't look it any more, because he's coming to stay with me to-morrow night. He'll be going up to Nobost by the boat and he'll be bringing back with him a young Irish lady. Joseph will be sending over the *Morning Star*, but in case of accidents you'll have the *Kittiwake* handy so that they don't get stranded on the pier at Snorvig."

"I'll do that, Father James."

On the way down to the diminutive harbour, Father Macalister took Hugh into the post-office and introduced him to Joseph Macroon. Joseph had shrunk a little with the years, and now with that knitted red cap of his he looked more like a troll than ever. His only son Kenny, who had been in the merchant navy for the last ten years, had come back to settle at home, and his father had bought a new boat for him, larger than the old *Morning Star*, and was still trying to persuade the Inverness-shire County Council to give Little Todday a lobster-pool, a proposal which the County Council resisted in the hope that the Government would extract it from the taxpayers instead of from the ratepayers. That the method of extraction was a distinction without a difference so far as the payer was concerned did not occur to them. Kenny Macroon and the Biffer, as the two chief representatives of the lobster world in these two islands, had been yarning together while Hugh was up at the chapel house.

"This is Uisdean MacAonghais," Father James announced. As this was the first time Hugh had heard his name in Gaelic, he didn't realize he was being presented until Father James continued sonorously "the Private Secretary of Mr Andrew Wishart, who is the Under-Secretary of State for Scotland. He is coming to stay with me to-morrow and I want the *Morning Star* to fetch him when the *Island Queen* gets back from Nobost. Miss Kinsella, an Irish singer, will be with him, and that reminds me. Somebody must tell Duncan Bàn I want to see him to-night. Miss Kinsella will be staying with Mistress Odd."

"We can make her quite comfortable here, Father James," put in Kate Anne Macdonald, the youngest of Joseph's five daughters and very much like him, with the same shrewd light blue eyes.

"No, no, Kate Anne, I want Miss Kinsella to be given some of Duncan Bàn's songs. Maybe she'll be staying here next Thursday night, when we will have a *cèilidh* in the hall. And now you're wanting to get back, Airchie."

The Biffer flatly refused to accept anything for the hire of the *Kittiwake*.

"No, no, I'll be in my grave before I take a penny from a friend of Father James to go and see him," he declared.

"Well, you'll come up to the hotel and have a dram?"

"Och, I'll do that right enough."

The bar was crowded that evening, and Hugh, telling himself that it was his duty to take back to Mr Wishart a faithful report of what the reaction in the Toddays would be to the establishment of a rocket range on them, mentioned to a group of crofters that Mr Waggett had been lamenting to him that afternoon the mistake the Ministry of Protection had made in not choosing Little Todday for the range and Great Todday for the training establishment instead of the three Uists.

"Wackett!" exclaimed Sammy MacCodrum, a small man with a large nose and a voice as squeaky as Captain MacKechnie's. "What is he after knowing about rockets? He's chust chock full of emptiness. *A Chruitheir*, what a man to be talking an opinion!"

"He may be right and all about this," said Angus MacCormac, a tall crofter with a white moustache that billowed like a crinoline. "Your brother Murdo was telling me that the lorry-drivers in Mid Uist were making money as fast as water. Just pouring out over them."

"Murdo's doing pretty well with his own lorry," said Sammy.

"Ay," said Calum MacKillop, another lorry owner, more generally known as the Gooch. "Ay, but that's no reason at all why he couldn't do better."

A couple of younger men now joined the group—a Maclean and a MacRurie.

"If you ask me," said the Maclean, "I think these *Uidhistich* who are making a fuss about these rockets are a lot of old *cailleachan*."

"Yes," the MacRurie agreed, "Old women who don't know the world's going on."

"Ach, don't talk so silly, Eachann," said the Biffer, scornfully.

"It's you that's talking silly, Airchie, if you think it wouldn't be the best thing that could happen to us here if the Government would spend millions. You're getting an old *bodach*, Airchie. You're living in the past. We want a future here. And when they're offered a future in West Uist they sit down and make a song about their way of life. A fine way of life. There have been too many songs. It's time to have a bit of plain-speaking for a change."

"Another dram, Eachann, and you'll be as full of wind as a Communist," the Biffer observed sardonically.

"Ach, I don't like these Communists at all," said Ruairidh Mór, entering the conversation, "but there's a lot in what Eachann is after saying. When I think of the way I've talked myself to the bone in Inverness, and now when there's twelf million pounds to be thrown away on a stupit place like West Uist they're so stupit that they don't want to pick it up. It makes me as sick as a dog."

"You're daft, Ruairidh. You're just plain daft," said the Biffer. "You'll soon be writing to the Government to ask them to give *us* rockets *gu leoir*. Is it yourself you're making as sick as a dog? And what are you making me? As sick as ten cats."

"If I make you as sick as twenty cats, Airchie, I tell you thiss. If I wass after thinking that they would do such a thing I would be after writing to them now," Roderick MacRurie declared.

Next day Hugh went to call on old Dr Maclaren.

"So you're Andrew Wishart's Private Secretary, eh? I hope he doesn't keep you in such strict order as Mrs Wishart keeps me," the doctor said. "For twenty years now I've been ruled by my housekeeper."

"I was rather surprised last night, Doctor, to hear most of the chaps in the hotel bar wishing that the Ministry of Protection had chosen the two Toddays for their rocket establishment. Do you think they would really welcome it here?"

"A few of the older people might object, but all the younger ones would be delighted," said Dr Maclaren. "You couldn't blame them. They've grown up to think of their home as a charity concern. Their fathers had looked upon the dole as a way of wangling something extra out of the Government. The young men who went to sea came home and let everybody know what a dead and alive place they were coming home to. The girls went out to service in Glasgow and wrote to tell their younger sisters what a paradise Glasgow was. There was still a chance to save the long-line fishing even twenty-five years ago, but vested interests managed to keep the fish for big business. In other words, the trawlers were allowed to carry on with the destruction of the whitefish spawning beds. If you walk along to Watasett you'll see a dozen rotting fishing-boats, high and dry these fifteen years or more. There might have been a chance during the last war to develop the tweed industry, but the Government clamped purchase tax on it and so the individual weaver had to put his work into the hands of those who knew better than he how to handle it commercially. But I mustn't bore you with might-have-beens. I wish they hadn't chosen an island like West Uist for these rockets, because West Uist was an island where the population was stable, indeed actually increasing. With kelp-gatherings and eggs and tweed and the best Highland cattle they were prosperous enough. I can only be thankful that they did not pick on Little Todday. That *would* be a disaster."

"Is Little Todday prosperous?"

"With such grazing? It certainly is. And now Norman Macleod . . . did you meet him? You will. He's the schoolmaster now in Kiltod. A splendid chap. He has persuaded them to grow onions and carrots. They're the finest in all Britain and free of the fly."

"Would Little Todday have resisted the rocket range?"

"To a man, with Father James to lead them. Oh yes, the Ministry of Protection would have found their rockets were just damp squibs on Little Todday."

Hugh's spirits rose. He looked forward to warning Mr Wishart that if the Ministry of Protection tried to take over Little Todday it was likely to find itself as much an object of contempt as even the Colonial Office.

When the *Island Queen* reached Nobost that Friday night and Hugh saw Jane Kinsella standing on the quay, he felt as if the forwards had heeled out the ball in their own twenty-five, that the scrum-half had sent him a swift clean pass and that he had run with the ball the full length of the field and touched down between the goal posts of the other side. The gangway rattled as he ran along it to greet her.

"By Jove, I am glad you were able to make it."

With Jane on the quay were two men and a woman.

"This is Mrs Macdonald, Hugh." He shook hands with a tall handsome dark woman who was wrapped in a Clanranald shawl. "And this is Joseph Macdonald." He shook hands with a stocky man with a square chin and a straightforward gaze. "And this is Michael Macdonald, Mr Macdonald's father." A tall old man with an aquiline profile and bright aquiline eyes stepped forward and stood straight as a pine to shake hands with Hugh.

"The Macdonalds had to give up their house this morning," Jane said. "And they've come to see me off because they are staying in Nobost to-night till they see what is going to be done to find them another home."

"I'm sorry to hear about this," said Hugh awkwardly, bitterly aware of how feeble the words sounded.

"Well, well, *ma tà*, you must be getting on board, *m'eudail*," Mrs Macdonald told Jane. "I would say what a pity it is that you would not be coming instead of going, but it is not a pity any more."

Jane flung her arms round Bean Iosaibh.

"Good-bye, good-bye, and thank you for being so kind

to me in spite of everything. And please do write to me and let me know what you are going to do."

"And where we are going," added Joseph Macdonald, his brow furrowed as his land never would be again.

"Good-bye," said Jane, clasping the hand of the old man. "And thank you again and again for those stories. Oh dear, I did not mean to cry," she said, fumbling for a handkerchief.

"*Beannachd leibh, beannachd leibh,*" said old Michael Macdonald in a voice of surprising richness for a man in his mid-eighties. "We will say a prayer together."

He pulled off his threadbare bonnet, crossed himself, and began in Gaelic a 'Hail, Mary', the response to which was made by the other three in the same language.

"All aboard! All aboard!"

The boat had few passengers that night. Hugh and Jane were able to pace the deck in solitude as the *Island Queen* glided southward over the tranquil sea shining in the light of the full May moon.

"Oh, Hugh, it was heartbreaking," she told him. "Joseph came to meet me at Nobost on Wednesday night and told me that on Friday the rocket people were taking possession of his house and croft, but he insisted on my coming back with him for the last two nights they would have. And last night—the last night—we had a ceilidh with others who were being evicted . . . what queer people the English are! They couldn't bear me to call it eviction. They'd asked me to sing for the poor exiles from England, and I told them I would as soon sing for a pack of Orange drummers on the Twelfth of July. 'But you must realize, Miss Kinsella,' said one of them, 'that these are not evictions. These crofters will be amply compensated and will be much better off on the mainland. They might even emigrate—assisted, of course, by the Government.' 'With their fare out,' I said, 'but not with their fare home.' Where was I? Oh yes, the room was full of people who would be evicted."

"And you sang to them, Jane," said Hugh.

"Oh yes, I sang . . . with my heart in my throat. It was dawn before the ceilidh broke up. And then this afternoon the furniture was taken out and put in two lorries. And isn't it funny, Hugh, the way what's not important at all seems so important sometimes? Do you know what upset me most when they were loading the lorries? It was the two china dogs on the mantelpiece being taken away from where they'd been sitting so long. One can be awfully silly, I think, when one's upset."

"I'm glad you didn't have to go back by yourself, Jane. I think you'll find the same atmosphere in Little Todday as you found in Balmuir, and I know that Father Macalister has a store of old songs. I'm staying with him, and you're staying with a Mrs Odd. I haven't met her, but apparently she's a great character. Her son was in the islands during the war and married one of the island girls. She's an old London woman who had a shop in Nottingham which her son and daughter-in-law run, and she lives on Little Todday for half the year."

Mrs Odd received a testimonial later from Captain MacKechnie, who invited Hugh and Jane to his cabin.

"Och, she and I have been friends for twelf years and more. She and her son Sarchant-major Odd gave me quite a new idea about the English. I neffer thought a great deal of them at all once upon a time. Too stuffed up in themselfs for my liking. And you'll be coming back with us next Friday? Ach, well, you're going to have the pick of our weather till then. Wasn't that old Michael Macdonald with you at Nobost?"

Jane told him what had happened.

"Look at that now for a tam shame right enough. I remember when I was a nipper hearing about the way the Lewis men piffed the Royal Scots in the eye when they were being put off their crofts by the Covernment. Those were the tays right enough, but I don't belief they'll come again. Och, we're run over with Ciffil Serfants chust the way a house is run over by peetles. And if we started poisoning

Ciffil Serfants, what a fuss there should be. And if we don't poison them off they'll be too many for us. So there you are."

On the pier at Snorvig Father Macalister was waiting for them with Kenny Macroon, who was just over thirty and the most eligible bachelor on Little Todday. His elder brother John had died in the Argentine soon after the end of the war, and he was now the heir to Joseph Macroon's complicated business. He had a merry eye and such an acute sense of the ridiculous that his face seemed to be perpetually crumpled with smiles that were not allowed to become laughter. Jane told Father Macalister about the plight of the Macdonalds.

"*A bhobh bhobh*," he sighed, if the gusty moan that shook his portly frame could be called a sigh. "Poor old Michael. To be turned out of his house at his age. I wonder, Kenny, could we find them anywhere on Todaidh Beag?"

"I don't believe we could, Father James."

Father Macalister sighed again.

"You'll like Duncan Bàn, Miss Kinsella. He'll drive you along to Bow Bells, which is what Mistress Odd calls her cottage. He gave up a career at Glasgow University to live here on his croft and write poetry. He's a really good bard, and a fine Gaelic scholar. No ambition of course, but I haven't a great deal of ambition myself and so we understand one another."

Duncan Macroon was at the harbour with his pony cart when the *Morning Star* came in about midnight. He was a rosy-cheeked man with a tumble of fair hair which, although he was now fifty, still kept much of the glint of youth.

"Ah, well, here's Duncan himself, Miss Kinsella," the parish priest exclaimed with a hint of relief in his voice because that lovable bard with eyes as blue as a kingfisher's wing did sometimes allow inspiration, both poetic and spirituous, to obliterate the memory of a promise he had made. I won't ask you up to the chapel house to-night, Miss Kinsella. I will come along to-morrow morning and see how you are. Be careful with that *clàrsach*, Duncan."

"I'll be as careful with it, Father, as I would be with my own self," Duncan Ban promised.

"Ah, well, Duncan, I'd rather you were a little more careful than that," the priest said. "And now, Miss Kinsella, *oidhche mhath agus cadal mhath*. Good night and good sleep."

"There's only one thing that could make me sleep better, Father," she said.

"And what's that at all?"

"Just for you to stop calling me Miss Kinsella and call me Jane."

"That's not at all a dangerous opiate to administer, Jane."

And to Hugh's great pleasure, when he and his host were sitting by a coal fire in the chapel house, Father Macalister praised Jane's beauty and modesty.

"And if she has as sweet a voice as she has warm a heart we're going to have a great treat, Uisdean. You don't mind if we get off the ceremony. We find it very difficult on Little Todday to stand on ceremony. Will you poke the fire and consider we have known each other seven years."

"I suppose you don't find peat on this island?"

"No, no, there's no peat at all, but we get a good deal of wood. You haven't seen our beaches yet."

"That's a beautiful beach at Balmuir," said Hugh.

"Ay, it is a beautiful beach right enough, and that fellow who was here last week spent a lot of his time on Tràigh Suis, which is the name of our most beautiful beach, and it's uncomfortably like the Balmuir beach. I think, Uisdean, that you know something," Father Macalister said, with a sharp look at his guest.

"None of us at the Scottish Office knows anything definite, I give you my word, Father James."

"But you sniff something in the air?"

"I'm anxious, yes. And frankly I was worried by the attitude of Roderick MacRurie, and by the way a lot of them were talking in the bar last night. Some of them actually seemed envious of what had happened in the Uists.

And to-night when I met these Macdonalds on the quay at Nobost I felt I could do anything to stop this infernal business."

"But this is progress, my boy. And that's the way mankind has been progressing ever since Adam and Eve. Oh, everything in the garden was going to be lovely, and what was the result? Poor old Adam and Eve were turned out of their croft."

"I made up my mind to-night, Father James, that if this sort of thing was going to happen I couldn't stay on as Mr Wishart's Private Secretary. It wouldn't be fair to him and it wouldn't be fair to myself. So when I get back I shall resign. Suppose, for instance, in my official capacity I hear that the Ministry of Protection intend to take over Great and Little Todday for their blasted rockets? I shouldn't be able to give you warning without disloyalty to my boss, and he's fundamentally a decent chap. I know he talked a lot of humbug at that Nobost meeting, but I must give him the credit for knowing that it was humbug, and he has been awfully decent to me. I simply couldn't let him down. So the only thing for me to do is to resign. We shall know fairly soon if these Protection people are making plans about the Toddays, and I hope I'll be out of my job by the time they do. Then with a clear conscience I'll be able to join the resistance. Meanwhile, I'm going to enjoy this week. Isn't Jane Kinsella a nice girl? You know, I haven't heard her sing yet. I hope she really can sing."

"We'll settle that problem to-morrow. What's the time? A quarter to one. That's a quarter to twelve by Almighty God's time and the time of Holy Church. So we can have a wee sensation before we go to bed and still let me say Mass to-morrow morning."

Five minutes later they were on their way upstairs to their rooms, under Father Macalister's arm the copy of a Western magazine. He tapped it affectionately.

"Good shooting, my boy. *Oidche mhath.*"

Chapter 5

LITTLE TODDAY

DUNCAN BÀN arrived with his trap just as Father Macalister and his guest were finishing breakfast. They drove west along the only metalled road in the island for a couple of miles before they turned off to take the track that led across the rolling machair to Duncan's own house, Tigh a' Bhàird, the House of the Bard, a couple of hundred yards beyond which was Bow Bells, a thatched cottage with thick white walls and small deepset windows. Mrs Odd's house was sheltered from the rage of the west by mounds of close-cropped grass starred with daisies and primroses, and above the silence in which Bow Bells was set the long sigh of the ocean was audible on this tranquil May morning, that long sigh which could sink to a whisper or rise to a moan and from a moan to a roar when the wind blew.

They had alighted from the trap by Duncan Bàn's house, and leaving the pony to nibble the sweet grass they walked along to Bow Bells.

"*Éisd,*" said Father James, putting a finger to his lips.

The three of them stood listening to a voice that came floating out from the open door of the cottage, a voice simple, pure and serene.

"It's herself," Duncan whispered.

"*Éisd, éisd,*" Father James insisted. And they stood there listening, the priest, the poet and the private secretary, until after a second song the voice was silent.

"*A Dhia,* Father, I don't believe the fairies could sing better than that," Duncan declared, as they walked along the path edged with scallop shells to the open door.

"Ah, there you are," exclaimed Mrs Odd, jumping out of her chair to greet them as if she had been nearer to thirty-five than eighty-five. What a lovely morning, eh? I was only saying to Jane just now how I wished I'd brought Luce and Kitty along with me. All this nonsense about school holidays. As if they wouldn't learn more here in this lovely weather than what they can in school. Don't you think this worriting about school is a lot of nonsense, Father James? My goodness, as if the kids hadn't got all their lives before them to be ejucated in. And this is Mr MacInnes, eh? I'm very pleased to meet you. What a set out over in West Uist! Jane's been telling me all about it. Well, if they tried to turn me out of my cottage for a lot of rockets I'd tell 'em they could put their rockets where the monkey put the nuts. Rockets! I ask you. I remember in the year dot when we was kids in dear old London my old dad—well, he wasn't so old then—he bought two Cathering wheels, two Roman candles as they call them and a rocket for Guy Fawkes, and my brother Ted, who's been under the daisies now for donkey's years, he set his heart on letting off this rocket. Well, it wasn't Ted's fault really because Dad had promised him he should light one of the Roman candles and hold it, but men being what they are, Dad of course had to light it himself, and when he did give it to pore Ted at last the stars had all shot out and all Ted got was a bit of fizzle at the end. So Ted was determined he'd light this rocket, but he didn't know nothing about rockets and he lit it, meaning to carry it out and show off with it in the garden, and of course it whizzed out of his hand in my mother's best parlour, knocked a candlestick off of the chimbley-piece *and* a vase *and* a statuette of Lord Nelson and then whizzed about all over the floor like a dog with a tin tied on to its tail, and just as my dad come running in to see what was the matter the rocket bust and one of the stars burnt my dad on the nose. What a commotion! And what a belting he gave pore Ted. Yes, *he* remembered the Fifth of November all right. But, good land alive, I don't know why I'm jabbering on like this. You want to hear Jane sing again, I'll be bound."

If Hugh had read more poetry and played less football

he would have been able to think of all sorts of wonderful romantic comparisons for Jane as he sat listening to those Irish ballads and Gaelic songs of hers. All he could think was that she was the loveliest girl he had ever seen and that he would like to sit for ever watching her slim fingers pluck the strings of her clarsach.

"*Briagh, briagh*," Father James murmured with a deep sigh of satisfaction. "You'll sing and play for us in the hall on Thursday evening. I'll make the announcement at Mass to-morrow."

"Thursday's Ascension Day, isn't it, Father?" said Duncan

"It is. And we'll have a glorious beautiful evening," said Father James. "And now, Duncan, you shall drive me back to Kiltod. You and Jane had better walk along to Tràigh Suis, and Mrs Odd will give you dinner and you can walk back to Kiltod in the afternoon, and to-morrow, Jane, you'll have supper at the chapel house. Come along, Duncan. Tingaloorie, all."

A minute later they saw his rolling stride moving over the machair toward Duncan's trap.

"One of the boys of the old brigade," Mrs Odd commented affectionately. "Well, if the Government started in trying to push people out of their homes on Little Todday I reckon they'd find Father Macalister a bit harder to push than what they bargained for. I remember my old dad saying when Lord Salisbury died as how the country would soon be in a bloody mess—excuse my dad's French—and I think he was right. He was always against Mr Gladstone. Sanctimonious old —, well, he went off into French again. Yes, that's what he used to call Mr Gladstone. And my husband was the same. Only he had it in for Campbell-Bannerman. Oh, he'd carry on alarming about Campbell-Bannerman. But my boy, Fred . . . well, boy's hardly the word for he's just on sixty now. Terrible, isn't it? . . . but as I was saying Fred hasn't a good word for any of these fellows in Parliament. Bottles of eyewash he calls them."

"Some of them are genuine, Mrs Odd," Hugh said.

"Oh, well, I suppose some of the advertisements you read are genuine. But if I started in believing every advertisement I read in the paper I'd very soon be putting crape on my nose, till it was as black as Newgate's knocker."

"Crape on your nose, Mrs Odd? Why?"

"Well, my brains would be dead, wouldn't they? But look here, if you're going to Try Swish you'd better be hopping. I've got a lovely bit of rump steak for dinner."

"Couldn't I stay and help with the table, Mrs Odd?" Jane suggested.

"No, no. Florag Van's in the kitchen. Flo's elder sister was with me till she got married, and from what I can see it won't be long before Florag Van goes the same way as her sister Florag Yocky. I love the dear people here, but they do have some strange notions. Fancy calling two sisters both Florag, and though Florag Yocky is now Mrs Mackinnon they still go on calling her Florag Yocky. That's because she's the daughter of Jocky Stewart. And his name isn't Jocky. It's good old-fashioned John. But I've never been able to make out why she isn't called Flora Jocky, instead of Yocky."

"I think it would be the genitive in Gaelic," said Jane.

"Well, I don't know what genitive is, but it sounds a contradictory sort of affair. But Garlic is all contradictions. Look at this word Bang, which means 'fair' so they tell me. That's why he's Duncan Bang. But if it's a girl she's got to be called Van. I said, 'fancy calling a girl with a pretty figure like Florag the Second a van. You might as well call her a carthorse while you're about it.' Well, I call her Flo. We often laugh over the old song.

Oh, Flo, such a change, you know
When she left the village she was shy.
But alas and alack, she's come back
With a naughty little twinkle in her eye
And her golden hair was hanging down her back.

"Only as I say to her you didn't have to leave the village, Flo. Your golden hair always has been hanging down your back."

At this moment Florag Bhàn, a pretty girl of about eighteen with hair that really was golden, came in to make some domestic enquiry.

"My goodness," Mrs Odd exclaimed, "It's high time I got cracking. I was always a chatterbox. My old mother used to say, 'Talk about talking the hindleg off of a donkey—you'd talk the jorebone off of an ass, Lucy, and that's a fact.' All right, Flo, I'll be with you in two two's."

"Bit of a character, Mrs Odd," Hugh said to Jane as they walked over the springy turf of the machair toward the ocean.

"She's a darling woman, Hugh. She made me marvellously comfortable, but I kept waking through the night thinking of the dear Macdonalds and wondering what was going to happen to them."

"I'll ask Mr Wishart to make enquiries from the Department of Agriculture when I get back. I can't get over it, Jane. I don't think I'll be able to stick it any longer at the Scottish Office."

They walked on for a while over the myriad minute stars of eyebright in the turf, and then after climbing the long range of dunes they ran down over the slope of powdery sand upon the other side and stood upon Tràigh Swish, as the map called Tràigh Suis.

"What a superb beach!" Hugh exclaimed, looking along the mile or more of white road to the high dark rock that guarded the northern end and then turning to look back along two miles or more to another high dark rock which guarded the southern boundary. He pulled a book out of his pocket.

"I borrowed this from MacRurie at the hotel."

It was a luscious piece of topography by Hector Hamish Mackay called *Fairie Lands Forlorn*.

"It's rather flowery, but shall I read you what this chap

says?" he asked. They sat down on the warm dry sand where the beach sloped up toward the rampart of dunes, and Hugh read to Jane.

"'Many and fair are the long white beaches that stretch beside the western shores of the islands at the edge of the mighty Atlantic, but none is fairer than lovely Tràigh Swish of Little Todday. Philologists differ about the origin of the name. So let us fly backwards out of the prosaic present upon "the viewless wings of poesy" and accept the derivation from Suis, a Norse princess of long ago who, legend relates, flung herself into the ocean from that dark rock which marks the southern boundary of the strand. Alas, her love for a young bard of Todaidh Beag, as Little Todday is called in the old sweet speech of the Gael, was foredoomed.

"'And while we are back in the faerie days of yester year let us ponder awhile that grey rock which marks the northern boundary of Tràigh Swish. Does it seem to resemble the outline of a great seal and justify its name—Carraig an Ròin? Some relate indeed that it is no mere likeness of a seal but the petrified shape of the seal-woman herself from whom the Macroons sprang. Who shall say? Upon this magical morning of spring when the short sweet turf of the machair is starred with multitudinous primroses, the morning-stars of the Hebridean flora as they have been well called, we yield our imagination to the influence of the season and are willing to believe anything. We stand entranced midway along Tràigh Swish and watch the placid ocean break gently upon the sand and dabble it with tender kisses. We listen to the sea-birds calling to one another as they wing their way to their nesting grounds on the two guardian isles of Poppay and Pillay. We gaze at the calm expanse of the Atlantic and try to forget its winter fury of which the heaped up tangle along the base of the dunes reminds us. We are at one with nature. We have the freedom of Tir nan Òg—the Land of Youth.'"

When Hugh's voice was silent, Jane began to croon a Gaelic lullaby she had just learnt from Mrs Joseph

Macdonald at Balmuir. [It is hard to have to use a word that has been so damnably debauched by croonuchs apparently incapable of debauching anything less defenceless than a word.] Somewhere in the marram grass that fringed the dunes the absent-minded little song of a rock-pipit was audible, and far away somewhere a cuckoo was calling, his notes already lacking the confidence of spring's prime.

"That was the last song Bean Iosaibh gave me," Jane said.

"And you sing it marvellously. I mean to say, it sort of takes my breath away," Hugh declared. She looked at him, and to him her eyes seemed larger and deeper than the ocean outspread beyond them.

"I mean, it's fantastic to think that when I boarded the boat last Wednesday morning I'd never seen you before. I feel as if I'd known you all my life."

He longed to add 'and loved you', but Fettes and Trinity College, Oxford, intervened. One couldn't say that sort of thing to a girl with whom one had merely spent a day on board a boat. She might suppose just exactly what he didn't want her to suppose. She might think he made a habit of telling girls he had scarcely met that he was in love with them.

"I've practically made up my mind, Jane, that I'm going to tell Mr Wishart I want to resign. I took his offer to be his Private Secretary because my father thought it would be useful for me if I went in for politics, and he's awfully keen on that. So's my mother. In fact, she has absolutely set her heart upon it."

"I don't care about politics at all," Jane said. "I think Dev's a grand man, but that's nearly all I know about politics."

"You don't care about politics?" Hugh pressed.

"Oh, it's all just talking and talking about nothing at all. It may be important, but it's terribly uninteresting."

"That settles it," Hugh declared firmly.

"Settles what?" Jane asked in surprise.

"That I shall give up this idea of going into politics," Hugh replied.

He hoped that this announcement would surprise her even more, because under the emotion of surprise Jane's eyes were larger and more lovely than ever.

"But why would my not being interested in politics make you give them up?" she asked.

Here was the perfect opening to tell her he loved her, but he fumbled the pass.

"Well, you were more or less expressing what was already in my mind. I mean, I'd more or less already decided to give them up."

"What will you do instead?"

"I'll offer to go into my father's business. He's in wool. It was really my mother's notion that I should go into Parliament. I think in his heart he'll be quite glad really."

"Is it a big business?"

"Oh yes, it's pretty big. One of the half-dozen biggest in Scotland. Yes, I'm sure my father will be glad. You see, I'm the only son—in fact, I haven't even got any sisters."

And for the first time in his life Hugh reflected what a severe deprivation that was when a vision of charming and amenable sisters all united in a resolve to become intimate friends of Jane passed across his fancy.

"But that's enough about me," he said. "What about you?"

"I haven't got a big business to go into. So I shall just hope to be a success as a singer."

"You certainly will be."

"Yes, but I'm ambitious, Hugh. I'd like to sing in opera. And that means I must get a good singing-master. I want to go to Italy. I believe I have the voice for opera, but it needs to be trained. Why are you looking so doubtful, Hugh? Don't you think I have the voice for opera?"

"No, no, I wasn't looking doubtful," Hugh assured her. "I'm sure you have the voice. I was only thinking that I can't imagine any singing I'd like to listen to more than your singing as it is now. And if you go off to Italy and become a prima donna I shall be rather out of it because I've always been bored by opera. I mean to say, all these trills and things always seem to me rather exaggerated. I'm sure your trill wouldn't make me feel that," he added hastily, for her eyes had clouded and he was afraid he had offended her.

"Folk-singers are all very well," Jane said. "But folk-singers in Ireland are two a penny."

"I'll bet not one of them is as good as you," he declared fervidly.

"But even if I were the best in Ireland, where would I get to? An occasional quarter of an hour—maybe even half an hour on Radio Eireann . . . and a concert in Dublin in the winter and another in the spring, and concerts in Cork and Limerick and one or two other places."

"And Scotland, of course," Hugh said hopefully.

"Yes, and maybe London."

"And gramophone records," Hugh reminded her.

"But what would all that be compared with singing at Covent Garden? Or in New York?"

"Oh, well," said Hugh with a sigh, "you'll have to be content this week with a grand concert in the Kiltod hall."

"I'm sure it *will* be grand," she said. "And now hadn't we better be going back to Bow Bells? I promised Mrs Odd we wouldn't be late for dinner."

The future of Jane's voice was not discussed again until she came to supper at the chapel house on Monday. Afterwards she sang to her own accompaniment on the clarsach simple song after simple song, most of them in English, but enough of them in Gaelic to evoke deep gusty sighs of approval and heartfelt pleasure from her host. Then she sang Madame Butterfly's *Un Bel Dì Vedremo*, at the end of which Father Macalister groaned "*A dhuine a dhuine*, and what's that all about at all?"

Jane explained, and he shook his head with a mournful long drawn out 'Oh' of protest.

"But you said you understood Italian, Father," she reminded him.

"So I do," he said. "And that's just why I think you're wrong to sing operatic nonsense like that."

"But I want to go to Milan and study singing. I want to sing in opera."

"Great sticks alive! What do you want to do that for?"

Hugh sat silent, making an effort not to let Jane see by the expression on his face how enthusiastically he was agreeing with Father James.

"I'd like to be a success in opera. They'd think much more of me at home. They don't think anything of folk-singers. They're all over the place in Ireland."

"And *you'd* be all over the place in opera," Father James averred.

"You don't think my voice is strong enough?" she exclaimed in dismay.

"Oh, it may be strong enough, but if you go to Milan and get taught to sing in the Italian style you'll be no more use for singing as you do now, and that would be a pity. It would be more than a pity, it would be a major calamity. No, no, no, stay as you are, *m'eudail.* I haven't had such a treat for years as you gave me to-night until you shot up into the air like a rocket with that operatic nonsense."

Hugh felt it was time for him to present Jane's case, if only for the pleasure of hearing him demolish it.

"Of course, it's quite understandable that she should want to make a name for herself as a singer," he said.

"She'll make a much better name for herself if she goes on singing as she sang this evening. If she goes to opera, she may be more successful than some poor souls I don't doubt, but she will find others more successful than she will ever be. She'll just be in a crowd of in betwixt and betweens. But I've heard nobody at all sing those songs so beautifully as she sang them to us this evening, and as she'll sing them again on Thursday night. A pure delight they were. And why? Because she sang them as simply and naturally as a *smeorach* at dawn."

"A smeorach?" Hugh echoed.

"A thrush. A mavis," the priest translated. "Simply and naturally without any of the fal-de-lals she'll learn from a singing-master whose business it is to take the wild rose from the hedge and turn it into a fat pink cabbage rose. Will she not have a much greater name as the last rose of Gaeldom than as one of a great bunch of well-trained performers squalling away at one another for dear life? You've heard of the lost Atlantis, Hugh?"

"Vaguely, yes."

"Well, there's still a little bit of it left in the Islands, but it won't last very long the way the world is going, and it is our duty to preserve it as long as we can. Jane, you saw the danger in Balmuir when you spent that last night with the Macdonalds. We have to fight against this damnable juggernaut they call progress. We are not going to let it roll right over us without a fight, and if you go chasing after opera in Italy you'll be running away from the fight. You'll be seeing on Thursday night what heart you can put into that fight. Mind you, they may not try to destroy Little Todday, but I feel in my bones that there are breakers ahead."

Those breakers were audible when the post reached Kiltod on Wednesday evening.

"A letter for me?" Hugh exclaimed to Joseph Macroon. He saw that it was from the Scottish Office and he slipped it into his pocket unopened, resolved not to read it until after the boat had left at midnight. If it was a summons from the Under-Secretary to return at once, he would be able to telegraph that he could not be in London before Monday.

"Will you take up Father James's letters to him?" Joseph Macroon asked.

Father Macalister was still in church when Hugh reached the chapel house; he was hearing confessions on the eve of the Feast of the Ascension. It was after eight when he came down into the sitting-room with an open letter.

"Well, well, well," he said as he gave Hugh the letter to read, "what a day to choose for a descent from the air!"

The letter was from the Ministry of Protection at 5 Whitehall Circus and was addressed to

The Rev. J. Macalister
Todday Island
near Obaig
Argyllshire
N.B.

A reproachful post-office official had scratched out Argyllshire and written *Inverness-shire* with a blue pencil.

Reverend and Dear Sir,

This is to notify you that Air Chief Marshal Sir William Windermere, G.C.B., K.B.E., D.S.O., D.F.C., A.F.C., Air Commodore J. T. Watchorn, C.B.E., D.S.O., D.F.C., Lieut.-Colonel W. C. Bullingham, O.B.E., and Dr Emil Hamburger will be visiting Todday Island on Thursday, May 20th, and the Minister will be grateful if you will afford them all the assistance you can render in the course of their inspection. The Minister instructs me to inform you that news of the visit of Air Chief Marshal Sir William Windermere, Air Commodore Watchorn, Lieut.-Colonel Bullingham and Dr Hamburger is not to be communicated to the Press for reasons connected with national security. Any premature speculation about the intentions of the Ministry of Protection in regard to any proposals now in the course of undergoing the most careful consideration will be highly prejudicial to the outcome of such consideration. The Minister instructs me to add that he is sure you will appreciate the importance of maintaining an attitude of the strictest discretion in regard to this visit and that he has implicit confidence in your willingness to offer your fullest co-operation both in regard to this proposed visit from an exploratory mission composed of Air Chief Marshal Sir William Windermere, Air Commodore Watchorn, Lieut.-Colonel Bullingham and Dr Hamburger, and furthermore in the implementation of any steps on which the Minister may find himself in a position to make a final decision after most careful consideration of the expert advice tendered to him.

I am, Reverend Sir,
Yours faithfully
Frederick L. Umpleby
Deputy Assistant Principal
Information Officer

"This looks as if they mean business," Hugh commented. "What will you do?"

"To-morrow is a holiday of obligation, Uisdean, and so I shan't be able to do anything at all. And nobody else will be able to do anything. I shall tell the people at Mass that nobody must hire a trap to them, and if they ask any questions nobody will be able to understand English. I think it will be just a wasted day for Sir William Windermere and his friends."

Hugh took his unopened letter. It was written by Mr Under-Secretary Wishart in his own hand.

Dear Hugh,

I'm sorry to cut short your holiday, but you must be back by Monday morning at latest. If you can get back before, so much the better. We have been having a lot of trouble with these Protection people. They cannot get it into their heads that Scots law is not the same as English law. I confess I'm worried. Fortunately the member for Inverness-shire (West) won't know how to take advantage of the situation or we might be faced with Labour gains all over the Highlands at the next General Election.

Yours sincerely,
Andrew Wishart

"You can't go away to-night, Uisdean," his host protested. "Besides, you'll be able to report to your chief on the situation here. Poor wee man, he's worried, is he? He'll be a lot more worried yet unless he can bring these up in the air marshals down to earth."

Chapter 6

ASCENSION DAY

THE Biffer was not at all anxious to bring the invaders over to Kiltod on that Thursday morning.

"I'll not be taking them in the *Kittiwake* at all. Drooby can take them," he told Roderick MacRurie, who had gone down early to negotiate a passage for his guests across the Coolish.

"Ach, now, Airchie, don't be so obastinate. They are big-tips; very important people from the Covernment. They'll bring a lot of money to Todaidh Mór and Todaidh Beag," the hotel-keeper pleaded.

"*Mic an diabhuil*, if they are here to bring us rockets, they can stay where they are," the Biffer declared.

"But they cannot be staying where they are when they are here," Roderick argued.

"Kenny Iosaibh was across early this morning. Why couldn't he take them over?"

"Och, it's what the *pàbanaich* on Todaidh Beag call a holiday of obbaligation. It's the same kind of thing as our Sabbath, Airchie."

At last the Biffer gave way and agreed to take the visitors over to Kiltod.

"But I'll not be sitting about all day waiting for them to go back to Snorvig," he insisted. "They'll say the time for me to come for them and if they're not there I'll not be waiting for them a minute. And the charge will be five pounds."

"*A Thighearna*, Airchie, that's a terrible price to be charging. I wass going to put it in the hotel pill."

"Ay, you were going to put five pounds in the bill, *a Ruairidh*, and give me three."

As this was exactly what Roderick had intended to do,

he had no retort, and with a sigh for the injustice of the suspicion he turned away to go back up to the hotel.

"Ten o'clock to the tot, Airchie," he called back.

However, the exploratory mission was not down on the pier at ten o'clock to the dot, because just as the members were getting ready to leave the hotel at a quarter-past, Paul Waggett arrived to introduce himself.

"Air Chief Marshal Sir William Windermere?" he asked.

The still yellowish moustache of the Air Chief Marshal ruffled itself like an aggressive canary.

"My name is Windermere, yes," he replied in a deep voice far removed from that of a canary.

"My name is Waggett. I am the owner of Snorvig House. I wondered if I could be of any help in showing you round the island?"

"The Air Chief Marshal is going over to Little Todday this morning," said the Air Commodore.

"Yes, I know, I was wondering if I could be of any help. I'm familiar with every inch of Little Todday. Wonderful for geese. I have the shooting, of course."

"I think we shall want to go round by ourselves," Dr Hamburger growled.

"Quite. Of course, everybody realizes why you are here," said Waggett with the knowing smile of a Port Said pimp. "And I thought you might like to know that everybody here hopes you will decide to make a rocket range here."

"Everybody seems to have more knowledge of our plans than we have ourselves," said the Air Chief Marshal gruffly.

"Little birds have long ears," said Paul Waggett, with what he believed was a knowledgeable smile. "But I thought after all that ridiculous fuss about the crofters at Balmuir you'd be glad to know that here in the two Toddays we should be delighted to be told that you had decided to make a rocket station here. Of course, there will be one or two people out of touch with what is happening in the world to-day who will try to make a fuss, but I can assure you the great majority will welcome you with open arms. They know what a little gold-mine for them it will be. Speaking for myself, although my sporting rights here have given me some of the best fishing and shooting in Scotland, I shall feel it is my duty to hand over Snorvig House for any purpose for which it may be required. I always say the country comes first every time."

"I'm afraid this is all rather premature," said the Air Chief Marshal. "We are here purely in an exploratory capacity."

"Quite, quite," Paul Waggett said, with that knowing smile. "Exploring every avenue, as they say. But I thought you'd like to know how keen the Todday people are. I commanded the Home Guard here during the war, and I can assure you there wasn't a keener body of men in the whole of Scotland. But, of course, I kept them on their toes. Well, I expect you're anxious to get across the Coolish. I don't know if you'd care to look in at Snorvig House when you get back for what we call a jockandorrus. Mrs Waggett and I would be delighted to welcome you."

"You speak Gaelic, Mr Waggett?" Dr Hamburger asked.

"Yes and no. I mean to say, I understand most of what the people here say to me, but they're unwilling to admit they can understand what I say to them. They're a bit slow, really. Mind you, I wouldn't actually call them stupid, but they are definitely slow in the uptake. They've been living out of touch with the world for so long. One must make allowances. They're lazy, too. Well, perhaps lazy is too harsh a word. But they procrastinate. For instance, if you want a window mended you may easily wait three years before you can get a carpenter to come along and do the job. I often say to Mrs Waggett how lucky it is that I'm pretty useful with my fingers. Otherwise we might have been without a roof by now. But I mustn't keep you back any longer. We'll expect you for drinks any time after six."

The Air Chief Marshal, the Air Commodore, Colonel Bullingham and Dr Hamburger set off with alacrity.

"That fellah's going to be a bit of a menace, Watchorn," said the Air Chief Marshal.

"Still, we have to keep in with fellahs like him, sir," the Air Commodore suggested. "He obviously has a good deal of influence here. I think we'd better go round for those drinks."

"You and Colonel Bullingham can go," said the Air Chief Marshal. "I think Dr Hamburger and I will give it a miss."

They hurried on down to the pier.

"Is this ten o'clock to the dot?" the Biffer asked.

"Yes, I'm afraid we're a few minutes late," said the Air Commodore. "But we were talking to your local laird."

"Local laird?" the Biffer repeated. "Who is *he* at all?"

"Mr Waggett of Snorvig House."

"Laird!" the Biffer ejaculated indignantly. "He's a fellow from London down in England."

"But he's been here a long time, hasn't he?"

"No time at all. Only just over twenty years. No time at all."

The party embarked in the *Kittiwake*, and soon she was chugging across the glassy Coolish in the warm May sunshine.

"You're even further from civilization here than they are in Balmuir," Colonel Bullingham observed.

"Where's that?" the Biffer asked.

"Where's what?"

"Civilization? Is that one of these new housing estates they have?"

"Civilization is not a place," the Colonel said with an obviously determined effort to be patient. Surely you must know what civilization is?"

"I know what civilization is here in the Islands. But I never heard you had that kind of civilization down in England."

The Colonel gave a glance at the Air Chief Marshal and shook his head. He hoped he was conveying to the higher peaks at 5 Whitehall Circus what a splendid job he was doing in trying to illuminate the darkness of these islanders' minds with the beams of official intelligence.

"So you don't think we're civilized down in London?" the Air Chief Marshal asked in that tone of indulgent condescension with which people in a position try to impress people not in a position with their keen sense of equality and fraternity without expecting any liberties to be taken as a result of such broad-mindedness.

"Och, it's not your fault," said the Biffer. "You're all too busy getting on in the world. You don't have any time for meditation."

"I'm afraid we shouldn't get very far in this world if we all went in for too much meditation," said the Air Chief Marshal.

"No, I believe you wouldn't," the Biffer agreed. "But you might get a great deal further in the next world."

A silence fell after this. Dr Hamburger looked balefully at Archie MacRurie. He had lived for many years in England, but he was still unable to understand why the English were so tolerant of backward peoples. And when they did try to behave like Germans, as in Ireland or Cyprus, they always feebly gave way in the end.

"There don't seem to be many people about," said Sir William Windermere as the *Kittiwake* drew near to the diminutive harbour.

"Ach, they'll all be in church," said the Biffer.

"In church?" Sir William echoed in amazement. "But it's Thursday."

"It's what they call a holiday of obligation in Little Todday," said the Biffer.

"What, a sort of Bank Holiday?" the Air Chief Marshal asked.

"No, no, it's something or other in their religion that the Roman Catholics have," the Biffer tried to explain.

"I tell you, sir," said Colonel Bullingham, flushing with indignation present and retrospective, "you've no idea what the Air Commodore and I have had to put up with at Balmuir with these so-called holidays of obligation. We have everything arranged for getting some of our stuff transported and nobody turns up. It's a holiday of obligation. And, mind you, the Protestants are just as bad. There's a minister at Gibberdale in East Uist who actually wants us to promise to abandon all work with guided missiles on Sunday. Yes, and not only that, but he has been successful so far in holding up work on the Mid Uist-East Uist bridge on Sunday. We might be working in the heart of Africa here, so remote are these people from—er—from . . ."

"Civilization," the Biffer muttered to himself.

"Of course, I know there has been a tradition in Scotland about doing no work on Sunday," the Colonel continued, "and so I suppose we have to expect a certain amount of old-fashioned opposition. But these holidays of obligation are just an excuse for rank laziness, and when I took the matter up with London, all I got was a rocket. . . ."

"A rocket?" the Biffer interjected. "If they have rockets in London, why do they want to have rockets in the Islands?"

"All I got was a reference to paragraph something or other in which it had been pointed out that it was the duty of every officer to do everything possible to avoid offending local religious feeling. No support of any kind."

"I'll enquire into that when I get back to the Circus," said the Air Chief Marshal. "We must try to see things in proper perspective."

"Quite, sir," the Colonel agreed.

"I mean to say, if we allow religious prejudice to upset our time-table we must get an Order in Council made compelling people to work on holidays of obligation, and on Sunday too if it comes to that."

"If you're after thinking that an order from the County Council will make the Wee Frees on East Uist work on the Sabbath you'd better be thinking all over again," the Biffer advised.

Before Sir William Windermere had been able to find a way of explaining in simple language to a native what an Order in Council was, the *Kittiwake* came alongside the steps of Kiltod harbour and it was time to disembark.

"We don't know exactly how long we shall be," Air Commodore Watchorn told the Biffer. "But we'll probably be ready after we've had a cup of tea this afternoon."

"Better say six o'clock. Don't forget, you and Bullingham are going to have drinks with that fellah, what's his name," Sir William turned to say. "Dr Hamburger and I will go straight back to the hotel," he added firmly.

"O.K. Six o'clock. Does that mean on the dot or off the dot like this morning?" the Biffer asked.

"Six o'clock sharp. We have to be back in Snorvig soon after half-past."

The Biffer watched the exploratory mission walking along the road toward the post-office, took his gurgling pipe out of his mouth and spat slowly into the water of the harbour. He was reflecting on the curiously low level of the Sasunnach mind.

"There doesn't seem to be anybody about," said Sir William when the exploratory mission reached the door of the post-office.

"Joseph Macroon, licensed to sell beer and spirits to be consumed off the premises," Colonel Bullingham read. "What's the next move, sir?"

From the towerless church of Our Lady Star of the Sea and St Tod on the top of the tallest brae in the island some sixty feet above the sea came the sound of singing.

"There's a bunch of people outside the church door," the Air Commodore pointed out. "Shall one of us go up and ask when the service is likely to be over?"

"I'll go," said Colonel Bullingham. He knew the responsibilities of junior rank.

Presently the Colonel returned, his countenance clouded, his prominent pale blue eyes popping.

"I can't get a word out of them. There were about a

couple of dozen chaps in jerseys kneeling round the open church door, and all I could get out of them was a shrug. And one old boy who was monkeying about with a lot of beads looked at me as if I was the devil incarnate and hissed at me. It sounded like 'whist'."

"Whist?" the Air Chief Marshal exclaimed. "They can't be having a whist drive at this hour of the morning."

"No, sir, of course not," said Colonel Bullingham, as irritably as a lieutenant-colonel can venture to be with an air Chief marshal. "I think he was trying to tell me to keep quiet because there was a service in progress."

"It looks like lack of co-operation, I'm afraid," said Sir William sadly. "What had we better do?"

"We might walk over to this beach on the other side of the island," Colonel Bullingham suggested. "Try Swish I'm told they call it."

"Ha-ha," Sir William guffawed. "Jolly good name for a rocket range, what?"

Dr Hamburger eyed the Air Chief Marshal sourly. He disliked extremely the English habit of making jokes about serious subjects.

"The trouble is," said the Air Commodore, "that this beach is about four miles away. We ought to hire a car."

"MacRurie, the hotel-keeper chap in Snorvig, told me there weren't any cars on Little Todday. There used to be a lorry, but the people complained because it upset their cattle," Colonel Bullingham said. "We'll have trouble here of course over the cattle unless . . ." he stopped.

"No, no, we mustn't mention that possibility yet," said the Air Chief Marshal quickly. "Well, what I suggest is that we wait until these people come out of church, get an early spot of lunch and hire a couple of traps to drive us over to Try Swish. Mind you, it isn't really necessary for us to see it. I accept the reports we've had about its suitability without hesitation. Our job to-day really is to tell the people here what a wonderful thing it would be for them if the Ministry decided to give them a rocket range. We still have to decide where the airfield is to be sited, but there again we shall have to accept the advice of our experts. Benthall, who was here for a day last week, said the whole island was an airfield. When do you reckon you'll get your first guided missiles off from Balmuir, Colonel?"

"I can't give you D Day for Operation Whizz yet, sir, but probably early next year."

"Jolly good! I shall try to come over myself. I think it encourages the chaps who get stationed on those outlandish places off the map if the people at the top show a practical interest in what they're doing. I don't suppose poor Wensleydale will still be Minister of Protection then—he's been at the Circus for nearly three months now—but there'll be his successor, of course, and I shall try to get him to come. Well, it took a long time to convince these politicians that the only way to get our chaps back from Germany was to let the Yanks see we really mean business with guided missiles. But I think Bermuda convinced them!"

"We may get a revival of that agitation we had over the Uists when the announcement is made about the Toddays," the Air Commodore observed.

"We may, but that announcement we made about protecting the St Kilda wrens and rats and what not did a lot to reassure people. No cats and dogs to be kept by the chaps stationed there. Yes, that announcement did more to reassure people than anything. They realized that we were absolutely aware of our responsibilities. Mind you, I think it was a mistake not to have provided alternative accommodation for these chaps we've had to turn off their crofts at Balmuir. After all, it oughtn't to have been difficult for the Scottish Office to provide them with a temporary place—I mean to say, prefabs aren't such a tremendous problem as all that."

"Quite," the Air Commodore agreed. "But these fellows at the Scottish Office have always been anxious to pass the buck to us."

"What surprises me," said Dr Hamburger, "is why you have a Scottish Office as you call it. Scotland is the same as England, isn't it?"

"Well, of course, it is really," Sir William agreed. "But Scotchmen are awfully touchy if you don't call them British. Americans hate calling us English because they call their own language English. But on the Continent they call us all English, which annoys the Scotch and the Welsh."

"But if you must have this Scotch Office," Dr Hamburger asked, "why must you call it Scottish?"

"I really haven't got the answer to that one, but, as you know, whisky is called Scotch, and that may have been the reason. I wish I knew when these people were coming out of church."

Sir William Windermere was beginning to feel mentally exhausted by his attempt to explain to Dr Hamburger the need for a Scottish Office, and like so many Englishmen he felt that his brain required the stimulus of a little physical exercise.

"We might take a stroll over beyond the church to see where we expect to site the airfield."

After strolling over the machair for half a mile, the exploratory mission paused to survey the pastoral scene.

"There's hardly a contour more than thirty feet high," the Air Commodore observed with satisfaction. "A couple of bulldozers will level this in next to no time. And at a rough guess I don't think it will mean knocking down more than about thirty houses."

"We've had rather unpleasant scenes in West Uist," Colonel Bullingham reminded the Air Commodore.

"Yes, I know, but the whole business was mishandled from the start," Air Commodore Watchorn argued. "The crofters at Balmuir were led to suppose we shouldn't want more than two hundred acres, and so of course when they found we wanted over two thousand they tried to dig their toes in, supported by a lot of cranks with nothing better to do than get their names in the papers. And now that we have started to put them out of their houses and wire off their grazing there has been a good deal of bitterness. If we'd made it clear from the start what we intended to do, the people in Balmuir wouldn't have had a leg to stand on. As it is, one Parliamentary Under-Secretary of Protection after another gets up and says we made it perfectly clear to the crofters from the first what we wanted, which makes it look as if Bullingham and I were a couple of liars. Luckily Macaulay, the Socialist member for West Inverness-shire, seems anxious to keep in with us. He may be hoping to be Parliamentary Under-Secretary for Protection when his party gets back into power, and so he's made it clear to Parliament that opposition to the rocket range has been cooked up by a lot of cranks."

"And the B.B.C. were helpful, weren't they?" asked Sir William.

"Oh, definitely," said the Air Commodore. "Nobody would have supposed from the B.B.C. that the people in West Uist were not all delighted by the prospect."

"But we should never have promised that public enquiry," said Colonel Bullingham. "After all, we knew perfectly well that for security reasons we couldn't ever consent to a public enquiry."

"Quite," Sir William agreed.

"Some busybody would have been bound to ask why if we were merely going to experiment with guided missiles we couldn't experiment somewhere else. We should have found it pretty difficult to avoid the suggestion of the real reason for choosing these islands. . . ."

Sir William put a chubby forefinger to his lips.

"The less said about that at present the better. It was difficult enough to get Operation Whizz accepted for these Uist islands, but it's going to be much more of a job to get Operation Buzz accepted. By the way, I hope there aren't any rare birds on these Todday islands. These bird-watchers are a fearful nuisance. Ever since they heard Lord Alanbrooke liked watching birds, they seem to think they can protest against the Services disturbing birds anywhere. Ah, there they are coming out of church. I think we'd better go along and call on the Reverend Macalister."

The exploratory mission made its way in the direction of the chapel house. At first the members offered greetings of synthetic cordiality to the natives who passed them, but the natives were so very native that they seemed unaware of being greeted and went on talking to one another in Gaelic.

"Extraordinary language, isn't it? I suppose you're getting quite used to it by now, Colonel?" Sir William asked.

"I can't think why it wasn't stamped out long ago," said the Colonel gloomily. "It may be a serious problem when security has to be tightened. I mean to say, a couple of Russians may come round trying to pry out what we're doing and our fellows will think they're talking Gaelic."

"Oh, well, of course the Ministry has wide powers," said the Air Chief Marshal soothingly. "And as soon as Operation Whizz is fully operative we can always make the three Uists a protected area, which will mean that nobody except those resident on the islands on a certain date will be able to land on them without applying for a permit a month in advance."

"Won't that cause more agitation?" Air Commodore Watchorn asked.

"I don't think so," said Sir William. "If the taxpayer has to pay for the Ministry of Protection, he'll want to feel sure that he is being protected. He can't be expected to worry because a few tourists get held up."

Soon after this confident prediction of public apathy about a few more rules and regulations, the exploratory mission reached the chapel house and the members were shown into Father Macalister's room, where Hugh and Jane were sitting.

"Father Macalister asked me to tell you that he will be with you very soon. He's still over in church at the moment," said Hugh.

"Haven't I seen you before somewhere?" Colonel Bullingham asked.

"Yes, I met you and Dr Hamburger at Nobost last March. I'm Mr Andrew Wishart's Private Secretary."

"Did he send you here to-day from the Scottish Office?" the Colonel asked suspiciously.

"No, I'm here on holiday. Oh, I'm sorry, gentlemen, let me introduce you to Miss Kinsella."

Sir William Windermere's moustache was still yellowish enough to respond gallantly to the sight of a pretty girl.

"Are you on holiday, too?"

"No, I'm here on business," said Jane.

"On business?" the Air Chief Marshal asked in amazement. "Business, did you say? There can't be any business here."

"I'm a folk-singer."

This was too much for the Air Chief Marshal altogether.

"I see," he murmured in bewilderment.

Luckily he was spared the strain of trying to look as if he understood what Miss Kinsella was talking about by the entrance of the parish priest, who was in his cassock.

"Ah, how d'ye do, padre. I'm Air Chief Marshal Windermere. I think you were notified by the Ministry of Protection of our visit."

The Air Chief Marshal looked doubtfully round at Hugh and Jane.

"You'd rather we were not present, sir?" Hugh asked quickly.

"Stay where you are, Uisdean," Father Macalister boomed. "What I say may be used in evidence against me, and I wish you to stay. But Jane, you'd better go along. Norman Macleod wants to talk to you about this evening."

Jane left the gathering, but the Air Chief Marshal was still worried by the presence of somebody who was not a member of the exploratory mission.

"This is not a Scottish Office matter, padre," he said.

"Just a matter for Scotland, and so you think that lets the Scottish Office out," the priest commented. "But I don't think so. And therefore either Mr MacInnes stays or I shut my mouth."

"I must make it clear to Mr MacInnes that he will not be entitled to make a report of our talk to the Under-Secretary," said Sir William. "We are an exploratory mission, and it would be highly irregular if anything that was discussed to-day was brought to the notice of the Scottish Office before we make our report."

"I'm afraid, sir, I cannot undertake not to give Mr Wishart an account of what happens here," Hugh said. "I am returning to-morrow night, and I shall be seeing Mr Wishart at the earliest possible moment."

"No final decisions have yet been taken by the Ministry, and it might be extremely prejudicial to a satisfactory solution of any problems that may arise out of such steps as the Ministry may feel compelled to take in the public interest if the various bodies concerned receive what may be an entirely inaccurate account of our intentions."

The Air Chief Marshal blew his nose.

"I'm sorry, sir," Hugh replied. "But if Father Macalister refuses to discuss matters with you unless I am present, I cannot withdraw. If in such circumstances you are unwilling to continue with the proceedings that will be your decision."

The Air Chief Marshal blew his nose again, and turned to Father Macalister.

"Well, padre, I'm afraid we arrived while you were holding a church service."

"It is the Feast of the Ascension," said the priest.

"Ah, yes, of course. I didn't realize you kept these sort of occasions on week-days, except of course Good Friday. The Ascension, eh? We must remember that another time."

"The Ascension of our Blessed Lord," the priest said sternly.

"Quite, quite."

"Not the ascension of rockets," he added. "And let me tell you, gentlemen, that you are going to find it very difficult indeed to make rockets ascend from Little Todday."

"Let us be clear about this, padre. Are you suggesting that you will obstruct the efforts which the Minister of Protection is making to ensure the safety of our country?" the Air Chief Marshal asked in tones of pained surprise.

"I am not suggesting it. I am stating it as a positive fact," said Father Macalister.

"You tried to make that clear at the meeting held in Nobost last March," said Colonel Bullingham, his pale blue eyes popping.

"I certainly did."

"Now, do not let us get worked up," Sir William urged. "Surely you realize, padre, that the Minister of Protection would not contemplate any interference with the life of an island, however small, unless he had been convinced by his expert advisers that such interference was necessary in the interest of the country at large?"

"But the Minister's expert advisers have not taken the trouble to convince the people of Little Todday," Father Macalister pointed out.

"Well, to be frank, that is one of the reasons why we thought it essential to pay a call on you and explain why it *is* necessary. The people of West and Mid and East Uist have recognized the paramount claims of security, and although we are all aware there was a feeling in West Uist that some of the crofters had been led to believe that the demands made upon their land would be smaller than in the event they have turned out to be, I am happy to tell you that there is no longer any opposition to our plans."

"Because you are going to evict all those who do object," said Father Macalister.

"Do not let us argue about that," Sir William pleaded. "We are anxious that in the case of Great and Little Todday there should be no misapprehension. Therefore we think it is right you should know that it is the intention of the Ministry of Protection to construct a rocket range on the west coast of Little Todday and an aerodrome across the centre of the island. However, it is not proposed to house the three or four thousand personnel on Little Todday. These will be stationed on Great Todday, where I am glad to say they seem to welcome the idea, realizing what financial and other benefits will accrue. I should add that compensation will be paid to those crofters on Little Todday who may have to give up their houses and land. There will of course be a certain amount of selected personnel stationed on Little Todday."

"The Americans," observed Father Macalister.

"The Americans?" repeated Sir William, trying to look as if he had never heard of America.

"The Americans who have to guard these rockets that are going to knock sparks out of Russia at fifteen hundred miles an hour."

"I'm not aware of any proposal to station American troops here," the Air Chief Marshal said.

"I believe you, Sir William, though thousands wouldn't. But no doubt those two Prosperos in the still-vex'd Bermoothes weren't aware of any such proposal until they met and talked it over."

Sir William Windermere, not being a Shakespearian scholar, had to admit he did not understand what Father Macalister meant by his last remark.

"Ah, well, well, the Greeks often didn't understand what the Oracle of Delphi was talking about and came to grief in consequence. But do you know what a dinosaur was, Sir William?"

"A large reptile now extinct."

"*Glè mhath.* Very good indeed. You ought to be in Round Britain Quiz on the B.B.C. Ay, ay, the dinosaur was just that. But why did it become extinct?"

"Ask me another, padre. I'm afraid I'm not a naturalist,"

said Sir William, trying not to feel as Henry II felt about Thomas à Becket.

"I'll tell you. The dinosaur became extinct because its body became too large and too heavily armoured for its tiny little head to manage. And every empire will go the way of the dinosaurs for the same reason."

"I always supposed that Roman Catholics were strongly anti-Communist," said the Air Chief Marshal.

"Oh, they don't like Communism at all. But we're not so much against common sense."

"That's the first time I ever heard Communism called common sense," Colonel Bullingham interjected. "But we live and learn."

"Ay, ay, Colonel, and very often we live and don't learn, but we shall certainly all die and learn. Well, I'm sure you'll be wanting to get on with your business. No doubt you'll soon be surveying Little Todday and we'll do all we can to hinder you to the best of our ability. You may find a few people on Great Todday to help you at first, but not the best of them. You weren't very clever in the way you handled the three Uists. You shouldn't have funked that public enquiry, because when you did, we all realized that you had an uncomfortable secret which couldn't be revealed until the two Prosperos had met on the still-vex'd Bermoothes. Well, well, gentlemen, good-morning to you."

"I suppose we can get a bite of lunch at that place near the harbour?" Air Commodore Watchorn asked a little anxiously.

"I really don't know," Father Macalister replied. "Joseph Macroon may not feel inclined to provide lunch on a holiday of obligation."

When the exploratory mission had left the chapel house, Father Macalister turned to Hugh with a profound sigh.

"Oh, well, well, Uisdean. God forgive me, that's the first time in all my life that I refused hospitality. Not even a dram did I offer them."

"There was no earthly reason why you should have offered them even a dram."

"But I had a terrible fight with myself not to. *A Dhia*, I felt like the Levite in the parable. And I doubt if Joseph is going to play the Good Samaritan."

Chapter 7

THE EXPLORATORY MISSION

FATHER MACALISTER'S forecast was correct. Joseph Macroon, as a great favour, offered the exploratory mission two 4-oz. packets of milk chocolate and a pound of digestive biscuits which had remained unsold since Christmas, when Joseph had bought them as an experiment. His customers had decided that they tasted more like chicken food than biscuits and the experiment had been a complete failure.

"And I suppose you can let us have four bottles of beer?" Air Commodore Watchorn asked.

Joseph Macroon tugged speculatively at his red woollen cap.

"Would you be promising to return the bottles?" he asked. "The pollis are very strict. I wouldn't like Sergeant MacGillivray to be thinking I'd been serving towrists with beer to be drinking all over the island."

With a promise that the empty bottles should be returned, the exploratory mission was provided with four bottles of ale.

"And what about a conveyance?" the Air Commodore asked. "We want to get across to Try Swish, as I believe you call it."

Joseph Macroon shook his head.

"I don't believe you'll find anybody to drive you to Tràigh Swish. It's a holiday of obligation, and the people don't like taking hires on such a day."

"But there were several traps waiting outside during the service," the Air Commodore said.

"Ay, but they've all driven away back home long ago. Ach, it's a very pleasant walk across the machair. You needn't be tiring your feet on the road."

So with the milk chocolate, the stale digestive biscuits and the four bottles of ale, the exploratory mission set out westward. After walking for about a mile, the members decided to sit on the side of a grassy knoll and eat their lunch.

"It's funny how one's tastes change," Sir William murmured pensively. "I remember at my prep. school, we thought there was nothing so jolly good as milk chocolate. It didn't seem at all sickly then."

Dr Hamburger was trying to dispose of a digestive biscuit, on his lip the vicious curl of a camel.

"These people are worse than the Poles," he growled. "You know, Sir William, that man Macalister is dangerous."

"Oh, I don't think he's dangerous. He may talk a lot, but in England we like agitators to talk; we find the more you let 'em talk the less they do."

"Colonel Bullingham and I heard that priest talking in Nobost last March," Dr Hamburger said. "And there's no doubt that the audience was paying attention to what he said."

"Far too much attention," Colonel Bullingham growled.

"What was he saying?" the Air Chief Marshal asked.

"He was talking to them in their own language. And in my opinion, sir, if we're going to have any security we shall have to forbid this Garlic being spoken," Colonel Bullingham declared.

"What we proposed to do here will be more secret than anything we are doing in Balmuir . . . at present," Dr Hamburger reminded the Air Chief Marshal, who looked nervously over his shoulder.

"I say, I hope there isn't anybody on the other side of this sand-dune," he murmured.

Colonel Bullingham jumped up and walked rapidly round to the other side, where he found a couple of crofters seated side by side in close conversation.

"How far is it from here to Try Swish?" he asked sternly.

The two crofters looked at him and shrugged their shoulders.

"Can't you understand English?" he demanded.

The two crofters looked at one another and then simultaneously turned their eyes on Colonel Bullingham with an expression of utter blankness, if such utter blankness could be called an expression. Colonel Bullingham returned to the other side of the knoll.

"There are two fellows there," he said angrily. "Both pretending they can't understand a word of English."

"Just like Poles, as I was telling you," Dr Hamburger commented.

"Perhaps we'd better be walking on," the Air Chief Marshal said. "I'm jolly glad we didn't say anything about Operation Buzz, what?"

An hour later the members of the exploratory mission were gazing down at the long white beach of Tràigh Swish from the top of the rolling line of dunes that barred the sand from encroaching on the machair.

"We couldn't have anything better, could we?" Sir William asked, almost in the tone of a pious diner saying grace after a good meal. "But don't let us be under any delusions. Operation Buzz is not going to be a joy ride. And of course we don't know yet if the Americans will agree to storing their nuclear warheads here, even if we do evacuate both islands. However, one thing is obvious. We must go ahead with our plans on the supposition that they will agree. The decision about evacuation won't have to be taken till next spring."

"What happens if this priest fellow stirs up the people to sabotage our work here during the next months?" Colonel Bullingham asked.

"We'll get his bishop to transfer him to some parish on the mainland," said Sir William. "Bishops are always anxious to work in with the authorities."

"This would be a Roman Catholic bishop, sir," the Air Commodore reminded him. "He may be another Archbishop Makarios."

"Well, if he's too troublesome we can always deport him," said Sir William jovially.

"I doubt if people in this country would stand for deporting an R.C. bishop," the Air Commodore demurred.

"I don't mean the bishop, Watchorn. I mean the padre here. But don't let's cross bridges before we have to. I think the people here will be perfectly amenable. But we mustn't make the mistake that was made at Balmuir. We must stir up these Scottish Office fellows to have alternative accommodation ready for them. You remember that chap in the boat thought civilization was one of the new housing estates. There's the answer. Why, it would be paradise for them to live on a new housing estate after the struggle for existence they've had for centuries in these islands."

"I think we might bury these damn bottles in the sand here," the Air Commodore suggested.

"No, no, better not," Sir William said. "We gave a promise to return these bottles, and it might make a bad impression if we went back on our word. But what I should like to do is to find a house where they'd make us a cup of tea. I always tease my wife about her insisting on tea, but I'd give anything for a cup now. It may be that milk chocolate."

"Or those biscuits," said Dr Hamburger, on his lip that camel's curling sneer again.

The exploratory mission had tried a couple of houses on the way back without being able to make the inhabitants understand what the members wanted. Then when they were beginning to despair of the refreshment they craved they met Duncan Bàn, who, noticing the bulges in their pockets, jumped to the conclusion that they were carrying flasks of whisky and at once answered their enquiries in English.

"Thank goodness to hear a civilized language again," Sir William ejaculated. "Aren't the children here taught English?"

"Och, yes, they're very well taught indeed by Mr Macleod the schoolmaster in Kiltod," Duncan assured him. "But they'll be shy of talking it to such great men as you'll be seeming to them. But if it's a cup of tea you're wanting, I'll take you to the house of Mistress Odd. She's an English woman."

"Oh, that's capital," said Sir William.

"I'd take you to Tigh a' Bhàird," said Duncan. "But there's not a drop in the house."

Duncan had hoped by this statement to see four hands simultaneously move in the direction of their pockets, but the hands did not respond, and presently the exploratory mission arrived at Bow Bells.

"Mistress Odd, Mistress Odd," Duncan shouted. "Here's four benighted rocketeers holding out their tongues for a cup of tea."

"But aren't we trespassing on your hospitality?" Sir William asked when the old lady opened the door and greeted them with, "It's a long way to Tipperary, but come right in, you wandering Willies."

"Well, well, *ma tà*, I'll be getting back," said Duncan. "I'll be round by seven to drive you and Jane down to Kiltod for the *cèilidh*."

"I wonder if it would be possible for you or anybody else to drive us down? The boat expects us at six," said the Air Commodore.

"I won't be able to," Duncan replied. "And I don't think anybody else will, unless maybe the fairies."

With a wave of his hand and one backward contemptuous glance at the bulges in the pockets of the exploratory mission, the bard vanished.

Mrs Odd went to the kitchen to tell Florag Bhàn about tea, and when she came back the members of the mission were still standing.

"Oh, for Pete's sake, do sit down," she exclaimed. "Make yourselves at home, even if you do have to hop off almost at once. I suppose you're here to sniff out the lay of the land, eh? It's a pity my son Fred isn't here. He used to be a sergeant-major in the Queen's Fusiliers, and during the war he was telling the Home Guard how to crawl about on their tummies and give that blinking Hitler what for. But what a pity Winnie isn't in charge any longer! What a man! The living spit he was of a bulldog my old dad won in a raffle, voice and all. Yes, they've been a poor lot lately. I didn't much care for Starling myself, but any old way he was a man. I don't reckon old Kruschen Salts is much good. And this Dulles. Well, he is dull, and that's a fact. And now you think you're going to put everythink right by shooting off a lot of rockets on Little Todday like a parcel of kids on Guy Fawkes night playing about in a waste ground. Ah, well, I suppose men never will grow up."

The Air Chief Marshal asked Mrs Odd if she lived on Little Todday all the year round.

"I usually go down for the winter to Nottingham, where my son Fred has his shop, but I shan't go away this winter. Oh no, if you think you're going to pull down my house while I'm away down in Nottingham, you're mistaken. Very much mistaken. I'm staying put, as they used to tell us in the war. And what's more, I'll stay put whatever you do. You'll have to tie me on to the tail end of one of your rockets if you want to see the last of me."

"But, Mrs Odd, if—and it's still very much if . . ."

"There's more sniff than if about it, I reckon," Mrs Odd interjected.

"If the Government should finally decide that the security of the free world . . ."

"Free world? With bus fares what they are to-day? Don't make me laugh."

"If the security of our own country made it absolutely necessary to put a rocket range on Little Todday, surely you as the mother of an old soldier would do all you could to set an example to the people here?"

"Security? Yes, I don't think. Do you suppose these Russians will be soppy enough to wait for you to start letting off rockets here to give them a Brock's benefit over in Moscow? Of course not. They'll start in first, won't they?"

"We are using guided missiles as a deterrent, Mrs Odd.

The Russians won't attack us if we are prepared. We can't afford to have them threatening us with guided missiles as they did during the Suez crisis," said Sir William.

"Yes, that was a nice disgrace. Tut-tut. Rule Britannia? Rule Britanniar I *don't* think!"

"I agree," said Sir William. "It mustn't be allowed to happen again."

"I've been hearing that ever since the Bore War. But it always does happen again, and if you think turning a happy island like this upside down is going to stop it happening again, well, that isn't thinking at all really, it's just being potty."

"Well, we musn't start an argument about that," said Sir William. "If the Government decides that Little Todday is vital for the defence of the country, you may feel sure, Mrs Odd, that wiser people than you *or* me have taken that decision. I'm appealing to you now to do all you can to persuade the people here that this project, *if* it comes off, will benefit them."

"Now, don't be silly, Mr . . . here, what *is* your name?"

"Windermere. Air Chief Marshal Sir William Windermere."

"How can it benefit anybody to be turned out of his house the same as you did to the people in West Uist? If I started in telling them it would be for their good they'd think I was crackers. And so I would be."

"But this project will give a lot of work to most of the people. Only some of the crofts might have to be taken over."

"Work? What kind of work? Navvies' work. Do you think a fellow with six good cows of his own wants to turn himself into a navvy for a year? I daresay there may be places in these islands where the people would be glad of extra work, but they wouldn't suit your convenience."

"It's not our convenience that is in question. It's the suitability of the site which we have to consider in the public interest. I couldn't explain to you why we have to choose Little Todday, because . . ."

"Because I'm an ignorant old woman. That may be so. But I'm not so ignorant as not to know when anybody's trying to use soft soap. And you can lather me all over, Mr Sir William Windermere, but you won't find I come out of the wash any different to what I am now. And, thank goodness, here comes your tea, because in another minute or two I might have said something a bit rude. So let's drop the subject. Sugar for you?"

"None for me, thanks," said Sir William.

"Sweet enough without it, eh?" Mrs Odd chuckled. "Yes, I bet you was a rare one for the girls before the silver threads started trickling into that moustache of yours. Sugar for you?" This was said to Dr Hamburger.

"Thank you, no."

"And you look as if three good lumps of sugar would do you a lot of good," Mrs Odd said. "You haven't got a motto always merry and bright, that's one sure thing."

"This is Dr Emil Hamburger," Colonel Bullingham said severely.

"Oh, he's a doctor, is he?"

"And this is Air Commodore Watchorn," the Colonel went on.

"Pleased to meet you. Sugar?"

"Two lumps, please," said the Air Commodore.

"And I am Lieutenant-Colonel Bullingham, commanding the 1st Ballistic Regiment."

"The what? I never heard of it. Any relation to the old A.S.C.? Ally Sloper's Cavalry as we used to call them."

"It is the Royal Army Service Corps to-day," said the Colonel.

"It is, is it? Well, I always heard my son Fred call it Ally Sloper's Cavalry."

"Mine is a new regiment raised only last year."

"Ah, I thought it sounded like an early turn. I must write

and tell my son Fred about that. He won't half laugh. Ballipstick Regiment, eh? How do you spell it."

"B-a-l-l- . . ."

"Yes, I got that bit," Mrs Odd chuckled, "it was the lipstick at the end I haven't got."

"B-A-L-L-I-S-T-I-C."

"And what's this new regiment for?" Mrs Odd asked.

"Guided missiles," said the Colonel sternly.

"I see. Her Majesty's Rocketeers. Well, if you want to be sure of being down in Kiltod by six o'clock, you ought to be getting a move on pretty soon."

"We are much obliged to you for giving us tea, Mrs Odd."

"Will you let us know how much we owe you?" the Air Chief Marshal asked.

"How much you owe me?" Mrs Odd exclaimed. "You don't owe me nothing. I'd give Old Nick himself a cup of tea, but you don't think I'd take his money? If you listen to an old woman's advice you'll think again before you start in knocking about Little Todday, because as sure as eggs is eggs you'll be in for trouble if you do."

"The people on Great Todday aren't of your opinion, Mrs Odd," said Air Commodore Watchorn.

"Oh, I don't doubt but what you'll get quite a few people on Great Todday to tell you that everything in the garden's lovely. I'll lay every lorry-driver in the island sees himself as Lord Nuffield the Second with the money coming to him. And I lay all the girls are rocking and rolling with joy already to think of American G.I.s handing out nylons and chewing-gum and cigarettes. But it won't be that easy on Little Todday. Little Todday's got Father Macalister, as you'll very soon find out. Well, tootle-oo, all. And I hope it is tootle-oo and not just or revore."

The exploratory mission left Bow Bells to find its way back to Kiltod.

"Quite a character, that old woman," the Air Chief Marshal commented pensively.

"A bit too much of a character, if you ask me," said the Colonel. "When do you think we shall be able to start work here, sir?"

"You'll be occupied with Operation Whizz for some months yet," Sir William reminded him.

"Quite, sir, but I hope they'll be getting on with the job here meanwhile. I'm hoping that we can announce Operation Buzz by next spring and get the islands emptied before the following winter. By the way, it's occurred to me that we might make Buzz appear as an act of consideration on the part of the Government."

"How do you mean?"

"The danger of radiation, sir."

"No," Dr Hamburger snapped. "We don't want to admit that there is the slightest danger of radiation. We don't yet know where we might not want to establish guided missile sites."

"Yes, I think Dr Hamburger is right there, Colonel. There's undoubtedly a growing prejudice all over the country against what these pacifists call making us an advance guided missile base for the United States. We know how unreasonable these pacifists are, but we don't want to give them any excuse for agitating. My own feeling is that we ought to have agreed to a public enquiry about what we were proposing to do in West, Mid and East Uist before the result of the Bermuda meeting was published. We could have denied any intention to do anything more than practise with our own guided missiles. Now we are not in a position to do that, and a public enquiry might be, indeed would be, a tricky business."

It was ten to six when the exploratory mission reached Kiltod. The first task for the members was to establish the reliability of their pledges by returning the empty ale bottles to Joseph Macroon.

"He was evidently rather surprised when we handed back his bottles," said Air Commodore Watchorn.

"Yes, but I think it made a distinctly good impression,"

Sir William agreed. "Trifles like that count for a lot with simple folk."

"Simple folk?" Dr Hamburger exclaimed. "They're as cunning as Polish peasants."

"I'm inclined to agree with Dr Hamburger, sir," said Colonel Bullingham. "I've learnt a lot about these simple people since I've been in Balmuir. Ah, there's the fellow with our boat. Punctual, too, for a wonder."

The members of the exploratory mission walked down the steps of the slipway and went on board the *Kittiwake* with a sense of relief. Little Todday had been a tiring and unprofitable experience.

"And how did you get along?" the Biffer asked.

"Oh, we managed to convey to Father Macalister what we wanted to convey," the Air Chief Marshal told him.

The crossing of the Coolish went by in silence. The exploratory mission was feeling tired by its eight or nine miles of walking on milk chocolate and digestive biscuits.

"Were you having your dinner with Maighstir Seumas?" the Biffer enquired.

"Is that some kind of local dish?" the Air Chief Marshal asked, with an effort to sound interested.

"Maighstir Seumas is Father James. He's not a dish."

"Oh, Father Macalister you mean? No, we didn't have a meal with him," said Sir William.

If the exploratory mission had been able to read the expression in the Biffer's eyes, it might have been shocked. Archie MacRurie, indeed, was reflecting to himself that Father James must have considered his passengers lower than hoodie crows if he had withheld from them his hospitality. He indulged in a slow thought-weighted spit overboard, and remained silent until they reached the Snorvig pier.

"Five pounds, eh?" said Air Commodore Watchorn. "Will you get it from the hotel? Mr MacRurie said he would put the hire on the bill."

"I'd rather be paid direct," the Biffer said. "I've nothing to do with the hotel."

Between them the members of the mission collected the money before they disembarked.

"I don't believe he even gave them a dram," the Biffer said to himself as he watched his passengers walking wearily up the steps to the top of the pier. "They must be terrible trash, right enough."

At the hotel, Sir William reminded the Air Commodore and the Colonel that they were expected at Snorvig House.

"You'll tell Mr Waggett how sorry Dr Hamburger and I were not to be able to take advantage of his hospitality. You can tell him that we had rather a strenuous day."

"Do you know what we call him in the R.A.F.?" the Air Commodore asked Colonel Bullingham, as they walked on up to Snorvig House. "We call him 'Bill Buttermere'."

Paul Waggett came to the door of Snorvig House to receive his visitors.

"Isn't the Air Chief Marshal coming?" he asked, in a tone faintly touched with pique.

The need for the Air Chief Marshal to rest after his strenuous day was dwelt on tactfully.

"Yes, I was rather afraid you might have difficulty over transport. The Roman Catholics over on Little Todday make quite a fetish of these holidays of obligation. I'm afraid they're just an excuse for old-fashioned slackness."

Mrs Waggett, a faded blonde with an expression of permanent appeasement, the result of being married to a husband like Paul Waggett for over thirty-five years, produced a tray on which was a bottle of gin, a bottle of Italian vermouth and a bottle of sherry, but no whisky. The Air Commodore and the Colonel thought enviously of the powerful whiskies and sodas that the Air Chief Marshal and Dr Hamburger were doubtless drinking at this moment down in the hotel.

"I'm considered rather a good hand at mixing a cocktail," said Waggett, pouring out three glasses half of gin and half of vermouth. "I'm afraid we've run out of ice. Our refrigerator has been misbehaving. Shall I pour you out a sherry, old lady?" he enquired, turning to his wife.

"Oh, thank you, Paul, that would be lovely," she gushed gratefully.

"Is Father Macalister a friend of yours, Mr Waggett?" the Colonel asked.

"Oh, of course I've known him for many years. You called on him?"

"He wasn't very co-operative," the Colonel said.

Waggett shook his head.

"I was afraid of that. He's hopelessly behind the times. I've tried to explain the difference between nuclear fission and nuclear fissure to him. There was a good article in the *Digest of Knowledge* which I offered to lend him, but it's hopeless, he just doesn't pay the slightest attention. And I've tried to explain to him the way a guided missile works, but it's no use; he's entirely wrapped up in his own ideas, and they were old-fashioned before the Kaiser's war. Yes, I'm afraid you'll find Father Macalister a strong opponent of any plan you may have to develop our defences on the two Toddays."

"Do you think Father Macalister could make things difficult for us?" the Air Commodore asked.

"He would certainly have a lot of influence with his own people. And even on Great Todday he would find support among the older people. We have a very stupid old doctor here called Maclaren, and George Campbell, the headmaster of Snorvig School, gets more and more stupid all the time. His brother-in-law, Norman Macleod, is the headmaster of Kiltod. Did you meet him? No? Well, he's definitely a disturbing influence. He used to be an open Bolshie, and then during the war when he was serving in the R.A.F.—on the ground, of course—he met a Roman Catholic girl in Preston and became a Roman Catholic himself to marry her. Of course, as a Roman Catholic he can't be an open Communist, but in my opinion he's fundamentally as much of a Bolshie as he ever was. He's absolutely Red inside."

"Was he ever a member of the Communist Party?" the Colonel asked, a gleam of hope in his prominent eyes.

"I wouldn't go so far as to say that positively, but you'll be wise to have him screened. When do you think you'll be starting work in these islands?"

"No decision has yet been taken whether we are going to bring the Toddays within the scope of the rocket scheme," said Air Commodore Watchorn.

"Oh, I'm not trying to pry into secret plans," Waggett protested. "But I thought you might be glad to know that if it is required I should be willing to let the Protection authorities take over Snorvig House. It would be a wrench for me to part with it, wouldn't it, old lady?"

Mrs Waggett, whose heart was beating a little faster at the prospect of being able to leave Great Todday to go and live near one of her married daughters, assumed a slightly strained expression of mental distress.

"Indeed it would be, Paul," she assured him.

"But, que voulez-vous?, as they say in France," Waggett continued. "In times like these we must put our personal feelings on one side. As soon as I read what the Prime Minister and the President had arranged in Bermuda I realized that no sentimental considerations could be allowed to stand in the way of making the Outer Isles the keypoint of our defence of the Free World. And do you know what Norman Macleod, that schoolmaster in Kiltod, called the communiqué the Prime Minister and the President issued from Bermuda? He called it a suicide pact. I heard him myself. I was so angry that I told him he was a disgrace to the teaching profession. I can assure you that when I'm angry I don't mince my words. Do I, old lady?"

"Indeed you don't, Paul."

He looked round at his visitors with a complacent smile.

"There you are," he told them. "And now let me give you both another of my cocktails."

Chapter 8

THE END OF THE DAY

HUGH and Jane had planned to picnic beside Tràigh Swish on the afternoon of that Ascension Day, but the arrival of the exploratory mission had made them choose instead a small remote beach on the north-easterly side of the island.

Duncan Bàn had driven them to where the track across the machair led to Bàgh Mhic Ròin, or Macroon's Bay, half a mile east of which was Tràigh nan Eun, or the Beach of the Birds.

"You'll find your own way back?" Duncan had asked. "I want to keep an eye on these suspicious characters from the outer darkness."

Hugh and Jane had told him they would find their way back to Bow Bells, where Jane would be changing her frock for the ceilidh and whence Duncan would drive herself and Mrs Odd to the Kiltod hall that night.

"He's a happy man, isn't he?" Hugh said as they stood for a moment or two watching Duncan's trap jogging south. "We take him for granted, but for a chap who was doing as well as he was doing at Glasgow University to chuck it all up and live on his own croft in order to write poetry was a bit of an achievement in the way of unworldliness. Father James thinks the world of him."

"I wish he weren't so fond of the glass," Jane sighed.

"It's only himself he harms," said Hugh.

"That's true enough, but it's such a lovable self, and I can't bear it to be knocked about."

They walked on until they came to Tràigh nan Eun, which was a small sandy beach formed by a semicircle of grassy knolls, to the top of one of which they climbed and there sat entranced by the solitude and beauty of the scene.

Northward the ocean was deep blue, but between them and the tiny island of Pillay the sea had the green of a cowslip's spathe. Pillay itself was a fantastic pile of basalt, the dark cliffs of its easterly face restless with a myriad guillemots, razor-bills, kittiwakes and fulmar petrels. Midway in the passage between Pillay and the pastoral expanse of Little Todday a black rock was upthrust. This was the Gobha, or Blacksmith, on which the famous whisky ship the *Cabinet Minister* had been wrecked during the last war. On the sand of Tràigh nan Eun oyster-catchers were whistling to hail the turn of the tide and the prospect of a meal.

"Jane?"

"What is it?"

"Will you marry me?"

She turned and looked at him with those blue eyes of hers which seemed to him as large as the ocean that was spread out beyond them.

"But we've only known each other for seven days."

"I could have asked you when we'd only known each other seven minutes, but I was afraid you'd think asking girls to marry me was a habit of mine to while away a sea-crossing."

"I'm sure I would have thought that."

"But you don't think that now? Jane, will you marry me?"

"I never meant to be married till I was at least twenty-five."

"But I shall be over thirty then," Hugh protested. "Jane, I really am madly in love with you. It's just one of those things."

"And there'll be such an argument about mixed marriages," she murmured. "It's one of Father Keegan's phobias."

"I suppose he's your parish priest at home?"

She nodded.

"Och, he's terribly narrow-minded over some things."

He took her hand.

"Jane, darling Jane. Do you love me? I've hoped you did

ever since you sent that telegram from Nobost. But I couldn't be sure it wasn't because I loved you so much that I couldn't imagine your not loving me. Jane, *do you* love me?"

"I suppose everybody will tell me I haven't yet grown up, but I just feel as if I'd known you all my life," she said with a little gesture of finality.

"Then you do love me, because that's exactly what I feel about you."

He drew her to him for their first kiss.

At that moment, three miles away, Air Chief Marshal Sir William Windermere was wondering why he had liked milk chocolate when he was at his prep. school.

"We'll tell Father Macalister, and he can announce our engagement at the ceilidh to-night," Hugh declared with enthusiasm.

"No, no," she protested. "I'd just faint with embarrassment."

"You wouldn't do anything of the kind. You'd sing one of your lovely songs better than you ever sang it before."

"You know, Hugh, for an Englishman . . ."

"I'm not an Englishman," he expostulated.

"For a Scotsman, then, you're awfully like an Irishman."

And certainly on that knoll above the sea Hugh was not conforming to the recognized behaviour of Fettes and Trinity College, Oxford, on such an occasion. To make the first announcement of his engagement to a gathering of Hebridean islanders was not what a Rugger international with that background might have been expected to do.

"Ethne Jane MacInnes! It sounds absolutely marvellous, doesn't it? I said to myself this morning when you were in church that if you did say you would marry me to-day I would suggest you came back with me on Saturday to our house so that you could meet my mother and father, but now I think it would be better if I told them about you and then my mother can write and ask you to come and stay with us. You see, I'd like them to simmer down after being told I'm going to marry a Catholic. Mind you, they're not a bit bigoted. We're Piskies, as a matter of fact."

"Piskies? What are Piskies?" Jane asked in bewilderment.

"Episcopalians. Yes, I think we'd both better break the news at home separately. Then I thought that perhaps I could come over to Dublin and show your people what I'm like. Your father's a doctor, isn't he? Do you think he'll object to me?"

"He's terribly interested in football."

"Oh, that's good," said Hugh in a tone of relief. "And on the material side I ought to be able to satisfy him, especially when I tell him I've decided to go into my father's business instead of taking up politics as a career. Then when I've been inspected and approved of I'll take you back with me to Greystones."

"To be inspected and perhaps disapproved of," Jane said.

"No, darling. They'll adore you. How could they help it? No, the only argument I'm likely to have with my father is over these rockets. He has a passion for thinking that people in the Government must be right. Let's face it, that's what they gave him a knighthood for last year."

"And your mother?"

"She's rather a pet. A little possessive. But I suppose mothers with only one child are often rather possessive."

"That doesn't sound too good for me," Jane murmured thoughtfully.

"Darling, she'll love you. I know that. But I say, don't let's waste any more of this marvellous day talking about other people. Let's talk about ourselves."

And this they continued to do until it was time for Jane to be going back to Bow Bells, where she was to rest for an hour before she put on a white dress to be driven with her hostess to the ceilidh.

"Well, Mrs Odd," said Hugh, "you're going to be the first person to hear some wonderful news. Jane and I are engaged to be married."

"I'm not a bit surprised," said the old lady. "I'd have

been very surprised if you hadn't have been. Well, this I will say. Never in all my life did I ever see two persons who was more cut out for one another than what you two are. Oh dear, it was May 1895 when Ernest Odd asked me to be his one and only, and I remember it like it was yesterday. We was walking along the Fulham Road and suddingly Ernest stopped and pointed to a playbill stuck in a shop window. 'See that, Lucy?' he said. 'The Importance of Being Earnest,' he said. 'So what about it, Lucy Eddowes?' he said. 'What about what?' I said. 'The banns go up next Sunday, that's what about it,' he said. And sure enough I was married in the first week of June. And except I got some rice down the back of my neck, it couldn't have been a nicer wedding. We went to Margate for our honeymoon, but Margate in June! It was just dead and alive. Still, we enjoyed ourselves. And you'll enjoy yourselves. But look here, young Jane, engaged to be married or not, what you'll do now is go and lay down for an hour before you tart yourself up for to-night. What an afternoon I had with those rocketeers. Duncan Bang brought them along and asked could I give 'em tea because they was starving. So I gave them tea and a bit of my mind with it. I didn't dislike the old geezer with the silver threads among the gold. He had a gay eye, oh, a very gay eye. But Percy Pop Eyes, oh, I didn't like him at all."

"Percy Pop Eyes?" Hugh repeated.

"Yes, you know, the fellow in Fred Karno's army who says he's a Colonel of the Ballipsticks."

"Colonel Bullingham," Hugh said. "No, I don't like him."

"Oh, he's a bad 'un. And I didn't like that peculiar fellow with a back of the head like a doorstep and nobs all over his forehead."

"Dr Hamburger. He's a German."

"A German, is he? We're a funny lot in England, aren't we? First of all we start saying the world won't be a fit place for anyone to live in till every German is dead. And then we turn round and treat them like pets. Yes, it's all very nice to say we must forgive our enemies, but that doesn't mean we must forget our friends, and which we very often do. But I mustn't go on yattering like this, and you'd better be hopping along back to Kiltod."

Hugh came near to following Mrs Odd's advice literally, with such elation was he filled; and half-way to Kiltod he had to make a detour in order to avoid overtaking the exploratory mission before its weary members reached the harbour. He and Father Macalister stood in the tiny garden of the chapel house to watch the *Kittiwake* carry them away.

"You'll be reporting to Mr Wishart on Monday, Uisdean?" the parish priest asked.

"Indeed I shall. But I'm afraid they're bent on going on," Hugh said. "It's a plan which they must have made long ago. Father James, I've something to tell you. Jane Kinsella has promised to marry me."

"Good shooting!" the priest boomed. "God's blessing on you both. Come right in, my boy, and we'll drink to your happiness with a dram of the old and bold."

"There's one thing which worries us both a bit," said Hugh when the drams had been emptied. "Jane's a Catholic and I'm a Protestant."

"You'll give an undertaking that any children of the marriage will be brought up as Catholics?"

"I will."

"And you'll hold fast by that promise?"

"I most certainly shall," Hugh declared emphatically.

"Then the Church will bless your marriage, and your wife will pray for your conversion."

"I couldn't become a Catholic myself unless I were convinced . . ." Hugh hesitated.

"I'm glad to hear it, my boy. We don't want people to become Catholics out of politeness."

"Jane is a bit worried about the attitude of her parish priest, Father Keegan."

"I'll write to Father Keegan," said Father James, in his deep tones as much assurance as if he were speaking for His

Holiness himself looking down benignly from his picture over the fireplace.

At this moment there was a knock on the door and Norman Macleod came in. The headmaster of Kiltod school was now in his mid-forties, but with his swirl of dark hair and bright brown eyes and clear-cut profile he did not seem much older than when he was the schoolmaster at Watasett in Great Todday and so light-hearted a poacher of Paul Waggett's sporting rights.

"Another mixed marriage, Norman," said Father James. "Uisdean here is going to marry Jane."

"Och, my marriage didn't stay mixed very long, Father. I was swallowed up pretty soon," he laughed. "But I'm glad," he said, offering Hugh his hand. "It's the only good bit of news I've heard to-day. Have you seen this dirty article in the *Inverness Times*, Father James?"

"Read it to me, Norman," said Father James.

"'The agitation started by a few sentimentalists against the Government's splendid project to help the economic life of the Western Isles has proved the fiasco that we confidently anticipated when it was first started nearly two years ago. The Government was well advised to reject the demand for a public enquiry after such responsible bodies as the Inverness-shire County Council, the Highland Panel and the Crofters' Commission had all refused to press for such an enquiry. Do these "Highlanders" from Edinburgh and London and Manchester consider that they are entitled to pit their sentimental politics against the judgement of men whose experience of Highland and Island problems has led them to welcome so gladly the prospect of many millions of pounds being spent upon bringing the Western Isles into close touch at last with modern life. Electricity, water, roads, bridges and perhaps even television, are these gift-horses to be looked at in the mouth? Are 4000 young National Service men doing their ballistic training in West, Mid and East Uists to be regarded as barbarian invaders from the world of to-day? We are happy to know that the people of the three Uists have no such feelings, and it was most unfortunate that a few crofters should have allowed themselves to be transported to an English television studio operating in the interests of advertisement in a misguided attempt to confuse public opinion.'"

"Ay, ay, misguided missiles," Father James murmured.

"'We have had occasion in the past to criticize the way in which the B.B.C. has sometimes presented Highland affairs, and therefore we are all the more pleased at being able to congratulate the B.B.C. on the care it has taken both in television and sound broadcasting to bring before the viewing and listening public of Scotland the wishes of the great majority of the Islesmen. Furthermore, we have no hesitation in stigmatizing as a mischievous fabrication the rumour that in refusing to air the petty grievances of the insignificant minority on the three Uists who set their personal feelings above their patriotic duty the B.B.C. was submitting to pressure from the Government.'

"'Those who had accused the Government of a piece of hasty and ill-considered vandalism must have wished that they had kept silent when they heard of the praiseworthy assistance afforded to the Ancient Monuments Department of the Ministry of Works by the Air Ministry. As a result numerous wheelhouses dating to the Iron Age in the first centuries of the Christian Era have been excavated, and also a Viking long house of the tenth century. It is hoped that some of these may be preserved, but should necessity dictate that launching-sites for guided missiles require their destruction archaeologists will have the gratification of knowing through photographs more about these remains of former inhabitants of the three Uists than they would otherwise have done because the requisite funds for excavation had not hitherto been available.'"

"Good shooting," commented Father James. "They'll destroy the houses of living crofters without mercy, but they'll do their best to preserve the houses of those who vanished fifteen hundred years ago. Yes, indeed, Norman, it will be a great consolation to us when they turn Todaidh Beag into a pancake that they'll be very careful to photograph any wheelhouses that lie under our machair."

"'Another instance of Government consideration,'" Norman Macleod read on, "'is to be found in the prohibition of all pets on St Kilda, where the personnel of the Radar station will not be allowed to keep dogs or cats in order to avoid any threat to the peculiar fauna of the island.'"

"I hope they won't interfere with that peculiar gun," Father James murmured, with a mocking expression of anxiety.

"Is there a gun on St Kilda?"

"Indeed there is, Norman. A huge great gun. It was landed on Armistice Day in 1918 to protect the island against German submarines. But I'm afraid it won't be a great deal of use against Russian rockets. Go on, my boy."

"'We do not overlook the temporary inconvenience that may be caused to a few crofters at Balmuir by the necessity to cut off some of their grazing and in one or two cases even to take over their houses. We are in sympathy with the hopes of Sir Robert Davidson, the member for North Sutherland, that they will receive ample compensation. We are, indeed, strongly in favour of generous financial assistance being afforded by the Government to enable any crofters deprived of their houses to emigrate to Canada. We repudiate with indignation the parallel that a few ignorant Socialist politicians in the Lowlands have drawn between the Sutherland evictions and the requisitioning "in the public interest" of a few crofts. There is no parallel to be drawn between sheep and guided missiles. It was well said recently by a Government speaker that the Western Isles should be proud of being chosen for the part they will play in the defence of the United Kingdom, and one may take this opportunity of congratulating Mr Thomas Macaulay, the Labour member for Inverness-shire (West), on his ability to convince the House of Commons that the opposition to the choice of the three Uists as a ballistical training-ground was inspired by a few sentimental cranks.'

"'We do not hesitate to affirm that the guided missile range on West Uist is the greatest contribution any Government has made to the economic prosperity of the Western Isles. A bright future hitherto undreamed of now stretches before them, which we hope that without irreverence we can compare to Moses' sight of the Promised Land.'"

"Ay, ay, poor old Moses," Father James put in. "But he had one great advantage. There was no Mr Dulles to obscure the view from Sinai. Go on, Norman."

"'The future is bright indeed, and the ratepayers of Inverness who have had to bear so much of the burden of the Island economy may feel without undue optimism that the weight of that burden may soon be lightened. We are not surprised that our friends in Ross-shire cast envious eyes upon this project, and we hasten to add that Invernessians will rejoice if future developments should enable the Government to extend to Lewis the benefits of this noble project for the defence of the Free World. This need not be considered an idle dream. Already we hear strong rumours of an extension of the Government's activities to islands south of the Uists, and we express our fervid hope that these rumours may prove to be founded on something more solid than wishful thinking.'

"'After that memorable meeting in Bermuda when the Prime Minister and the President of the United States, addressing one another affectionately as "Mac" and "Ike", decided to make the Western Isles the first line of defence for the Free World, there was no patriotic Scotsman whose heart did not beat proudly at the news. Not again will Bulganin threaten us with Muscovite missiles and by such a threat suggest to the world that we had cleared out of Suez because we were frightened. Thanks to the foresight of the Ministry of Protection, the Prime Minister was able to convince the President that we were in a position to make use of any guided missiles the United States would send us.

That the nuclear warheads are to be guarded at first by American soldiers is not surprising. However, we have every confidence that as the mighty project grows our American friends will see that the Western Isles afford opportunities for security unmatched anywhere in the Free World, and we may expect that the British Government will rightly take the fullest advantage of such opportunities. We are proud to remember that Mr Macmillan is the great-grandson of a Highland crofter.'"

"Oh, well, well," Father James exclaimed with a sigh that was like a coronach. "*A Dhia nan Gràs*, we must have a snifter to take away the taste of all that oil."

"Oil, is it, Father?" Norman Macleod jeered. "Not at all. It is boot-blacking you're after tasting. The *Inverness Times* has been licking the boots of those in authority for so long that I believe the paper is printed nowadays with boot-blacking instead of printers' ink."

Father James poured out three drams of malt whisky.

"It's pretty clear they've got something up their sleeves for Todaidh Mór and Todaidh Beag," Norman Macleod said. "We mustn't make the mistake they made at Balmuir by not getting a clear-cut statement about what they intended to do. We mustn't let ourselves be led up the garden path."

"After their success in the Uists," Hugh said, "they're feeling much more sure of themselves. They made no bones about what they intended to do here. But I'm worried about that frankness. I think they may be hoping that there will be resistance here, in which case they will find an excuse to make their great experiment."

"And what is that?" Father James asked.

"I'm afraid I can't tell you, because I got to hear of it in my capacity as Mr Wishart's Private Secretary and it wouldn't be fair to him if I told you. What's worrying me is whether you will be playing into their hands by resisting or whether if you don't resist you will find yourselves in the same position as they're in now at Balmuir. Don't forget that when those chaps get back to London they'll be able to say that Great Todday is delighted at the notion of being turned into a training-camp. Look how they've cashed in on the welcome they will receive from Mid Uist and East Uist, and even from those in West Uist whose future has not been directly jeopardized by the rocket range. I'm really in a bit of a fix at the moment. I'm going back now to give my resignation to Mr Wishart because, valuable though it might be, if I had inside information about what is going on behind the scenes I couldn't use such information without feeling I wasn't quite playing the game."

"No, no, it wouldn't be cricket," Father Macalister agreed. "That's where the English have always got the better of us. They always play cricket. But they take good care to have a couple of umpires in white coats to see that nobody cheats. I'm not going to press you to tell me what you've heard, Uisdean. But on Little Todday we shall resist from the start. Your conscience is as clear as a bell, my boy. There's nothing you could say would change that resolve."

"Nothing," Norman Macleod affirmed.

"And now let's forget about these Barbarians from the outer darkness. We're going to have a great evening. Music and love—*ceòl agus gaol*—will come from the West till the day of the seven whirlwinds. But, by Jingo, the day of the seven whirlwinds may not be far away when the world is full of guided missiles. The *seachd siann*. I've always translated it as the seven whirlwinds, but *sian* also means a whizzing sound through the air. *A bhobh bhobh*, we must make the best of *ceòl agus gaol* to-night. It may be the last chance we will have."

The ceilidh had been announced to begin at eight, and so by half-past nine one of the Todday pipers was able to open the proceedings to a packed hall. Hugh had thought every day during this magical week that Jane had never sung so exquisitely as she was singing at whatever moment he was listening to her, but to-night, with a large audience to support his opinion, he could feel justly convinced that indeed she never had sung so well. Yet with all the elation of a successful lover, with all the pride he felt in the delight that the audience took in his loved one, Hugh could not shake off the apprehension that haunted the back of his mind throughout. While Jane was singing he could escape from it into what seemed a world of impregnable beauty and peace, but when her voice was silent the leaden cloud upon the future of this island weighed his spirit down. The very enthusiasm that greeted Father Macalister's announcement of the betrothal was poignant, and the murmured response of the people when he bade them pray for the happiness of Uisdean and Seonaid brought him not far away from tears.

It was hard on midnight when Father Macalister stepped forward to bring the ceilidh to an end with a few words. It had been a wonderful evening. Apart from the delight that Jane had given with her songs, the performers of the island had all excelled themselves. The story-tellers had never told their stories so vividly. The pipers had never piped with such fire. The other singers, although all protesting against being asked to sing when there was such a singer as Jane to hear, had never sung so well themselves.

When Father Macalister began to speak in Gaelic, Hugh caught hold of Jane's hand and held it.

"Oh, if only I could follow what he was saying," he almost groaned.

That his hearers were spellbound by their parish priest's eloquence was obvious in the way that they seemed to rise and fall upon his words like a boat upon the water, and when he ceased there was complete silence before they rose simultaneously to their feet and acclaimed him.

But before he brought the evening to a close Father Macalister turned to Hugh and Jane:

"I have told them, Uisdean, that we will resist having our island murdered by the powers that be for the sake of making it easier for them to murder other people. We have seen other islands surrender: we will never surrender. We will not be bribed by promises of the wonderful glorious wealth that will come to us. When I was in the arms of my mother, God rest her soul, the men and women of Skye fought the Marines sent by the Royal Navy to frighten them, and the men of Lewis beat off the Royal Scots with sticks and stones. What the crofters of Lewis and Skye did once upon a time, we can do again. Like them, we can go to prison, and I'll be the first to go. You can tell them that in the Scottish Office. Little Todday belongs as they think to the Department of Agriculture, and so the notices to quit our crofts will certainly be served; but the real owners of Little Todday are the crofters themselves, and that's a lesson the Department will have to learn."

Yes, it all sounded wonderful, Hugh thought as he walked up towards the chapel house after seeing Jane off with Mrs Odd in Duncan Bàn's trap, and he had no doubt that Father Macalister with the unanimous support of his parishioners would prove a hard nut to crack. But the nut *would* be cracked. How could one little community hold out to-day against an implacable bureaucracy supported when required by subservient Members of Parliament?

There was still even at midnight a dim afterglow in the west, but black night was coming up over the bens of Great Todday. Against that glow the figures of the islanders bound for home seemed unsubstantial as ghosts.

Chapter 9

HUGH AND JANE

MUCH to Hugh's relief, the members of the exploratory mission had left Snorvig for Nobost on the following afternoon. So he and Jane did not have to bother about them when they boarded the *Island Queen*.

"By Chinko, that wass pretty quick, right enough," Captain MacKechnie squeaked when they told him that they were engaged. "And you'd never seen one another in your life till you sailed with me last Wednesday week. When are you going to marry yourselfs?"

"We hope, this autumn."

"Well, I'll be marrying myself to the land next October," said Captain MacKechnie. "Ay, ay, that'll be the end of me in the old *Island Queen*. Forty-fife years, and in October I'll be taking her across to Snorvig and to Nobost for the last time. Ach, I'm not looking forward to it at all. How wass Father Chames?"

"He was in splendid form," said Hugh. "I think these rocketeers will find him a bit of a handful if they try to turn Little Todday into a rocket range."

"Ach, the country's gone mad," Captain MacKechnie spluttered. "Well, well, I wish you both the old wish. May all your troubles be little ones, though my goodness, what a world to bring little ones into!"

Jane and Hugh parted next day at Renfrew Airport, whence she was to fly by Aer Lingus to Ireland.

"You don't think you'll wake up in Dublin, darling, and tell yourself it was all a dream?" he asked anxiously.

"I may sound a bit vague sometimes, but I'm not so vague as all that, Hugh," she assured him. "But is it yourself you're thinking of? Are *you* going to wake up at home to-morrow morning and think it was all a dream?"

Hugh's countenance tried to display compassion for the temporary derangement of his young love's brain, and then the loud-speaker was heard announcing the number of Jane's flight. He held her in his arms for a moment, and sat waiting alone until the droning of the Eire plane died away on the bright air.

It was tea-time when Hugh reached Greystones, a long low house which stood on the slope of a wooded hill overlooking the village of Langley with a wide view of the lush Border country beyond.

"Your father's not back yet from golf," Lady MacInnes told him.

Hugh looked a little apprehensively at that exquisitely dressed little woman presiding over the tea-table and pulled himself together to take the plunge.

"Mother, I'm engaged to be married."

"Hugh! But why didn't you tell us before you went off on this island trip of yours?"

"Because I only met her last week on the boat from Obaig."

"I never heard of anything so . . . so . . . well, really I can't find a word for it. Who is she?"

"Her name is Ethne Jane Kinsella. . . ."

"She's not an Italian?" Lady MacInnes broke in.

"No, no, she's Irish."

"Irish? Not a Roman Catholic, I hope?"

"As a matter of fact she is," Hugh said.

"Oh, Hugh, Hugh, what will you be doing next?"

"Marrying her, I hope," said Hugh.

"But who is she? What is she?" his mother asked, blowing through a silver instrument like a pea-shooter and extinguishing the flame of the spirit-lamp over which the tea-kettle was suspended.

"She's tall and very slim and extraordinary beautiful . . ."

"Yes, yes," Lady MacInnes interrupted sharply. "That's not so important."

"I think it's extremely important," her son insisted.

"She's the daughter of a Dublin doctor, and she's a wonderful singer. She accompanies herself on the clarsach."

"On the what?"

"It's a small harp."

Lady MacInnes turned up her powder-blue eyes with a sigh of maternal despair for her only child's sanity.

"Is she a professional singer?"

"Well, she is and she isn't, if you know what I mean," Hugh said.

"I haven't a notion what you mean," his mother declared.

"Well, Jane has had some engagements to sing folk-songs, and until she met me she was hoping to go to Milan and be trained for opera. But she has more or less given up that idea now. She's only twenty. Oh, and I've decided to give up politics. I'm going to tell Andrew Wishart when I get to London on Monday that I'm resigning as his Private Secretary."

"I suppose this young woman objects to politics," Lady MacInnes commented bitterly.

"It's nothing whatever to do with Jane," Hugh assured her. "Absolutely nothing. I can't stand the humbug that politics let you in for if you expect to get anywhere in politics. I'm going to ask Father to let me go into the business. I hope he'll be pleased."

"You know he'd set his heart on your having a political career," Lady MacInnes said reproachfully.

"Mother, do let's be honest with one another. It was you who had set your heart on that political career, and Father has always done what you wanted."

"I don't understand the younger generation," she declared.

"Mother darling, you're not so old as all that. You're not fifty yet. You were a bright young thing in the mid-twenties when parents were all saying they couldn't understand the younger generation. I'm sorry to disappoint you about politics, but I've seen enough of them since I was at the Scottish Office to know that I shouldn't get anywhere. Oh yes, I should be given a safe Tory seat in due course because of Father's money and commercial influence, but I'm not prepared to spend my life voting as I'm told to vote."

"You've not become a Communist?"

"No, no, no," Hugh said impatiently. "You don't have to become a Communist to feel misgivings about the future of the Conservative Party. What has finally made up my mind is this outrageous plan to make the Outer Isles a base for guided missiles. I think it's a crime against the people of Scotland . . ."

"So you've become one of these idiotic Scottish Nationalists, have you? Really, Hugh, I do think you might have a little consideration for your father and me."

"I haven't become anything at all politically. I think I can do more for my country and myself as an exporter of spun wool. I should have come to that decision if I'd never set eyes on Jane. I'm fond of Andrew Wishart, but as his P.S. I hear of projects which I consider will be disastrous for the country and I cannot stand the strain of having to be officially ignorant of them."

"I don't know what your father is going to say. You're not proposing to get married as fast as you got engaged?". Lady MacInnes asked anxiously.

"I'd rather counted on September," her son replied. "But that'll depend on how Father takes to the notion of my going into the business. I want to earn money, not just live on an allowance."

"And when are we to be allowed to meet—Jane you call her—it's not my favourite name for a girl—and you say she's tall?"

"Taller than you, Mother darling. But that's not difficult to be. I'm sorry you don't like 'Jane'. She uses her first name when she sings."

"Yes, what was that?"

"Ethne."

"I never heard the name before."

"It's Irish."

"It would be," said Lady MacInnes. "But you haven't answered my question. When are we to be allowed to meet her?"

"I thought of going over to Dublin in a month's time. I'll have to give Andrew Wishart a month to find another P.S. And then if Jane's family approves of me I suggest I bring her back here for you to get to know her. Of course, she may have difficulty over this mixed-marriage business. Catholics don't like them much."

"I see you're already half-way to Rome yourself, Hugh. Catholics indeed! *We* are Catholics. You mean Roman Catholics. Well, I never thought I might one day be the grandmother of a lot of little Roman Catholics. Hugh dear, are you sure this engagement isn't just the result of a sudden infatuation?"

"I fell in love with Jane at first sight," said Hugh gravely. "And I am absolutely positive that I shall always love her."

"Oh well, I suppose we must just make the best of it," his mother sighed.

He jumped up and sat down on the floor beside her knee. "I knew you'd understand, Mother darling." He caught hold of her hand, and she leant over to kiss his forehead.

"Hullo, hullo. You two look very happy," said Sir Robert MacInnes, coming into the room at that moment. "I've just had a wonderful round. Seventy-eight, Hugh. I haven't been round in seventy-eight for three years."

"I say, that's splendid, Father."

"Hugh's got engaged and wants to be married in September, Bob," Lady MacInnes announced.

"And I want to go into the business," Hugh added.

"What, and give up your political ambitions?" Sir Robert exclaimed with a quick look in the direction of his wife. "Well, we must discuss this bombshell of yours later."

That evening father and son talked over the future together, and at the end of it they were in accord.

"It's no use my pretending I'm not glad you're coming into 'MacInnes', old chap," said the head of the firm. "Your mother has been awfully good about it, but it's no use pretending it hasn't been a blow to her."

"It won't be when she sees Jane," Hugh prophesied confidently.

"Mothers always have great ideas for their sons, especially for an only son. Still, it's your life, and if you choose wool instead of Whitehall I'm not going to say you haven't made the better choice for a MacInnes. After all, you *have* played for Scotland. We have had that satisfaction. You know, everything went right for me this afternoon, Hugh, and strictly between you and me—don't breathe a word to anybody—I'm told they're likely to make me Captain of the Royal and Ancient next year."

"That would be marvellous, Father. I say, my knees will tremble for you when you drive off from the first tee at St Andrews."

"I shall feel a bit wobbly myself. You know our sixteenth? Well, believe it or not, Hugh, I was down in three. Tom Fletcher couldn't get over it. 'You're growing younger, Bob, instead of older,' he said to me."

"I shall take up golf seriously when I'm married," Hugh vowed.

"Does—er—Jane play golf?"

"I never heard her say so. You'll have to teach her."

"I never could get your mother keen on golf. I suppose she hadn't really got the reach."

"Jane's pretty tall."

"Ah, then, we ought to be able to make a golfer of her."

And on that optimistic note father and son parted for the night.

Hugh caught the night train at Kirkshiels; and next morning at Euston, preoccupied with the news he had to break to Mr Andrew Wishart in two or three hours' time, he left an ivory shoe-horn in the sleeper, which, on the principle of British Railways that anything left in a sleeper is a natural perquisite for the cleaners, he never saw again.

The Under-Secretary was obviously delighted to have him back.

"Ah, there you are, Hugh. We've been having a terrific battle with these Protection people. They're definitely going to take over the two Toddays for their rockets, and almost at once, but they're still hankering after evacuating the islands. Not at once, but next spring . . ."

"Sir," Hugh broke in, "please don't tell me any more."

"Why, what's the matter?"

"I'm afraid I must ask you to accept my resignation. I won't go for a month, though if you could get another P.S. before that I'd be grateful. I'm engaged to be married."

Hugh explained the circumstances to his chief, who tried to sound as congratulatory as a harassed Under-Secretary can who foresees that his next Private Secretary will almost certainly be some promising junior Civil Servant from St Andrew's House.

"And so I'd be grateful, sir," Hugh said, "if you didn't confide in me any secret intentions you may have heard about. In point of fact, what was called an exploratory mission arrived in Little Todday last Thursday: Air Chief Marshal Sir William Windermere, the Air Commodore and that pop-eyed Colonel from Balmuir, and that humourless Teuton, Dr Emil Hamburger. They've been talking over with Father Macalister—you remember him at the Nobost meeting—the project to put an aerodrome and a rocket range on Little Todday. I was told by Sir William that I mustn't tell you anything of what was said until they had sent in their report to the Scottish Office. I refused to give him any such assurance, but as Father Macalister refused to discuss matters unless I was present, they had to put up with my hearing what they had to say."

"You didn't say a word to Mr Macalister about this plan to evacuate the people from both islands?" Mr Wishart asked anxiously.

"No, sir, of course not, and that's why I don't want to hear anything more about it. In any case, I think the Government will have trouble enough on their hands when they try to start operations in Little Todday, for there's not a man, woman or child in the place who won't do all that's possible to make things difficult. Great Todday at the moment is rather enamoured of the idea, but of course they won't be having the range and they won't be having the aerodrome, and everybody will be trying to dispose of unsuitable land for cultivation as suitable sites for barracks, with handsome compensation. The spokesmen for the Government may get up in the House one after another and assure Parliament that the Western Isles acclaim the Government's plan with gratitude, but they won't be able to hide from the country what Little Todday thinks, because Little Todday will act. Of that I am absolutely certain. The people at Balmuir were tricked at the beginning, but Sir William and his friends have been quite frank about their plans for Little Todday—except of course about the possibility of evacuating the entire population."

"I'm afraid there's no doubt about these plans," Mr Wishart said. "The Government have decided to gamble on guided missiles, and they have put forward a plausible case. After all, we cannot afford to have the Russians threatening us as they did at the time of the Suez business. We must be in a position to threaten them. I wish with all my heart . . . dear me, I made a quite involuntary pun on my own name . . . I regret very much that the Western Isles have been chosen as the site for this deterrent, but we must bow to expert opinion. *Si vis pacem bellum para*, as the old Latin tag says."

"I remember another Latin tag, sir. *Solitudinem faciunt pacem appellant*. I remember it because I once had to write it out a hundred times for hitting the chap who was construing Tacitus at that moment with a paper dart which was intended for the back row of the form, but turned itself into a misguided missile. *Solitudinem faciunt pacem appellant*. Yes, they're going to make a desert of the Western Isles and call it peace."

"I think desert will be the last word you'll be able to apply to the Islands when they're full of these chaps training for ballistic warfare," said Mr Wishart. "But don't misunderstand me, Hugh. I feel just as strongly as you do about this rocket business, but what can we do? If we could trust the Russians . . . but we can't. They mean to rule the world, and we and the United States have got to stop them."

"And by the time they're ruling what's left of the world, the Chinese will step in and rule them."

"I never heard you talk like this, Hugh."

"No, but one or two people on Little Todday started me off thinking last week. And I suppose I was in the mood to be started off because I'd met the girl I was going to marry, and I began to wonder what the world would be like by the time my children were grown up. However, sir, you won't have to put up with my struggles to start educating myself, and please believe me when I say how really sorry I am to leave you. You've been more than decent to me. But now it's about time I got down to answering a few letters. I saw a formidable pile in my room."

Mr Wishart shook off the menacing question that lay at the back of the minds of so many Conservative politicians at this time. Was he the member of a Government which one day would be blamed by history for the ruin of their country?

"Well, they may accuse us of premature senile decay," he said to himself, "but they'll find that a Labour Government will be suffering from rickets."

He was pleased with this epigram, which he noted down for a future speech to the electors of North Lennox.

Luckily for Hugh, Mr Wishart was reconciled to the idea of a Civil Servant as his Private Secretary, and so he was able to go over to Dublin a fortnight sooner than he had hoped and face the ordeal of approval by Jane's family. It turned out to be no kind of an ordeal at all. Dr Kinsella was a popular Dublin physician whose Georgian home was a resort of good conversation almost every evening. His wife, from whom Jane had inherited her figure and her looks, had decided in her mid-forties that the secret of a comfortable middle-age was not to worry about anything. Jane was the eldest of a family of five. One brother was at the National University: another brother was still at school; her two sisters were at school. Father Keegan, who no doubt had been prepared to be critical, was completely reassured by Hugh's obvious honesty of purpose. The engagement was announced. Two or three columnists interviewed the happy pair, and there were photographs of them in two or three of the Dublin papers.

Hugh had wanted to arrive in Dublin with the ring, but Jane had asked him to wait until their engagement was announced.

"We must get one before we're photographed," he insisted.

So they went to a jeweller's, where they had their first argument.

"But I don't want a grand ring, Hugh."

He had set his heart on an oblong sapphire.

"This isn't at all grand," he insisted.

"Hugh darling, look at the price!"

The jeweller was naturally on Hugh's side.

"It's really a lovely stone, Miss Kinsella. You wouldn't see a lovelier stone anywhere in Dublin. You wouldn't see a lovelier stone in New York."

But Jane was firm.

"That's the ring I want," she said, pointing to a small sapphire on a slim platinum ring.

"That's hardly an engagement ring, Miss Kinsella. It's more of a ring for a young lady going to her first ball."

"I do think Mr O'Shea is right, darling," Hugh said.

"Is he going to wear the ring?" she asked. Both the jeweller and Hugh had to admit that he was not.

"Very well then, that's the ring for me. And it fits my

finger perfectly. I don't want to be plucking the strings of my harp and have everybody saying 'Look at Jane Kinsella showing off the fine ring she was given by that Protestant fellow she's going to marry.'"

"They're much more likely to say 'Look at the miserable little ring that Protestant fellow gave Jane Kinsella. It's easy enough to see it's a Scotsman she's going to marry,'" Hugh countered.

Jane shook her head.

"It's no use, Hugh. And surely I might be allowed to choose my own engagement ring?"

He surrendered.

A week later Jane and Hugh were on their way to Scotland. Hugh looked round the airport affectionately.

"This is the only airport I know where one feels that the formalities are indulged in with a good-natured contempt for them. Oh, they can be strict enough, but they don't give the impression they are enjoying it. People in Dublin were inclined to suggest that they felt out of things in the world of to-day, and when I told them that Eire gave me a sense of freedom I had never felt in another country they all seemed to think I was just trying to say something I thought would please them."

"But one does feel cut off in Eire, Hugh. It's too small a place to-day."

"But everybody who isn't in one of these ant-heap cities thinks he's in too small a place," Hugh exclaimed. "If I had my way I'd put our rocket ranges in Hyde Park. An enemy will drop H-bombs on London if he can in any case. Why should they be challenged to destroy parts of Britain they would otherwise let alone? And why people in Eire should fret about being cut off I really cannot understand."

When the train from Glasgow stopped at Kirkshiels, Hugh saw Sir Robert MacInnes on the platform.

"Oh, good, there's my father," he cried.

"Hugh, I'm shaking with fright."

"Don't forget to say you're terribly keen to play golf

properly. I mean to say, if he asks you whether you like golf say you like it but you've never had a chance to play it properly. Then he'll offer to coach you, and, darling, you must try to look bucked by his offer."

By this time they had reached Sir Robert.

"Father, this is Jane."

The tall upstanding man with grizzled hair eyed his future daughter-in-law and decided in that moment that his only son had chosen well. He shook her cordially by the hand.

"By Jove, you must be five foot nine," he observed.

"Five eight and a half, Sir Robert."

"I was pretty near it, wasn't I?"

The porter was putting the luggage in the boot of the dark-crimson Jaguar.

"You'll sit by me, Jane. We have about twelve miles to go."

Hugh sat behind in a state of euphory; the purring of the Jaguar as it swept between the rose-starred green of the fresh June hedgerows seemed to be expressing his own content.

"You're feeling a bit shy, aren't you?" he heard his father ask Jane.

"Yes, I'm feeling terribly shy," she admitted.

"So am I," said Sir Robert. "Are you keen on golf?"

"I would be if I could play it properly."

"I'll give you lessons. You ought to be jolly good. You'll have the swing. I hope you left your people fit and well."

"Oh yes, they were all very well."

"I had a very nice letter from your father about Hugh. I appreciated it very much. So did my wife."

"I was always on at my mother to write to Lady MacInnes. But she's terrible about writing letters. She's always going to, but she never does."

"I know, I know. I'm not too fond of writing letters myself. However, I did write and thank Dr Kinsella for his letter to me."

"I know. He showed me your letter. He said he thought I was a lucky girl to have found such a sympathetic father-in-law."

"Did he? Did he really? Does he play golf?"

"He does sometimes, when he has time, but what he really likes is football. He remembered well seeing Hugh play at Lansdowne Park. He said he scored one of the best goals he ever saw scored. Ah, no, now wait a minute, it was a try. That's right, isn't it?"

"Yes, we were all very proud of that try. Unfortunately I couldn't get over to Dublin because I had a business conference. Well, you mustn't be too disappointed, Jane, if Hugh doesn't play Rugger again. I'm afraid that leg of his will keep him out of the Scottish team, and there's no point in taking risks to play for a club side."

"I'm very glad he's going to give up football, Sir Robert. It would be terrible for me if he had scored a goal—I mean a try to beat Ireland."

"Divided loyalties, what? Ah, well, don't worry. He's going to take up golf seriously. But don't let him start trying to teach you golf. He's got some shocking bad tricks of his own he must get rid of before he does that."

"What a wonderful girl she is," Hugh was telling himself. "She's bored to death by Rugger and golf and yet the old boy thinks she's as keen as mustard on both."

A few minutes later the Jaguar was sweeping up the drive to Greystones. The mistress of the house must have been on the look out in the drawing-room, for she was in the hall to greet Jane. Hugh thought with a smile she was like a little girl as she put up her cheek for Jane to bend over and kiss.

When Jane went back to Dublin a fortnight later, the date of the wedding had been fixed for September 18th.

"And now you're man and wife," Captain MacKechnie squeaked, when Hugh and Jane came aboard the *Island Queen* two days after the wedding. "Isn't that wonderful now? It wass only last May you came aboard, Mr MacInnes, and you were talking to me up in the wheelhouse, and I'm telling you, Mistress MacInnes, he had an eye on you away up in the bows all the time. Yess indeed, and by Chinko, in four months you married yourselfs. Och, we must tap the steward for this, right enough."

"It's a bit early in the morning for whisky, Captain MacKechnie," Hugh suggested.

"Not at all. It'll put the motion of the train out of your stomacks, and we'll have a beautiful crossing to Snorvig."

So in his cabin the Captain wished the bride and bridegroom long life and happiness.

"And if you'd waited another ten days you wouldn't have had me to take you to Snorvig. Yess, I'll be on the peach in Skye in another ten days. I hope none of these rockets will fall out of the sky in Skye. We had a comic on board here last week and he wass singing 'Speed bonny bomb like a bird on the wing over the sky to sea.' Ah well, I wonder what they'll be saying to themselfs on Little Todday this morning?"

"Why this morning particularly?" Hugh asked.

"Did you not hear the wireless last night?" Captain MacKechnie squeaked.

"No, we were in the train."

"Och, the Ministry of Protection is going to put a rocket range and an aerodrome on Todaidh Beag and a training centre on Todaidh Mór to show them how to let the rockets off. And you'd have thought by the way that announcer down in London put out the news he wass telling the people in Todday they'd won a pick football-pool."

"Little Todday won't take this lying down," Hugh said.

"Ach, I don't know." Captain MacKechnie shook his head sadly. "There'll be a lot of talk, but nobody fights any longer. The spirit is gone. I must be getting up to the bridge."

Hugh and Jane wandered away to the bows.

"I didn't know your name. I hadn't heard you sing the last time we stood here in the early morning," Hugh said. "What are you thinking, my Jane?"

"I was thinking it's too bad of us to be turning Mrs Odd out of her cottage in this lovely weather."

"It's nothing of the kind," Mrs Odd declared, when about twelve hours later Hugh and Jane were greeted by her at the door of Bow Bells. "I'm starting back for Nottingham to-night, and I'm well looked after. Peggy has gone on first with Luce and Kitty and Joe. I'm sorry you've missed them. But Fred stayed behind to take me back with him. You haven't met Fred yet. Fred, where are you? Come and meet Mr and Mrs MacInnes."

A brisk lean man with grey hair and keen eyes stepped forward and clicked his heels as he shook hands.

"Still the Sergeant-major," his mother commented. "They never get over it. Just a walking ramrod."

"I hope you had a pleasant voyage, sir," said Mr Alfred Ernest Odd. "We had a treat of a holiday out here. No rain at all most of the time, and England was in a proper drench."

"We do feel awfully guilty at depriving Mrs Odd of such lovely weather," said Hugh.

"Don't mention it, sir. She set her heart on you spending your honeymoon in Bow Bells. As soon as Mrs MacInnes wrote and told her you were going to be married, she was all het up as you might say for you to spend your honeymoon here. And when Ma makes up her mind to anything, well, it's made up. Yes, she and me are going by the boat to-night."

"What did you think of the news on the wireless last night?" Hugh asked.

"About this rocket range and aerodrome? It's the most chronic bit of news I ever heard in my life. Well, if I'd have been told I'd live to see the day when the Army was . . . but I won't start in on that. I don't know what's going to happen here. I think they're going to have trouble. However, we'll see what happens when they start in sending the notices to quit. For all I know they'll want to take Bow Bells."

"I do hope not," Jane exclaimed in dismay.

"Ah, well, miss—I beg pardon, Mrs MacInnes . . . Ma's getting on, you know. She can't go on making that journey much longer. Still . . . she'll feel it, pore Ma will, if they do take Bow Bells."

Late that evening, before Mrs Odd set out with her son in Duncan Bàn's trap, she took Jane aside.

"Now listen," she said, "if these loopy ballipsticks say they're going to take Bow Bells you're to send me a telegram right away to Nottingham, and I'm coming back. Now promise me that, Jane. I know Fred has been saying to your hubby that perhaps it'll be all for the best because I'm getting too doddery to travel all the way from Nottingham to Little Todday. But if they're going to take Bow Bells they'll have to put me out by force, because I want to show them up. So that's a promise, Jane."

"I promise," said Jane.

"And I hope I die of the pneumonia. That'll give 'em something to write about in the Sunday papers. 'Otto-generarian thrown out of home by rocketeers found wandering about in the macker and not expected to live.' Good-bye, duckie, and enjoy yourselves. Oh dear, if I'd have brought Ernest to Little Todday for our honeymoon, what a scream! He said Margate in June was more of a funeral than a honeymoon. What he'd have thought of Little Todday. Well, we must be moving along. I'll have a lot of good-byes to say."

Chapter 10

NOTICE TO QUIT

THE announcement that the Ministry of Protection had decided to include the two Toddays in their ballistic plans disturbed public opinion. Much capital had been made by the Government out of the fact that the rocket range at Balmuir was purely an experimental station for guided missiles and that the only suitable site for such an experimental station in the whole of Britain was in West Uist, where there would be no danger to shipping and where the necessary provision of an area of level land by the sea backed by a range of hills was available. To this was added the final justification of the choice in the suitability of Mid and East Uist with their convenient aerodromes as a training-ground for the new ballistic forces with which it was hoped to render the Royal Navy, the Army and the R.A.F. in due course obsolete, or at any rate unrecognizable as what they once were.

As presented to the public by one of the Under-Secretaries deputed to expound the attitude of the Government, that attitude had been one of almost straining its back in an endeavour to make the whole business more beneficial to the Western Isles than to the defence of the country as a whole. Protests against the eviction of crofters were answered by pointing out the care that was going to be taken of the St Kilda mouse and the St Kilda wren. Protests against the destruction of an immemorial way of life were rebutted by pointing out the help that had been given to archaeologists to excavate and photograph wheelhouses two thousand years old and Vikings' long houses a thousand years old. When ornithologists complained of the disturbance to the swans, the Government spokesman countered by pointing out its paternal solicitude for the puffins and fulmar petrels of St Kilda. Indeed, by that September it can be said that everybody had settled down to accept the inevitable with the apathetic docility characteristic of almost everybody in Britain except shop stewards in large factories.

And then this news about the Toddays. Could those alarmists who had forecast the intention of the Government to make the whole length of the Western Isles a base for guided missiles to be used against Russia be right? Of course, nobody except the Russians themselves believed that they would be used against Russia unless the Russians used them first. That was equally the view in Russia about their own guided missile bases. If both sides could go on believing that the more terrible the weapons of their own invention became the less likelihood there was of their ever being used, it might be an expensive waste of the world's nuclear energy, but it could be an effective way of preventing the calamity of another war. Yet suppose war did come in spite of every fancied deterrent?

It was a disagreeable reflection for the people of Scotland to feel that the British Government had successfully managed to put them in the line of fire because that rocket range in the Western Isles was likely to be the first military objective of the enemy before he turned his attention to London. So this news about the two Toddays was disquieting. *The Caledonian* wrote a powerful and gloomy leader about the prospect, and even the *Glasgow Trumpeter* seemed less certain than usual that everything was for the best in the best possible Scotland so long as a Conservative administration was in power. Only the *Inverness Times*, with the prospect of the burden of the Inverness-shire rates being still further lightened, expressed warm approval of the Government's decision with the usual patriotic trimmings.

A week after Hugh and Jane arrived on Little Todday, two representatives of the Department of Agriculture arrived on the island to serve the notice of the resumption of certain crofts by the owner "in the public interest", those four apparently harmless little words which had slipped unnoticed into the Smallholders Act a year or two ago in order to put them at the mercy of an ever more greedy bureaucracy. The Land Commissioners might sit in majesty to hear an appeal against the owner's action in resuming possession of a croft, but the Land Commissioners who had protected the crofter against the private interest of the landlord were impotent against an Act of Parliament. The Land Commissioners might try to assert themselves by inviting the owner to prove that a proposed resumption was in the public interest. Evidence would be given by officials of this or that Ministry to declare that it was, but under the plea of national security all of those officials would refuse to say why and the apathetic British public, as ductile as the public believe the public behind the Iron Curtain to be, would turn on the television and dismiss a disagreeable subject. Britons, after proclaiming for so long that they never would be slaves, had succumbed to slavery in a coma of mental inertia.

The representatives of the Department of Agriculture were both known and were both well liked on the island. Alasdair MacIver, who was an Ullapool man, had tried for the last twenty years to see the crofter's point of view, and in spite of an endless volume of advice and instruction from the theoretical agriculturists at their desks in St Andrew's House he had done a valuable job. He had been able to discourage the notion that an extensive planting of Austrian pines in sandy soil on the edge of the Atlantic would stand up to the wintry storms and allow the islanders to grow crops where no crops would grow. He had kept a watchful eye on the need for planting marram grass where the wintry gales had skimmed the surface of the machair and encouraged the sand to spread. He had persuaded the theorists in Edinburgh that a vicious Shorthorn bull was not the most suitable husband for the Ayrshire cows favoured by the islanders. He had supported Norman Macleod's plan to grow onions and carrots, and had even managed to persuade the Department to make an order forbidding the importation of onion sets and insisting that the islanders should grow seed, thereby preventing the fly from making the cultivation of onions an unprofitable labour. He had tactfully smoothed over the occasional disputes about boundaries which are inevitable in a crofting community and so spared the Land Commissioners a lot of trouble. He never led the Catholics of Little Todday to believe that he was favouring the Protestants of Great Todday, and he was successful in keeping the latter equally confident of his fairness. He was a good singer of Gaelic songs, and whenever his business for the Department brought him to the Toddays he was in popular demand at any ceilidh that was going.

The other representative of the Department was John Bain, who hailed from the Black Isle and had a good-natured contempt for the Highlander and Islander of the West as agriculturists, cattle-breeders and fishermen. He regarded them as lazy, casual and unpunctual whose main rule of life was never to do to-day what could possibly be postponed until to-morrow, and on that morrow to procrastinate until the day after. Nevertheless, he was respected and liked, for if he made a promise he kept it, and if he said "yes" he did not mean "no".

Neither Alasdair MacIver nor John Bain was pleased with the job he had been given. Indeed, they both hated it; and when they stepped ashore at Kiltod on a golden September morning, Alasdair MacIver in cigar-brown plus-fours of crotal-dyed Harris tweed and John Bain in plus-fours of Glen Urquhart check, both of them looked and felt gloomy.

"You'd better do the talking, John," said Alasdair MacIver. "They're more used to hearing unwelcome news from you than they are from me."

"No, I don't think that even you could coat this pill with sugar," John Bain agreed. "Well, they've made me jumping mad over and over again, Alec, but I just hate doing this to them. Where'll we tackle them first?"

"We'd better begin with the croft furthest away," MacIver suggested.

"That's either Hugh Macroon or John Stewart."

"Hugh Macroon will be a tough nut."

"Then we'd better crack him first," Bain decided.

"Mightn't it be a good idea to call on Father Macalister first?" MacIver suggested.

"That's right, Alec. Put it off as long as you can," Bain jeered. "Man, you're just as Hieland as you can be."

"It's not procrastination, John. It's tact. We don't want to have him too much against us."

"You've got a hope," John Bain laughed derisively.

However, he agreed to the preliminary call at the chapel house.

"Come in, come in," the parish priest urged with a great appearance of expansive hospitality. But when they were seated in his cosy room he asked suddenly, "And what brings you two birds of ill-omen to Little Todday on this lovely morning?"

"You're right, Father Macalister. We *are* birds of ill-omen," said John Bain. "We have to serve notices on twenty-two crofters that the Department must exercise their rights as owners and resume the twenty-two crofts in three months from now."

"On Christmas Day?" Father Macalister asked.

"No, it will probably be at the beginning of the New Year."

"Ay, ay. A merry Christmas but not quite such a happy New Year."

"We don't feel very merry or very happy about it, Maighstir Seumas," said Alasdair MacIver. And then he added something in Gaelic.

"I know what you said, Alec," John Bain put in. "And I agree with you, but there it is. Would you care to see a list of those on whom we have to serve the notices?"

Father Macalister read through the list.

"Ay, as I expected, the best run crofts in the island," he

commented with a deep sigh. "And where will they go to celebrate the New Year?"

"I believe the Department are going to acquire a certain property on the mainland with the object of re-settling the Little Todday crofters," said John Bain.

"You have great faith, Mr Bain," the priest told him.

"Well, perhaps I should say the Department are hoping to acquire this property."

"Ay, I think hoping would be the right word."

"But meanwhile I understand they will receive compensation."

"And I understand that the necessary finance to assist them to emigrate to Canada will be forthcoming for those who wish to do so," Alasdair MacIver added.

"You won't find a man on Little Todday willing to go to Canada," Father Macalister declared with sonorous fervour. "Not a single man. In 1920, at the time of the land-raiders, there was a big drive to get people to go out to Canada from the Islands. There were a lot of poor souls from West Uist and Barra who were taken in and, dash it, I was taken in myself, for I offered to go out with them. We had a terrible time, and I made such a nuisance of myself that the Canadian Government deported me . . . well, they didn't do that literally, but they raised the matter in London and the people in London persuaded the Bishop to advise me to come back to Scotland. A good few of the people came back with me. God knows how we raised the money for their fares. Nobody from Little Todday went, but they've heard all about that terrible time in Canada and you won't be able to dangle that carrot in front of the donkey. Well, go along and serve out your notices, but you can make up your minds that the only way you'll ever put the Macroons of Little Todday out of the land of their fathers is by force. I see Duncan Bàn's croft has been marked down. Does that mean they'll be putting Mrs Odd out of her house, because that's a part of Duncan Bàn's croft?"

"I'm afraid it does, Father James," said Alasdair MacIver.

"You've got a dirty job to do," Father James told the two representatives of the Department of Agriculture. "But I'll say this to your credit. You neither of you called it a patriotic necessity. And so, birds of ill-omen though you both may be, I'll offer you a dram. Now don't argue about it. Drink it down. You'll be feeling pretty chilly presently."

MacIver and Bain looked at one another.

"Well, just to show there's no ill-will, Father Macalister," said John Bain.

"There's a powerful amount of ill-will, Mr Bain," said their host. "But you need not take it personally."

"Let's hope the Government will change their mind," said Alasdair MacIver, draining his glass.

"The Devil never changes his mind, Mr MacIver. That's one of the reasons why he is so successful. And the Devil at this moment is sitting at every meeting of the Cabinet prodding the members not to change such poor insignificant little minds as they've got."

"Come, come, Father Macalister, I won't agree with that," said John Bain. "They were badly let down first by the Americans and then by the United Nations, and I think they've made it clear that from now on we must rely on ourselves."

"But if the Russians already have such wonderful rockets of their own, are they going to wait until we have bigger and better rockets before the fireworks start?"

"Now, we mustn't start a political argument," said Mr Bain. "We have a job of work to do."

"Ay, ay, a miserable job of dirty work."

So on one croft after another did the two representatives of the Department of Agriculture serve the notices of the owner's intention to resume possession of a croft after paying due compensation.

The last one they visited was Tigh a' Bhàird, where the bard himself was fast asleep after spending the night on

Tràigh Swish with a bottle of whisky in the company of the fairies. He had staggered home at sunrise to swallow six raw eggs and thus offset the effect of his vigil.

"He doesn't seem to be at home," said MacIver after knocking on the door several times without receiving any answer.

"He may be along in his other house," Bain suggested.

So the Department representatives walked along to Bow Bells, where Hugh and Jane were sitting in the minute front garden. Asked if they had seen Duncan Macroon anywhere around, they shook their heads.

"I wonder if you'd be kind enough to give him this paper when you see him?" MacIver asked. "Mr Bain and I have to get along to Kiltod for our lunch. We're going back to Snorvig in the *Morning Star* at two."

Alasdair MacIver and John Bain went on their way.

"Hullo, this is it," Hugh said to Jane, passing the paper to her.

"We never pay any attention to bits of paper like this in Eire," Jane declared.

"Oh, come, Jane, you must pay attention occasionally to official communications and notices."

"We pay least attention of all to suchlike."

"Well, we'd better stroll along to Tigh a' Bhàird and see if Duncan is back," Hugh suggested.

Perhaps the knocking on his door by the Department representations had roused him. At any rate Duncan Bàn shouted "*Thig a stigh*" when his next visitors arrived, and he presently emerged from his bedroom with touzled hair but with those kingfisher-blue eyes of his as clear as the day itself.

"There are two fellows from the Department of Agriculture who couldn't manage to wake you, Duncan. So they came along to Bow Bells and asked me to give you this. They'll be away by two in the *Morning Star*."

Hugh handed Duncan the scrap of paper. "I fancy you were the last to be given this."

A vivid flush of anger suffused the countenance of the bard. "They'll put me out of a croft that I and my forefathers have held for three hundred and forty-two years? What Clan Ruairidh could never do, what MacNeil of Barra couldn't do once upon a time, what John Knox couldn't do four hundred years ago and hasn't been able to do yet, what the bloody Redcoats couldn't do after Culloden, what that poor dandy of a degenerate Clanranald couldn't do when he sold his heritage to pay his gambling debts in London, what Sir Moses Hoggenheimer couldn't do when he tried to make Little Todday a goose preserve for his aristocratic friends, *a Dhià nan Gràs*, does the Department of Agriculture, St Andrew's House, Edinburgh 1, Waverley 5371, think it can put us out?" He tore up the notice of resumption into small pieces.

"Nobody would be more pleased than I to see them fail, Duncan. But don't forget the Government is behind them," Hugh reminded him.

"That doesn't say we're going to let the Department of Agriculture, St Andrew's House, Edinburgh 1, Waverley 5371, roll right over us, not even if they're led by the Chief Egg Officer."

"The Chief Egg Officer?"

"That's the way he signed himself when I received a great heap of forms to sign about the eggs my own fowls were laying."

Duncan bent down, gathered up the pieces of the resumption notice, and put them in his pocket.

"I'll go round and find what the others have done," he announced. He rushed out of his cottage, and a minute or two later Hugh and Jane saw him astride his favourite dun pony galloping off to the next croft. "I'll see you in Kiltod," he shouted back.

"I wonder what he's going to do?" Hugh said. "Anyway, we may as well walk along to Kiltod."

Hugh and Jane reached the post-office just as the Department officials were coming out after lunch with Joseph.

"We gave your paper to Duncan Macroon," Hugh told them. "It wasn't received very cordially."

"I don't suppose it was," said John Bain.

"Ah, poor Duncan," said Joseph. "He's been in committee with the fairies ever since that announcement on the wireless. Well, well, I'd sooner the Government had left Little Todday out of their reckoning, but I think I'll go along to Glasgow to-night and see about a lorry."

"A lorry?" Hugh repeated.

"Ay, or maybe two," said Joseph, tugging his red knitted cap resolutely down over his forehead.

Mr MacIver and Mr Bain had just boarded the *Morning Star* when Duncan Bàn came galloping down to the little harbour.

"Wait a moment, *a mhic an diabhuil*," he shouted.

"That's not a very friendly way to greet old friends," Alasdair MacIver protested.

"You're no longer friends of mine," Duncan Bàn told them. "And it's me that's sorry I was not a minute sooner, for if I had been you'd both have been in the water instead of looking up at me from the *Morning Star*. However, I'll have to baptize you with paper instead."

With this Duncan Bàn took a small box from his pocket and emptied a shower of scraps over the representatives of the Department.

"These are your notices to quit. Take them back to St Andrew's House, Edinburgh 1, Waverley 5371, and tell them that every crofter in Little Todday who received one of their notices tore it up. Ay, and you can tell the Chief Egg Officer he'd better come along with you next time and I'll baptize you all with eggs."

"Our job, Duncan, was to serve the notices," said John Bain. "It's no job of ours what you do with them. But take a warning from me. You're up against the Government, and nothing you or any of you do on Little Todday will stop them from going on with what they intend to do. You'd better be philosophical about it like Joseph Macroon and buy yourself a lorry."

This diverted Duncan Bàn's wrath to Joseph Macroon, who started to walk away from the harbour, in his eyes that remote expression which always indicated that Joseph's mind was working busily upon a plan.

"You're going to get a lorry?" Duncan demanded fiercely. Joseph raised his hand to hush the question as he might have raised his hand to brush away a midge. "If you do," Duncan continued, "we'll push it over into the Coolish when they try to land it."

With this the bard remounted his dun pony and galloped away.

"Ah, poor Duncan," Joseph said to Hugh and Jane, "these committee meetings with the fairies go to his head."

Hugh and Jane went up to the chapel house, where Father Macalister rubbed his hands with glee when he heard of the baptism of paper.

"Good shooting!" he boomed. "Oh, well, well, we must just do our best to do our worst."

"Don't misunderstand what I'm going to say, Father James, and don't think I wouldn't do almost anything except give up Jane if I could help to upset this rocket scheme." Hugh paused to think how he could express himself without seeming to be trimming to the prevailing wind. "Did you read a full account of what was said when the Land Commission sat in Nobost last year?"

"I certainly did."

"Well, when Air Commodore Watchorn was giving evidence he was always careful to say 'at present' when asked awkward questions. There was no intention at present to use the range for anything except training. There was no intention at present to use the range for offence or defence. There was no intention at present to fire anything but blank rockets. There was no question at present of having foreign troops in West or Mid or East Uist. There was no intention at present of stationing more than four thousand trainees on the three islands. And so on, and so on. Now I am positive that the ultimate plan is to use the whole of the Long Island. I think Lewis may very well become ultimately the strategic centre of our defence against guided missiles from the East, and if this be true, then nothing is going to divert the Government from doing step by step what they plan to do."

"And therefore we are to lie down and let them roll right over us?" Father Macalister asked reproachfully.

"The best hope is that the Government may go too far and provoke a really strong public reaction."

"But meanwhile we are to lie down in Little Todday?"

"No, I won't say that. What I do say is that I'm positive no resistance here will divert the Government from their plan. They want to press forward so that if they are defeated at the next Election the Labour people won't have the courage to scrap a scheme on which so much money will already have been spent. However, as I say, in their hurry to press on they may press on a little too quickly. And now I'll have to say something that will make you angry. My feeling is that active resistance will lead to a lot of sectarian propaganda and counter-propaganda in which Little Todday will be presented as a nest of Papists behaving like the I.R.A. in Ireland. As much passive resistance as you like, Father James, but I know what the official reaction would be to the slightest display of violence."

"Does the Sasunnach ever believe that anybody else is serious till that anybody kicks him in the pants? And just because of that belief patriotic young soldiers ordered to suppress patriotic young rebels have to die before the Sasunnach in authority surrenders to the inevitable."

"But, Father James, you couldn't hope to avert the catastrophe here by violence," Hugh urged. "How could an almost level island of some twenty square miles without a hiding-place anywhere hope to hold out against what might be military force?"

"Uisdean," said Father James solemnly, "Todaidh Beag

kept the Faith for sixty years without a priest to administer the Sacraments. Todaidh Beag was loyal to its rightful King in the Forty-five. In the years of the potato famine the men of Todaidh Beag were offered the free maize that was being distributed if they would renounce their Faith. And what did an old man of eighty reply to the temptation? 'No, no, Almighty God has put a ring of gold round Todaidh Beag and I would not be the one to break it.' And only a hundred years ago the men of Todaidh Beag were being hunted with dogs to compel them to go aboard the emigrant ship that was waiting in the Coolish to carry them away to Canada. Through the years since, except for the Crofters Act, which was passed in a panic by Parliament after the resistance to the soldiers in Lewis and the Marines landed in Skye, nothing was done for the Western Isles. Their fishing was destroyed by English trawlers. The shipping companies were allowed to impose villainous freights which we pronounce here as 'frights'. When the Government for its own purposes has decided to spend millions of pounds, which if spent once upon a time would have made the Western Isles happy and prosperous, the people are expected to be grateful for the money they earn as navvies. Let them surrender in the other rocket islands. We will not surrender here. If they try to lay violent hands on our crofts, we will lay violent hands on the invaders."

"You won't be able to make a Cyprus out of Little Todday. You can't be an Archbishop Makarios."

"Ah, there's a man. By all the holy crows, when I heard that a Greek Orthodox Archbishop had put an Anglican Orthodox Cecil out of the Cabinet I laughed so heartily that Kirstag came in thinking I was going to expire of cerebral combustion."

"I won't say any more, Father James. But I beg you once again to discourage actual violence. The Government in their present mood are quite capable of getting you off the island; and without you, what would the people do?"

"They would stand fast, Uisdean."

That evening Hugh and Jane were sitting above their favourite beach, Tràigh nan Eun, watching an equinoxial sunset of fiery splendour.

"Jane, do look at those birds on Pillay," Hugh exclaimed. "They're the colour of flamingoes in the sunset."

"Don't they look beautiful! You would think they were really pink instead of white."

"In another week we'll be away from Little Todday and our honeymoon will be over. Darling, it has been so wonderful. You're not beginning to regret that operatic career you might have had?"

"I'm happy, Hugh. You must know how happy I am."

"It's a pretty grim thought that when we come back to Little Todday we shall probably find bulldozers at work and gangs of contractors' navvies and perhaps the houses in which you have sung to your harp all pulled down. Jane, were you surprised this afternoon by the way I was talking to Father James?"

"I was a little surprised to hear you being so cautious."

"I'll tell you something. I know that these devils in the Ministry of Protection want to evacuate the people from Great and Little Todday entirely. But at present they're a little nervous of public opinion, and the Government are more than a little nervous of the effect it might have in an Election. But if the Little Todday people get too obstreperous they may jump at the excuse, and public opinion is so easily swayed that they might be able to carry their scheme through, especially if they can find an excuse for getting rid of Father James first so as to suggest a potential danger to security. That's why I was trying to counsel restraint."

"Why don't you tell him what you know?"

"I can't, Jane. It came to my knowledge when I was P.S. with Andrew Wishart."

"Well, you've told me," Jane pointed out. "And I could tell Father James and your conscience would be quite clear."

"No, Jane darling, you mustn't. I know women don't look at this sort of thing in the same way as men. But I should feel I'd done something dishonourable. You won't say a word to Father James? Promise me, Jane darling."

"I think you're being too high-minded altogether, but I could not do something you didn't want me to do on our honeymoon," she said tenderly.

"Jane, you are so sweet. Look, the birds are white again."

"Like your conscience, Hugh darling, now that I've promised to keep your secret."

On the morning of the day when the honeymoon was over, four men in black coats and pin-striped trousers reached Kiltod from one of the Snorvig boats. Each was armed with a theodolite.

"They *are* like black beetles, aren't they?" Hugh said when he and Jane were watching them at work on the machair. "Oh dear, we shan't see Captain MacKechnie to-night."

There was no moon when they went on board the *Morning Star* to cross the Coolish after an exhausting round of farewells, all the more exhausting because at the back of everyone's mind there was the thought that they might never again see Little Todday as it was.

Just as the *Morning Star* was about to cast off, a bundle of white rods was dropped into the boat.

"Put that little lot overboard. The tide will carry them out," said the voice of Norman Macleod.

"What are they at all?" Kenny Macroon asked.

"The aerodrome," said Norman Macleod, with a chuckle. "And it was all so beautifully measured out. Good-bye, Jane. Good-bye, Uisdean."

Chapter 11

THE PORTENT

IT would be dishonest to suggest that a large majority of the people of Great Todday did not respond with something like elation to the news that the Ministry of Protection had decided upon including Great Todday and Little Todday in their grand plan to secure the safety of Britain by letting the Russians know that as soon as possible we should be in a position to fire back at them bigger and better rockets from the West than any they possessed in the East. That the Russians might not feel inclined to wait for the Ministry of Protection's rockets to be ready did not seem to occur to anybody. Just as before World War Two the phrase "collective security" was worn hopefully like an amulet to protect the country against the Germans, so now the single word "deterrent" was being sported with equal optimism as an amulet to protect the country against the Russians. The cool observer might feel saddened by the pathetic credulity of this trust in a phrase or a word, but cool observers could always be discredited in the popular mind by suggesting that they were pacifist cranks or fellow-travellers, or merely unpatriotic blighters.

"I hear you've been having trouble on Little Todday over the surveyors," Paul Waggett said to Group Captain Oakenbotham, who had arrived to overlook the Ministry of Protection's plans for the future of both islands and who not being forewarned had accepted an invitation to dine at Snorvig House.

"Yes, but the Air Commodore told me I might find the people there a little sticky at first."

The Group Captain was a man with a long chin and a loud voice who sounded just as enthusiastic when he was referring to difficulties as when he was reporting that all was going well.

"I was talking yesterday to Mr Meeching, who told me that all his marks have been removed for the third time," Paul Waggett said.

"Yes, it is rather annoying," the Group Captain admitted boisterously. "But I'm going over to see Father Macalister and explain to him that if this sort of thing goes on we shall have to take a serious view of it. The trouble is that for some reason or other we have to wait until the New Year before we can really get going. Apparently the crofters obstructing our work cannot be put out of their holdings until then. However, next week the contractor's men are going over to blow up the harbour at Kiltod so that they can carry on with the construction of the new pier. We can't get on with landing a lot of our equipment until that is ready."

"Well, I hope the Little Todday people will be reasonable," said Paul Waggett. "But I doubt it. I had a good deal of difficulty with them during the war. You may have heard of the *Cabinet Minister* wreck with a cargo of whisky?"

"I have indeed. That must have been a wonderful time for you all out here," Group Captain Oakenbotham trumpeted.

"It was disastrous," said his host.

"Disastrous?" the Group Captain exclaimed in amazement.

"Complete demoralization," Waggett sighed. "Utter and complete. Do you know that our P.S.I., Sergeant-major Odd, actually took a case of whisky back with him to Colonel Lindsay-Wolseley, the commanding officer of the 8th Inverness-shire West Home Guard Battalion."

"Lucky chap," commented Group Captain Oakenbotham with resonant envy of the Colonel's good fortune.

"But I don't think you realize, Group Captain, that they were all helping themselves to this whisky, quite regardless of the Excise."

"I'm not surprised."

"I couldn't trust even my own men. It was a bitter experience for an Old Contemptible like myself. The wreck occurred on a Sunday afternoon and the Little Toddayites, being Roman Catholics, were the first to start looting the ship. The Great Toddayites, who are very strict about observing Sunday, didn't start till after midnight. But I'm bound to say that when they did start they were just as bad as the Little Toddayites."

"Oh, that reminds me," said the Group Captain. "I'm told there will be strong local objection here to the contractors working on Sunday."

"Yes, you'll certainly find that."

"But I understand Roman Catholics don't pay the same attention to Sunday."

"They go to church in the morning, of course," Paul Waggett said.

"Quite, quite. But they wouldn't object to other people working."

"They object to work on Little Todday on any day of the week," Paul Waggett assured his guest.

"But not to others working?"

"Oh no. They're always delighted to watch other people working."

"Ah, that's very satisfactory. I'll tell the contractors they'd better start on Kiltod next Sunday."

Thus it befell that as the sacring-bell tinkled at the consecration of the Host upon that quiet Sunday in October the holy sound was blasted by the roar of the explosion that was loosening half of the harbour wall in Kiltod. The rest of it was loosened when the last words of the *Agnus Dei* were being sung.

> *Agnus Dei qui tollis peccata mundi,*
> *Dona nobis pacem.*
> *O Lamb of God that takest away the sins of the world,*
> *Grant us peace.*

The bangs were heard not so loudly, but loudly enough,

by the congregation of the Reverend Angus Morrison, the Church of Scotland minister in Great Todday, and on that Sunday perhaps for the first time in his ministry he preached a sermon to which he had not devoted the greater part of Saturday in preparation.

"*A dhuine a dhuine*," said Ruairidh Môr to his cousin Simon when the service was finished and the congregation was decorously leaving the church, "I never heard the Reverend Angus so fierce."

"I don't believe I ever did myself," said Simon MacRurie, elder and prosperous merchant. "But he was a bit too fierce to my thinking. We don't want to upset the Government by grumbling about working on the Sabbath. It wasn't here they were working. The Reverend Angus would do better to keep a quiet tongue about Todaidh Beag. The Wee Free minister at Gibberdale was saying to me in Nobost that he'd heard the Church of Scotland minister was too friendly altogether with the *pàbanaich* on Todaidh Beag. I'm minded to give him a word of advice."

"Ay, it might be chust as well, *a Shimidh*. I was minded to do the ferry same thing myself, but it would come petter from one of his elders."

So that evening Mrs Morrison came into her husband's study at the manse to say that Mr Simon MacRurie wanted to see him. She was so nervous that the refined Kelvinside accent she usually cherished with such care slipped back into a purer Glasgow.

"I hope he's not going to complain about anything, Angus. He's looking terribly solemn."

The Reverend Angus Morrison was a small man, a native of Harris who had been called to Great Todday just before the start of the last war. He had made himself respected and loved, but there had always been an inclination to treat the *duine beag bochd*, the poor wee man, with a kind of affectionate compassion. His friendship with Father Macalister was regarded with suspicion by some of his influential parishioners, and his steady attempts to promote a closer relationship with Little Todday was considered a sign of weakness, not of broadmindedness.

"This is an unexpected pleasure, Mr MacRurie," said the minister when his leading elder came into the small study. "Will you please sit down. What a beautiful day it has been. I don't remember finer October weather than we've been enjoying."

"Ay," Simon MacRurie agreed, "it has been a fine day right enough, and the Government took the opportunity to do that job of work they were wanting to do over at Kiltod."

"The Government?" Mr Morrison repeated sharply. "You mean the contractors, don't you, Mr MacRurie? And I hope I made it quite clear this morning in my sermon that I considered their behaviour an insult to the Lord, Whose day it is."

"But the bang was not on Great Todday, Mr Morrison," the elder pointed out with an attempt at severity.

"Are you trying to teach me what I must and must not say in the pulpit, Mr MacRurie?"

"No, no, I would never do that, Mr Morrison. No, no, no, not at all. But I'm sure you woudn't want to be offending the Government."

"So rather than offend the Government, Mr MacRurie, you would offend the Lord by profaning the Sabbath?"

"I would never profane the Sabbath, Mr Morrison. The idea of such a thing is terrible to me. But we are all anxious to help the Government. It is an opportunity such as we've never had in Great Todday. There will be thousands and thousands of pounds coming to Great Todday. We all feel unworthy that the Lord would show us such favour and we are humbly grateful for it. And I'm sure the contractors were after being very considerate when they made the bang on Little Todday where they think nothing at all about the Sabbath."

"Mr MacRurie," said the minister sternly, "I am really surprised to hear one of my elders talking such un-Christian nonsense as you are talking to me at this moment."

And in describing the scene later, Roderick MacRurie would declare that his cousin Simon had compared the minister's appearance during this interview as that of a little cock-hen ready to fly at anybody.

"But they are not Christians in Little Todday," Simon protested. "They are *pàbanaich.*"

"Mr MacRurie, I am not only surprised but I am deeply ashamed to hear one of my elders talking as ignorantly as you are talking now. The people of Little Todday may be better Christians than you or I. And I will tell you this, Mr MacRurie, that if you suppose I will check my tongue because you or Ruairidh Mór or anybody else thinks he will be losing money by what I say you had better be thinking again. Do you suppose that I will encourage the girls of Great Todday to be doing this rocking and rolling about with a lot of young navvies from the mainland dressed up as Teddy-boys?"

"I don't approve of dancing at all, Mr Morrison, and I've always been against letting them have the hall for these dances, but it was always you who let them have the hall."

"For our old Highland dances, yes," said the minister. "And I'll continue to let them have the hall for such dances. And now, Mr MacRurie, I'll be glad if you will let me have my Sabbath evening to myself, for I wish to pray to the Lord that He will turn the hearts of my congregation to His purpose when I go into the pulpit on the next Sabbath morning."

"What will you be preaching about, Mr Morrison?" Simon MacRurie asked in a tone that sounded almost propitiatory.

"I will be preaching about the Mammon of Unrighteousness, Mr MacRurie."

On his way home, Simon MacRurie turned into the hotel, where he found his cousin in his snug little parlour. On the elder's entrance the hotel-keeper hastily pushed a bundle of accounts into a drawer of his desk.

"Chust reading through a few pills, not working," said Big Roderick.

And then the conversation between the two cousins turned for awhile from English to Gaelic, before it emerged into English again.

"Well, well, *ma tá*, I'm glad you told him to mind his steps, Simon," said Big Roderick. "I'll tell Group Captain Oceanbottom not to be listening to what the poor wee man says. Wackett wass in this afternoon and he's to call a meeting in the hall to egsplain to the people about kided mussels."

"What are you saying, Roderick? It's guided missiles, not guided mussels."

"*Seadh, seadh,*" said Roderick huffily, "I never had the chance to get the English like yourself. What about Wackett?"

"He'd better have his meeting. I was thinking, Roderick, it might be a good idea for you or me to make him an offer for Snorvig House before he sells it to the Government. They'll be wanting it next year and we might get a better price than Waggett."

"Ay, and if we didn't I might be making something of it for the hotel."

"Yes, yes," Simon MacRurie agreed, "we'd better be letting Wackett have his meeting. If we have it on Saturday maybe the wee man will not be preaching that sermon of his on the Sabbath."

However, the Reverend Angus Morrison declined to sit on the platform that night in support of Paul Waggett and Group Captain Oakenbotham. News had reached Father Macalister of his sermon, and on Monday afternoon he came over to Snorvig and called at the manse.

"I've come to thank you, Mr Morrison, for what you said yesterday morning. It was a noble and generous and brave thing that you did."

"It was my duty, *a Mhaighstir Sheumais,*" the minister replied.

The priest brushed away a tear.

"We will not forget it in Todaidh Beag. The future for us is dark. You have heard that twenty-two crofts have been served with notices to quit in the New Year. We will appeal to the Land Commissioners, but I have no hopes of them. They will do what they have been told to do behind the scenes. We will resist eviction and I'll do my best to stir up their courage, but in my heart I know that it is a losing battle. If Great Todday were with us we might be able to put up a better fight, but there it is. Are they going to take over much of the land here?"

"I believe they will be taking quite a lot, but it is none of it land of any value for agriculture or grazing, and we are to have water laid on everywhere and electric light . . ."

"And television, I hope."

"Oh, yes, they're talking of television for next year when the four thousand troops arrive."

"Ah, then you'll soon be quite civilized in Great Todday," said Father Macalister.

"I expect you'll be getting the same amenities in Little Todday."

"Och, yes, we'll soon be able to watch England beating Scotland at Rugger," Father Macalister said. "But even if we had a chance to see Scotland beating England at Rugger it wouldn't make up for the whoosh of these rockets going up. That's all it is, so Air Chief Field Marshal Sir William Windermere told me, just a little whoosh, no more. But to set off that harmless little whoosh they are going to destroy . . ." Father Macalister broke off abruptly. "I wonder why they did not choose Iona. Never mind, Iona may be next on the list for a rocket range. Ah, well, I just wanted to thank you, Mr Morrison, before Sir John Harding arrives and deports me to Timbuctoo."

"I will do whatever I can to support you, Mr Macalister," the minister promised as the priest took his departure.

A few days later Joseph Macroon's new lorry arrived simultaneously with a bulldozer. The blowing up of Kiltod harbour made the landing of both a difficult matter, but the contractor's navvies managed to get both safely ashore on Tràigh Tod, the beach south of the harbour.

During the night there was a curious accident. The lorry, according to one or two people who saw it happen, suddenly of its own accord careered off across the machair and hit the bulldozer such a thump that both of them were unfit for further action. That was all Sergeant MacGillivray could find out when under pressure from the contractor's head man in Snorvig he went over to Little Todday to investigate the strange occurrence.

"Och, Sarchant, I was standing here talking to Hugh Macroon, when suddenly the lorry chumped up in the air and went off like a stirk with the wobble fly and then we heard a pang down by Tràigh Tod, and Hugh and me walked along and saw the pulltozer with the lorry in the middle of herself."

Thus Jocky Stewart.

The Sergeant turned to Hugh Macroon, a crofter with a dome of a forehead and unblinking eyes who was not given to words. Hugh Macroon took his pipe out of his mouth and spat a solemn affirmation.

"That's how it was," he said, and put the pipe back in his mouth again.

"And there was nobody driving the lorry?" the Sergeant pressed.

"Not a single crayture," Jocky Stewart declared. "Hugh and me were chust after saying would it be Kenny Iosaibh who would be driving the lorry or would Iosaibh be hiring a shafoor to drife it for him, when all of a moment the lorry went off like I wass telling you. Ach, I wouldn't say she mightn't be thinking she wass a rocket herself."

Sergeant MacGillivray shook his head and put the notebook back in his pocket. His round red face was impassive.

"It's a pretty queer kind of a story," he observed.

Then in Gaelic he warned the two crofters that a repetition of such incidents might lead to trouble.

"Ach, I don't believe Joseph's lorry will ever start off again like that, Sarchant. I don't believe there's any life left in the poor crayture," Jocky Stewart assured him.

Sergeant MacGillivray uttered a few more words in Gaelic nicely balanced between the monitory and the minatory and walked slowly back to the boat which had brought him over from Snorvig and was now lying by the wooden landing-stage the workmen had improvised in the sheltered harbour.

"*A Dhia*, Hugh," said Jocky Stewart, "that wass terrible Gaelic the Sarchant wass speaking."

Hugh Macroon's pipe gurgled agreement.

"Would that be Lochaber Gaelic, Hugh?"

Hugh Macroon nodded.

"Och, well, well, I don't believe Argyll Gaelic would be more terrible than that."

While Jocky Stewart was animadverting on the inferior quality of Argyll and Lochaber Gaelic, up in the chapel house Father Macalister was listening to Joseph Macroon's moans about the financial loss he had suffered from his lorry's irrational behaviour.

"It was either Duncan Bàn or Norman Macleod, or both, Father James."

"Or the fairies. I told Sergeant MacGillivray I was pretty sure it was the fairies. And he put that down in his notebook."

"Ah, Father, please don't be joking. I'm after losing the best part of £300 by this caper," Joseph Macroon groaned.

"Ah, well, there it is, Joseph. You must see to it that the next lorry you buy cheap is not a bronco."

"But suppose the contractors sue me for the damage to their bulldozer?"

"That'll just be a lesson to you, Joseph."

"Will you not say something from the altar on Sunday, Father James?"

"What would I be saying, Joseph?"

"You could be saying that such behaviour was a disgrace to the island's good name," Joseph urged.

"But you don't really want me to be rebuking you from the altar, Joseph?"

"Rebuking me?" Joseph Macroon gasped.

"Oh, yes! It was you that brought this peculiar lorry to Todaidh Beag."

"Won't there be plenty work for a lorry presently?"

"Not for any lorry belonging to anybody on Todaidh Beag," said Father Macalister gravely. Then he put a hand on Joseph Macroon's shoulder. "It has cost you £300 to learn that lesson. Don't be wasting any more of your money, my old friend. We may not be so smart as they are in Todaidh Mór, but at least there won't be anybody able to write in the papers that the people of Little Todday are grateful to the Government for spending millions of pounds to civilize them."

Joseph Macroon shook his head sadly.

"*A bhobh bhobh,*" he sighed hopelessly. "I'm thinking you would be one too many for the Devil himself, Father James."

"I wouldn't say I would be able to knock him out, Joseph, but I believe the referee might give me the verdict on points."

That evening Norman Macleod came up to the chapel house to ask Father Macalister if he intended to go over to Snorvig on Saturday to hear Waggett explain the mysteries of atomic warfare.

"No, no, Norman. It wouldn't do any good," he was told. "Besides, if Mr Morrison isn't going it would give the Free Church *Monthly Record* an opportunity to say that he was as much priest-ridden as the poor benighted heathen in Little Todday."

"I believe Duncan Bàn and I and maybe one or two others will go over and do a bit of heckling," said Norman Macleod.

On that Saturday night in October Roderick MacRurie

took the chair with Paul Waggett and Group Captain Oakenbotham on either side of him, the latter in R.A.F. uniform and the former in the dinner-jacket he always donned on what he considered occasions of national importance. The Snorvig Hall was full, but there was no sign either of Norman Macleod or Duncan Bàn Macroon.

Big Roderick opened the proceedings with a speech in Gaelic which was received with less than the usual warmth to which he was accustomed. This was partly due to the anxiety of the audience to know more about the proposal to make Great Todday the hostelry for four thousand trainees with accommodation for wives and families and partly to his self-confidence being sapped by the steady punctuation of his remarks by sonorous "pahs!" from Dr Maclaren in the front row, and one contemptuous comment of "*ah, cachd!*" from the Biffer at the back of the hall.

When the chairman had finished what he had had to say in Gaelic, he went into English for the benefit of "Croup Captain Oceanbottom and Mr Wackett," to the annoyance of Paul Waggett, who had been laughing at the chairman's humour only about a second behind in his appreciation and who had supposed he had successfully created the impression that he had been following every word of the Gaelic. However, he felt he had recaptured the impression by laughing at the notion of not being able to follow every word of what Roderick Mór had been saying.

"We are cathered here to-night to give a great welcome to Croup Captain Oceanbottom, who has been ferry pleassed by the way the people of Todaidh Mór are showing their patriotic devotion to the great new plan to defend our country against these Russians who we did all we could to help in the war and who are turning round now to kick us in the pack. I will call upon Croup Captain Oceanbottom to address us presently, but first of all I will call on Mr Wackett to egsplain all about nuclose energy. Mr Wackett, pleasse."

It would be as tedious for the reader as it was for his audience that night to attempt to follow Paul Waggett's meanderings through a subject of which he knew rather less than the oldest boy of any team in a B.B.C. general knowledge competition for schools.

"And before I sit down." The shuffling of feet died away to a whisper in the audience's grateful expectation of that blessed moment. "Before I sit down, it is my pleasant duty to assure Group Captain Oakenbotham that the people of Great Todday look forward eagerly to co-operating with the Ministry of Protection in their great project for national defence. We are proud of their confidence in our loyalty. Some of us may lose a little from having four thousand ballistic troops stationed on our island. I myself am only too well aware that the sporting rights I have now enjoyed for nearly twenty-five years cannot be the same in such circumstances. But shall I weigh my grouse and salmon and sea-trout . . ."

"And eggs," somebody shouted from the back of the hall, probably the Biffer.

"Shall I weigh my grouse and my salmon and sea-trout against my country's need? I wish that the same spirit was being shown by our friends on the other side of the Coolish. I have been shocked to hear from many of the workmen employed by the contractors to prepare the way for the fulfilment of the Government's plans that they have been exposed to every kind of petty annoyance in Little Todday, including a refusal even by the children to admit that they can understand a word of English. I have been shocked to hear from the Government surveyors that as fast as they mark out sites, the pegs they put in disappear immediately. The Reverend Morrison, who I regret to see is not with us to-night, spoke last Sunday about the desecration of the Sabbath day by blowing up the harbour at Kiltod. If I wished to enter into a theological argument with Mr Morrison I should remind him of the saying that the Sabbath was made for man not man for the Sabbath, but

I do not believe in making matters worse by theological controversy. I shall content myself by reminding Mr Morrison that the poor taxpayer has a right to expect the Government will do everything possible to encourage the contractors to get on with the job, and I consider it Mr Morrison's duty as a minister to remember that other saying in the Bible—charity begins at home, and not to oppose the contractors' praiseworthy determination to get on with the job."

As soon as Paul Waggett sat down, Dr Maclaren rose.

"Doctor Maclaren, please," the chairman protested. "I wass going to call on Croup Captain . . ."

"You'll call upon him, Roderick, when I've said a few words to Mr Waggett," and the loud applause from the audience warned Big Roderick that he would be wiser to submit if he wished the meeting to remain orderly.

"Mr Waggett," Doctor Maclaren began, "we've known one another now for a quarter of a century." Waggett inclined his head in acceptance of this statement. "And in that time I have heard you talk a great deal of nonsense, but never since we first met have I heard you talk quite so much clotted nonsense as you have talked to-night. You know nothing about nuclear energy."

"I beg your pardon?" Paul Waggett said, the superior smile and the tilted nose vanishing in a flushed expression of amazement.

"Nothing at all," the Doctor continued inexorably, "except the scraps you pick up from the popular weeklies you read, and even those scraps you've managed to mix up. You don't even know the difference between 'fission' and 'fissure', and in fact your lecture to-night was the most notable demonstration of a fool rushing in where angels fear to tread that I have ever heard."

"I must call on the chairman for protection," said Waggett angrily. "You are not behaving like a gentleman, Dr Maclaren."

"Perhaps not, but I'm talking like a sensible man."

"Doctor, Doctor, please," the chairman rose to plead.

"Sit down, Roderick," the Doctor snapped, and Big Roderick obeyed. Then the Doctor turned to the audience. "I'll speak in English because I want Group Captain Oakenbotham to understand what I say. What you must all try to understand is that behind this rocket range business as put forward by the Government there is a much bigger scheme, and that bigger scheme is gradually to occupy and develop the whole of the Long Island from the Butt of Lewis to Barra Head to serve as a threat to Russia. Whether that is a good or bad strategic plan I am not qualified to argue. But in your anxiety to cash in on the money that will be yours in the immediate future you will do well to remember your ultimate future. This plan will mean that in the event of war the Outer Isles will be the first objective for Russian rockets. The Government says that the three Uists and the two Toddays are to be merely a training-ground for what they call ballistic warfare. It was announced first that they were preparing to spend twelve million pounds on this training-ground. They announced later that they were going to spend seventeen million pounds upon it. They may announce to-morrow an even larger sum. Do you suppose they would spend these huge amounts on a mere training-ground? You have heard from Mr Waggett to-night that the people of Little Todday are refusing to co-operate. Have you in your hope of money flowing in Great Todday thought what it means for the future of Little Todday to have an aerodrome right across the island and to have a rocket range on Tràigh Swish? Have you thought what it means to a crofter to be told that he has to give up his house and his land in this coming New Year? Whatever may happen to you here, Little Todday is condemned to be extinguished by the Government as surely as if a Russian rocket had blown it to pieces. I do not suppose you paid much attention to anything Mr Waggett said to-night, but if after to-night I hear anybody in Great Todday criticizing the efforts of Little Todday to obstruct this damnable attempt to destroy them, that man may remain a patient of mine but he will never again be my friend."

Dr Maclaren sat down amid loud applause and shouts from the Biffer, Drooby and several others of "*Suas Todaidh Beag!*"

"I will now call upon Croup Captain Oceanbottom," said the chairman.

The Group Captain smiled tolerantly at Dr Maclaren before he began to speak in hearty tones:

"My friends, for even after my short stay on your beautiful island I feel I can call you 'my friends', I cannot follow Dr Maclaren in his wild speculations about the future. I can only assure him that I have never heard a whisper of any of these future plans about which he talked so confidently. The plain facts are that the Government has made a revolution in our defence system in order to economize. That we shall in due course have rocket ranges elsewhere than those at present under construction is no doubt true, but the reason why we have chosen the three Uists and the two Toddays for our plans is their suitability as a training-ground for ballistic warfare. I regret that Colonel Bullingham, who commands the 1st Ballistic Regiment which will be stationed at Balmuir, is not with us to-night, but I do not think I shall be saying anything that might endanger security if I let you into a secret. To-day, my friends, the first guided missile made an experimental flight, and naturally Colonel Bullingham could not leave Balmuir."

At this moment the door at the back of the hall burst open and half a dozen women entered wailing.

"The Clach Mhôr has fallen. The Clach Mhór has fallen into Loch Tod."

And round the audience ran a murmur of apprehension, for the Clach Mhôr for hundreds of years had been a pledge of the island's safety. The great stone had stood balanced on a granite ledge of Ben Bustival from time immemorial. That it never fell had been a perpetual miracle. Tradition said that St Tod sailed from Donegal on a log to Little Todday, his monkish habit providing the sail, his arm uplifted in benediction, the mast. On Little Todday he had built a church, the foundations of which beside a holy well were still visible above Tràigh Tod. He then went on to bring the Gospel to the people of Great Todday, much to the annoyance of the Evil One, who rolled a huge stone down Ben Bustival with the object of knocking out St Tod when he was preaching on the brae below. However, the saint saw the stone coming and stopped it in mid career by holding up his hand. And where it stopped that day it had remained ever since, but so miraculously balanced that it could be moved round by a touch of the hand. The saint, in gratitude for his defeat of the Evil One, promised that the stone would remain where it was until some great calamity was threatening Great Todday, when it would fall as an omen of disaster.

And now the Clach Mhôr had fallen. It had fallen, moreover, on the day that the first rocket had been fired from Balmuir.

Nobody wanted to listen to what Group Captain Oakenbotham had to say. The meeting broke up.

"Extraordinary," Paul Waggett said to his wife when he returned home. "Sunk in superstition. They think something terrible's going to happen to the island just because a stone falls. The only person who suffers is me, because it fell into my best brown trout lock on Ben Bustival."

"All the same, Paul, I hope you will be able to sell our house to the rocket people," said Mrs Waggett tremulously.

"Look here, don't you start getting superstitious, old lady," said her husband with playful severity.

Norman Macleod and Duncan Bàn brought the news of the portent to Father Macalister.

"Well, we want all the help we can get from St Tod on Todaidh Beag, boys. It's just as well we haven't got to bother about Todaidh Môr. Indeed, I wonder the holy man put up with them so long. What was the meeting like?"

"We didn't go to the meeting, Father James," Norman Macleod told him.

The priest looked at him sharply.

"Did you not, Norman?"

"No, we had a crack with George Campbell and my sister Catriona."

"Ay, ay, good shooting."

Chapter 12

THE LAND COMMISSION

THE young people of Great Todday displayed a manly scepticism about St Tod's prophecy, but the older islanders, in spite of so many years of effort by the ministers who had given them their spiritual services to root out superstition, were oppressed by a sense of impending disaster. When the Land Commissioners arrived in a November gale to hear the arguments for and against the resumption of the landlord's rights over crofts and common grazing, instead of the eager agre ment which the Department of Agriculture had confid ntly expected from the crofters of Great Todday, their P incipal Assistant Deputy Chief Lands Officer, Mr Walter Scott, who had been entrusted with the presentation of the Department's case for resumption, was taken aback to find that almost every application he made was being opposed. Fortunately for him, the three Land Commissioners were suffering as much as himself from the tempestuous crossing. So Mr Walter Scott was granted a day's respite before the Land Commission sat in the Snorvig hall, and he was able to put his case together without his head swimming.

The President of the Land Commission was Sir Alexander Rossie, Q.C., the author of two books about mediaeval Scotland. Lawyers thought he was a better historian than lawyer: historians were sure that he was a better lawyer. He was a small shrivelled Fifer with a high piping voice, and although only in his mid-fifties gave the impression of being much older. Sir Alexander was filled with a strong sense of his own constitutional importance as President of the Land Commission, the rulings of which he regarded with veneration. Most of the disputes that he and his fellow Commissioners were called upon to settle were concerned with the boundaries of neighbouring crofts, and Sir Alexander had been known to sit a whole day hearing evidence whether John Mackenzie was justified in claiming that Colin Campbell had placed his fence two inches inside land that properly belonged to John Mackenzie. Sir Alexander's decision, supported by the other two Commissioners, who had never been known to dissent from his rulings, had for himself the sanctity of Domesday Book.

"I don't think we shall have any real bother with the opposition to-morrow," the Principal Assistant Deputy Chief Lands Officer of the Department of Agriculture observed happily to the President of the Land Commission.

Sir Alexander held up a protesting hand.

"Please, Mr Scott, I would prefer not to discuss what will happen to-morrow. I am anxious to keep a perfectly open mind."

"Yes, yes, I apologize, Sir Alexander," said Mr Scott quickly.

"There are very important issues at stake, Mr Scott. I know that the country is waiting anxiously to hear what the decision of the Land Commission will be. You must have noticed how many newspaper correspondents were in the boat."

"I'm afraid I felt much too sea-sick to notice anything on the boat," Mr Scott admitted.

"Yes, it was a nasty crossing. Mr MacTaggart and Mr Fletcher, my fellow Commissioners, were both prostrated, and even I was not sorry when we reached Snorvig. However, Captain MacKellaig, who has taken Captain MacKechnie's place, handled the *Island Queen* as well as his famous predecessor."

At this moment Big Roderick came into the hotel sitting-room.

"I've chust had a telegraph from Mr Macaulay to say he will be crossing the Sound from Nobost this morning."

"No doubt he wants to report the result of the Land Commission's findings to Parliament," said Sir Alexander.

"I like to see a Member looking after the interests of his constituents."

Mr Thomas Macaulay, the Labour member for West Inverness-shire, arrived just before one o'clock, and feeling it was his duty to impress the company with his lively interest in what was happening in the world, he asked for the wireless to be turned on in order to listen to the one o'clock news.

"Before I read the news," said the announcer, "here is a guided missile warning. Attention all shipping. At ten minutes past twelve the Ministry of Protection issued the following guided missile warning. A guided missile of the British Borzoi type which was launched from Balmuir shortly before noon has not returned to its base. Any ship in sea area Hebrides which has sighted this guided missile should communicate as soon as possible with the Director of Ballistic Warfare, Ministry of Protection, 5 Whitehall Circus. Telephone, Whitehall 9999.

"I hope it won't come down here," Sir Alexander Rossie piped.

"I hope not indeed," said Mr Walter Scott. "That might entail really serious opposition from the crofters."

Mr Macaulay frowned.

"We can't have these things roaming about all over my constituency," he said sternly. "I shall ask a question about it in the House."

"Ay, I believe you will, Mr Macaulay," Big Roderick averred. He had never hitherto held Mr Macaulay in much respect as the Parliamentary representative of Great Todday, but he looked so fierce over the undemocratic behaviour of this rocket that Roderick began to wonder if he might not have misjudged Mr Macaulay's apparent lack of interest in this remote corner of his constituency where votes were comparatively few. Roderick did not know that the other members of the House of Commons paid even less attention to Mr Macaulay than Mr Macaulay himself paid to Great and Little Todday.

Group Captain Oakenbotham coming into the room just then was at once invited to reassure the company on the subject of wandering rockets.

"I've been trying to get through to Balmuir," he said, "but telephonic communication with Balmuir has broken down."

"Do you think the whole range may have been blown up?" Sir Alexander asked, his voice even higher than usual with anxiety.

"No, no, no, one of those confounded swans has probably bust the wire. They're always doing it. Personally I think it was a mistake for the Ministry to issue that guided missile warning. It puts ideas into people's heads."

"It's rather an uncomfortable idea," Mr Walter Scott murmured. "I mean to say, the idea that one of these rockets may be wandering about all over Scotland is definitely uncomfortable."

"Oh, that's out of the question," Group Captain Oakenbotham assured him heartily. "These British Borzois only have a range of about fifty miles. They're tactical weapons: they're not strategic. What we're anxious to find out is where this Borzoi came down in the sea. They're expensive, you know, and we can't afford to lose them."

The Group Captain's words may have been successful in convincing the company at the Snorvig Hotel that a rocket was unlikely to land on the table in the middle of lunch, but over the rest of the island that wireless warning produced something like a panic. Even those who had scoffed at the threat of disaster foretold by the fall of the Clach Mhór began to wonder if there might not be something in it. The schools at Snorvig, Watasett, Bobanish and Garryboo were besieged by anxious mothers determined to get their children back home. That fierce sermon which the Reverend Angus Morrison had preached about the profanation of the Sabbath by those bangs the contractor's men made when they were blowing up the wall of Kiltod harbour came back to his parishioners, and he was approached almost humbly by Simon MacRurie himself to ask if he would hold a service to intercede with the Almighty and beg Him not to punish the island for that profanation. The immediate panic was allayed by an announcement from the Ministry of Protection in the six o'clock news to say it had now been established that the British Borzoi had sunk in the sea between St Kilda and West Uist, to which the B.B.C. appended an almost emotional appeal to listeners not to ring them up any more with reports of having sighted the rocket over various parts of Scotland. Nevertheless, when the Land Commission sat in the Snorvig hall to hear the Principal Assistant Deputy Chief Lands Officer make his request for the Department of Agriculture to resume one or two crofts and a considerable area of inferior grazing land in the public interest under the provisions of the Smallholders Act, 1955, it was apparent that instead of the willingness to cooperate which had hitherto been so enthusiastically evident there was now a spirit of sullen resistance in the air.

Sir Alexander Rossie became more and more aware of this spirit as Mr Walter Scott put forward the advantages to the island economy of its being used as a training-ground for ballistic troops. When Group Captain Oakenbotham offered evidence in greater detail of the Ministry's plans, in the course of which the assurances given a year ago at Nobost were repeated, the President of the Land Commission felt that it was his patriotic duty to play upon the romantic feelings of the islanders by which his study of history had led him to believe they were ruled.

"I myself hail from the Kingdom of Fife, Group Captain Oakenbotham," he piped, "and if the Land Commission were sitting this morning in the Kingdom of Fife I should take a different view of the situation, but it is the duty of the Land Commission to pay due regard to the responsibility it owes to every part of Scotland. It cannot ignore the special conditions which exist in the Outer Isles, and it must bear in mind that the way of life there is found nowhere else in Great Britain to-day. You are no doubt aware,

Group Captain Oakenbotham, that the language here is Gaelic. Are you able to give an undertaking that the troops who are situated here will be required to learn Gaelic?"

"I'm afraid I am not in a position to do that, sir," said the Group Captain in that loud and cheerful voice with which he was accustomed to conceal any doubts he might feel about his own adequacy to answer a question.

"But you are in a position to put such a recommendation by the Land Commission before the Ministry of Protection?" Sir Alexander piped.

"I will certainly do that, sir," the Group Captain promised.

"And I am sure that Mr Macaulay will do his utmost to obtain Parliamentary approval for such a recommendation," Sir Alexander went on, turning to the Member. Mr Macaulay nearly toppled off the fence on which he was sitting so gingerly during this hearing to answer with a firm negative, but he regained his balance just in time and stayed on the fence.

"I think it would be inadvisable to say anything in Parliament, Sir Alexander, until the Services had either approved or disapproved of such a recommendation. I am as you know a Gaelic speaker myself, but it has never been the policy of the Labour Party to . . ."

"Labour Party *cachd*!" the Biffer shouted from the back of the hall.

"*Suas* the Liberals!" his friend Drooby cried. "*Suas* Lloyd George!"

"Och, what a pity he is not here to-day," an old *cailleach* wailed. "What a fine man he was. He gave me my old age pension."

"Order, order!" piped the President of the Land Commission. "This is not a political meeting. Well, have I your assurance, Group Captain Oakenbotham, that you will place my recommendation before the Ministry of Protection?"

"I shall do that, sir."

"And would it not be a good idea," Sir Alexander continued, "if a special Highland uniform were devised for these ballistic troops?"

Even Group Captain Oakenbotham's easy cheerfulness was shaken by this question. He could think of nothing to say.

"You will remember," Sir Alexander piped on, "that when the kilt and the tartan were proscribed after the Forty-five the garb of old Gaul was restored to those Highlanders who enlisted in the Highland regiments that were being raised for the defence of their country."

"I didn't know that, sir," the Group Captain had to admit.

"Dear me, you didn't know that?" Sir Alexander piped on a high note of astonishment. "Well, I suggest that a special Highland uniform should be devised for these ballistic troops as a recognition of the sacrifices that the people of these islands will have to make in surrendering their way of life to the country's needs. I have a friend in Edinburgh who would be glad to design an appropriate uniform. I am not suggesting that these troops should wear kilts. No, no. I am merely suggesting that their uniform should adumbrate a Celtic background."

"Adumbrate" was a new word to the Group Captain, and he made a mental note of it as a useful long word for use in official communications.

"Adumbrate, sir. Quite," he repeated to impress the word on his memory.

"Yes, yes," Sir Alexander piped on. "I am sure that this friend of mine in Edinburgh could evolve something really distinctive."

If Sir Alexander Rossie hoped that the report of his attempt to romanticize the effect of the Government's plans on Great and Little Todday would soften the attitude of Little Todday, he was to be sadly disappointed when on the following day he crossed the Coolish to hear the objections of the Little Todday crofters to being put out of their crofts.

"It's really a beautiful morning," he observed to his fellow Commissioners, when they boarded the tug that the contractors for the new pier at Kiltod had put at their disposal. "We ought to get a calm crossing to-morrow."

Mr MacTaggart and Mr Fletcher assented gloomily to this statement. They were filled with apprehension of what their President might say at the sitting of the Land Commission in Little Todday. After his performance in Snorvig, the Press correspondents had crowded round him like wasps round a jampot, and Sir Alexander had elaborated so garrulously what the other two Commissioners considered his preposterous suggestion for turning the ballistic troops into wraiths of the Celtic twilight that the thought of them in cold print presently had made them feel as queasy as the prospect of the crossing back to the mainland.

Mr MacTaggart and Mr Fletcher shuddered when they recalled the highlight of that Press conference:

"An allusion was made to the possibility of emigration to Canada for crofters who may have to give up their houses and land," the *Daily Tale* had said. "What are your feelings about that, Mr President?"

"I hope that the Department of Agriculture will take steps to provide accommodation nearer home. You may recall that the Moona Islands two miles north of Barra Head were recently evacuated by the three ailing elderly inhabitants left on them. Why should not half a dozen young and energetic crofters from Great and Little Todday get married and build up a thriving community on the Moona Islands? They might become known as the Honey-moona Islands."

For Mr MacTaggart and Mr Fletcher the remembrance of those words turned the pale blue November sky this morning to a leaden grey.

The Principal Assistant Deputy Chief Lands Officer of the Department of Agriculture was waiting for the Land Commissioners at the end of the half-built new pier; with him were Group Captain Oakenbotham and Mr Thomas Macaulay, M.P.

"There seems to have been some misunderstanding, Sir

Alexander," said Mr Walter Scott. "There is nobody in the hall, and there are no chairs or tables either. It is completely bare. I went up to the chapel house, but there was no sign of Father Macalister. Then I went along to the school, and that was as empty as the hall."

"But surely the crofters of Little Todday were notified that the Land Commissioner would be sitting here to-day?" Sir Alexander piped irritably.

"They were certainly notified," Mr Walter Scott assured the President.

"This amounts to a contempt of court," Sir Alexander declared.

"I'll go along and find out from Mr Joseph Macroon if there has been some misunderstanding," the M.P. volunteered.

He came back a few minutes later to say that the post-office was closed and that he could get no reply from any of the houses in Kiltod.

"The place is absolutely deserted."

The foreman of the contractor's gang working on the new pier was now consulted.

"Where is everybody? Don't ask me. I've been on some queer jobs in my time, but this is the queerest job I ever was on. It's not like working among human beings at all. Jabbering away among themselves in this Garlic of theirs, and if you ask a civil question all you get is a stare as if you was something left behind by the tide. And every evening when we go back to Snorvig we have to make certain we take every tool we've got back with us because if we don't it's a sure thing we'll never see it again. 'What's the good of rounding on us?' I ask them. 'We're paid to do a job of work. It isn't our fault they want to turn you into a blinking rocket range.'"

"But have they definitely tried to interfere with your work?" Group Captain Oakenbotham asked.

"They haven't tried to push us into the water yet, if that's what you mean. But then we haven't had to interfere with their land. After that bulldozer was hit by Macroon's lorry there hasn't been another bulldozer landed, but I reckon when the next one does arrive it won't be much use for work a few hours later."

"I think we'd better go up to the hall," said Sir Alexander. "The Land Commission can't sit where we are now."

Nor could the Land Commission sit in the hall unless the Commissioners were prepared to sit on the floor.

"Where *can* everybody be?" Mr Walter Scott exclaimed.

"Well, we certainly can't go wandering about all over the island looking for them," said Sir Alexander.

"The Air Commodore warned me before I came to Little Todday that I should find the padre here very unco-operative," said Group Captain Oakenbotham. "What do you think we ought to do, Sir Alexander?"

"The only thing to do is for Mr Scott to put his request formally to the Land Commission and for us to grant resumption. We shan't trouble you to give any further evidence, Group Captain Oakenbotham."

There was a sound of voices outside the hall.

"Ah," Sir Alexander piped with satisfaction, "here they come at last. No idea of time, as usual."

But the voices were not the voices of the crofters of Little Todday arriving to plead their case before the Land Commission. They were the voices of the Press correspondents, who had pooled their financial resources to bribe the Biffer and his friend Drooby to bring them across the Coolish in the *Kittiwake* and the *Flying Fish*.

"Would you care to give us a statement, Sir Alexander?" asked the two bright lads of the *Daily Excess* and the *Daily Tale*. "We understand there has been a boycott here."

Mr MacTaggart and Mr Fletcher shivered. What might not Sir Alexander Rossie say to create in the public mind an impression that the Land Commission was a kind of judicial harlequinade?

"I have no statement to make for the Press," Sir Alexander piped with dignity.

"But you will make a statement, Mr Macaulay?" asked the *Glasgow Trumpeter*, who hoped for ammunition with which the leader-writers of his paper might do some damage to the Labour Party.

"I have no statement to make," said Mr Macaulay.

Those six simple words were hardly recognizable in a leader of the *Glasgow Trumpeter* next day.

"Mr Thomas Macaulay, the Labour member for West Inverness-shire, was obviously bewildered by the humiliating position in which he found himself. Asked to offer some explanation of the extraordinary behaviour of his constituents he refused, and if by adopting this attitude he has lost whatever negligible political influence he has been able to exert in this remote corner of his constituency Mr Macaulay has only himself to thank. It is abundantly clear that he and his Party are not regarded seriously either in Great or Little Todday. Indeed, Mr Macaulay's whole attitude represented in miniature the present unhappy position of Labour without a leader and without a policy. Mr Aneurin Bevan may be a wandering rocket; Mr Thomas Macaulay is merely a damp squib."

Two of the Press correspondents volunteered to go on a scouting expedition to see if they could find the missing audience. This suggestion ruffled Sir Alexander Rossie's sense of his own importance.

"The Land Commission has been treated by the crofters of Little Todday with a discourtesy for which I cannot find a parallel in the whole of my experience. I propose here and now to hear the landlord's request for resumption of the twenty-two crofts. Mr Scott, please."

The Principal Assistant Deputy Chief Lands Officer read out his list, and the President of the Land Commission immediately granted every application for resumption and confirmed the right of the landlord subject to the payment of due compensation to resume possession one week after January 1st of the following year.

"This sitting by the Land Commission is now terminated,"

the President declared not before time, everybody thought, because it had been no fun to have to stand in a chilly hall listening to the Principal Assistant Deputy Chief Lands Officer of the Department of Agriculture reading out the specifications of twenty-two crofts.

When the boats were midway between Kiltod and Snorvig, the sound of a mighty "boo!" came travelling across the calm waters of the Coolish.

"I don't know what they're cheering about," the *Daily Excess* said to the *Daily Tale*. "They surely don't think they've beaten the Government."

"I wouldn't call it 'cheering'," said the *Daily Tale*. "I would call it 'jeering'."

"Saying 'boo' to a gaggle of geese," *The Caledonian* commented. "I wish they *could* beat the Government."

Chapter 13

THE SHERIFF'S PARTY

"I WONDER what the end of it is going to be?" Hugh said to Jane when they were sitting at breakfast in what had once been the coachman's cottage at Greystones. He had just been reading the account of the Land Commission's visit to Great and Little Todday. "I think we must go over and see what happens in January when the Department intends to resume its rights as landlord."

A week or two later Hugh had a letter from Norman Macleod to say that the Little Todday crofters had been warned by the Department of Agriculture that their obstructive attitude had compelled the Department to take the unwelcome step of calling upon the Sheriff to enforce the resumption of the landlord's rights.

"That means the police will be with the Sheriff," Hugh said. "Oh, we must be there, Jane. We must certainly be there."

So two days after Hogmanay Hugh and Jane set out for Little Todday to stay with Father Macalister.

"Hugh, look!" Jane cried as they were walking along the platform at Buchanan Street to catch the Obaig train. "It's Mrs Odd."

Both of them shouted to her just as the old lady was getting into a second-class compartment.

"Well! Only last week I sore an empty hearse, and here's the pleasant surprise and which you always get if you see an empty hearse." There was a brief argument on the subject of first or second class.

"Now, look here, Mrs Odd," said Hugh. "I don't see why Jane and I should present British Railways with the difference between two first- and second-class tickets just because you're too obstinate to let me stand you the difference on one ticket. Because whatever you say, we are determined to have your company."

So presently the three of them were in a first-class compartment, looking comfortably out at the grey wintry afternoon. Mrs Odd was talkative.

"There was a bit of an argy-bargy before Fred and Peggy let me go off on my ownsome. But, as I said, 'If you think you're going to stop me standing by Duncan Bang when we tell the bluebottles sent to put us out to buzz off back to where they come from, you'd better give your brains a rest. I'm going,' I said, 'and nobody's going to stop me!' Oh dear, what a set out when that rocket started off on its ownsome. 'Well,' I said, when I heard that warning on the wireless, 'what a pity it can't land on the head of Colonel Ballipstick Bullingham. I reckon those pop-eyes of his would both come out on stalks like a shrimp's.'"

Some of the dignity of the Sheriff's arrival at Snorvig on January 7th was marred by his having to be assisted ashore by a couple of constables, the crossing having been a severe one and the Sheriff having been retching without cessation from the time that the *Island Queen* left Tobermory. Fortunately it was dark and there were not many about on the pier to see the arrival of the Law. Sergeant MacGillivray, whose red cheeks contrasted almost brutally with the eau-de-Nil complexion of the Sheriff, had a car waiting to drive the tottery avatar of the Law up to the hotel.

"Ah, there you are, Siorram, welcome, come in," said the host, swelling with hospitality. "Will you take a tram?"

The Sheriff shook a feeble head.

"Thank you, no," Mr MacRurie. I think I would like to go straight up to my room."

"Ferry good, Siorram. Ferry good. Will you be taking kippers with your tea?"

The Sheriff's countenance was momentarily convulsed.

"Thank you, I'll take a cup of tea and some dry toast in my room," he replied.

"The boat will be at the pier to-morrow morning at ten o'clock to cross over to Kiltod," Sergeant MacGillivray said. "Do you wish to see me, sir, this evening?"

"No, thank you, Sergeant."

"I've made all arrangements for Sergeant Macrae and the two constables. Sergeant Macrae was very pleased to be back in Snorvig. He was here as constable before I came."

The Sheriff closed his eyes wearily.

"Yes, yes, I've no doubt he was. Good-evening, Sergeant."

Sergeant MacGillivray clicked his heels and retired.

The new pier at Kiltod had made considerable progress during the last seven or eight weeks, and the workmen were hard at work when the Sheriff, with Sergeant MacGillivray, Sergeant Macrae and the two constables, reached Kiltod next morning.

With them was a bunch of officials from the Department of Agriculture, which included Mr Edward Dalrymple the Deputy Assistant Chief Lands Officer, the Deputy Assistant Chief Executive Officer, the Assistant Senior Inspector of Livestock, the Assistant Senior Inspector of Potatoes, and the Deputy Chief Egg Officer, their united salaries adding up to a mere £8000 out of the Department of Agriculture's total salary list of over £130,000 annually, excluding clerks, stenographers, and various odds and ends.

The wind was still blowing hard, but it had veered to the west from the south-west and the tug had reached the shelter of Little Todday in time to spare the Sheriff any more qualms.

"None of the Little Todday men about," Sergeant MacGillivray remarked.

Curly-headed Sergeant Macrae chuckled.

"It puts me in mind of the time when the Exciseman and me searched the island for the whisky from the *Cabinet Minister*. It was just as quiet as it is this morning, and not a bottle did we find."

The Sheriff asked how far away were the crofts that they had come to take possession of.

"About two miles," he commented. "We'd better get hold of a car."

"There isn't a motor-car on the island," Sergeant MacGillivray told him.

"Then we'd better get a trap," the Sheriff decided.

"Ay, if we can," the Sergeant muttered doubtfully.

Sergeant Macrae chuckled again.

"There won't be any trap. I know them here," he prophesied.

"Ay, I'm thinking we will have to walk," Sergeant MacGillivray agreed.

And walk they did for over two miles in the teeth of the wind before they came in sight of Duncan Bàn's house, Tigh a' Bhàird, round which were gathered the whole population of the island except the aged, infirm and the very youngest of the children.

"None of these newspaper fellows about anyway," the Sheriff observed with satisfaction in his tone. He was remembering the reports in the Press of Sir Alexander Rossie's romantic eloquence.

The Sheriff spoke too soon. Father Macalister had arranged for the Dot to bring them over to Bàgh Mhic Ròin, Macroon's Bay, on the north side of the island in case the police should try to prevent their crossing over to Kiltod. The Sheriff had no sooner congratulated himself on the absence of the Press than *The Caledonian*, the *Glasgow Trumpeter*, the *Daily Tale*, the *Daily Excess*, half a dozen other correspondents and several camera-men appeared on the other side of the crowd and were already busy among them with their notebooks and photography when the official party reached the gathering.

The loud cheer with which their arrival was greeted made the Sheriff hopeful of a peaceable reception, but, alas for his optimism, the cheer was for Sergeant Macrae.

Father Macalister stepped forward to speak to the invaders.

"Before you read your rigmarole, Sheriff," he said, "it is

my duty to warn you that nobody on Little Todday will pay any attention to it. I'm sure you'll agree with me that four policemen will never be able to put twenty-two families out of their houses if more than a hundred able-bodied men are determined to prevent it. Therefore take my advice, Sheriff, and don't give the order to roll right over us, because if you do we will have to roll right over you. We will just put you on the tug and take you back to Snorvig. No violence will be used. Just gentle persuasion. And I'm sure everybody will have a good laugh when they see the pictures of the Sheriff and the officials of the Department of Agriculture being put on board an emigrant ship with four policemen, including our old friend Sergeant Macrae, of whom we always speak with affection. If the Ministry of Protection sends an Expeditionary Force against us, we may be defeated in action, but we will then appeal to the United Nations. The United Nations's plate is pretty full, but we'll just add a little salt to it. And now, Sheriff, I've said my rigmarole and we'll all listen very inattentively to yours."

There was a colloquy among the invaders, at the conclusion of which the Sheriff stepped forward:

"I do not propose to call upon the police," he began.

This was greeted by a loud cheer and cries of "*Suas an t-Siorram!*"

The Sheriff held up his hand.

"I shall not call upon the police because I want to give you a last opportunity to realize that the Law must be obeyed. The Department of Agriculture has no desire to inflict undue hardships upon its tenants. The Department recognizes that some hardship might be entailed by leaving your homes in mid-winter, and therefore after consultation with the representatives of the Department I have decided to grant you a further six weeks before you are compelled to hand over your crofts to the Department as the landlord."

There was an angry murmur, which died away when Father Macalister spoke again.

"The people of Little Todday will adopt the same attitude six weeks hence as they have adopted this morning. They can only be evicted from their crofts by military force, and if the Government decides to use such force it will be disgraced in the eyes of the world. We are glad you have decided not to inflict on the police the humiliation of being carried off the island and dumped in a boat, because Sergeant MacGillivray and Sergeant Macrae are old friends of ours. And we wouldn't have liked to carry you gentlemen from the Department off the island in such an undignified position because we know that your hearts are not really in this business. We know that your consciences must be troubling you. We know that you must be asking yourselves whether or not you have sold your country for a salary and a pension. We are sorry for you. And I would be glad," Father Macalister went on, turning to the Press correspondents, "if the newspapers would not present us people of Little Todday as enjoying a temporary triumph this morning. We have enjoyed no triumph. We have given that triumph to the Sheriff and the officials of the Department of Agriculture and the police, who have prevented any display of violence by the moderation of their own behaviour. One last word. We are fighting for our own homes in a small island on the outermost edge of Western Europe, but we are fighting at the same time for millions in Western Europe who have been betrayed by the example that Great Britain is setting in starting this insensate and suicidal project to fight the Devil with the Devil's own weapons. In the Dark Ages there were many years during which the light of Faith in Europe was almost extinguished except in Ireland and in these Western Isles. The Devil has been waiting for a long while to pay us back for that, and now he thinks his chance has come. Yet I believe that we are going to beat him, and that belief is the most formidable feat of faith I have ever performed."

That night, when the wind which had veered to the north-west was booming round the chapel house, Hugh and

Jane were sitting with their host round a rich fire in the sitting-room.

"Well, Hugh," he said, "we must be really grateful to our visitors for the way they behaved."

"I doubt if the rocketeers will behave as sensibly," said Hugh. "Do you really believe you will beat them in the end, Father James?"

"I do, and now, Seonaid, sing to us. We are in need of tranquillity."

Above the ground bass of the wind she sang old Gaelic lullabies and songs of love.

The wind had died down by midday on the morrow, and after lunch Hugh and Jane walked over to Bow Bells.

"Well, I'd made up my mind I'd be sleeping on the macker last night," said Mrs Odd, "and in fact I put on two pairs of knickers to keep out the draught. But yesterday won't be the end of it, and I'm going to stay here till either I see the end of it or it sees the end of me. I was glad Sergeant Macrae came over with them. That quietened down Duncan Bang, because he and Macrae were always great friends. Before that he was charging about all over the place like the Light Brigade. Wasn't Father James grand?"

"He was indeed," Hugh agreed. "I only hope the authorities will realize that. But they are so, so stupid. Look, Mrs Odd, Jane and I are going to walk over to Tràigh nan Eun. Can we come in and have tea with you on the way back?"

"Yes, I'll meet you when the sun goes down—now who was it used to sing that song? Oh dear, my brainbox is in the lost property office nowadays."

Hugh and Jane reached that small cove just before sunset. Although the wind had dropped, a heavy sea was running through the narrow strait between Little Todday and Pillay and seething over the black rock of the Gobha. A flock of gulls which had been scavenging on the sandy brae rose screaming and as they flew across to Pillay they were tinged by a carmine glow in the west to the same hue.

"What a pity there are no rare birds on Little Todday," Hugh said. "That's the only way to stir up public opinion. People don't get worked up about the ways of human beings anything like as much as they do about the ways of birds. The Nature Conservancy people can get a grant of two or three hundred thousand, but when a few scholars asked the Government to contribute to the expenses of preserving the oral traditions and songs of these islands whose oral traditions and songs will inevitably be destroyed by these rocketeers, not a farthing could be found."

When Hugh and Jane got back to Greystones two days later there was a letter for Hugh from Andrew Wishart at the Scottish Office:

Dear Hugh,

I read in the Caledonian's report of the Sheriff's visit to Little Todday that you were among those present. I have to address a conservative rally at Selwick next Wednesday and it might be helpful if I could hear from you exactly what did happen. Perhaps you could manage to come in to Selwick. I shall be staying at the Blue Bonnet Hotel. I shall be going to Edinburgh next day.

Yours sincerely,

Andrew Wishart

Hugh rang up his old chief at the Scottish Office to suggest he should stay next Wednesday night at Greystones, whence he could be driven next day to Edinburgh.

"And don't eat too much high tea at the Blue Bonnet, sir, We can get back to a decent supper here after the meeting. There won't be anybody except my father and mother and Jane, who's looking forward to meeting you."

Mr Wishart accepted Hugh's invitation with alacrity. So Wednesday evening found Sir Robert MacInnes and his son sitting on the platform behind the Scottish Under-Secretary, who produced the stock eloquence of such an occasion. Hugh wondered how he could have possibly been taken in by it once upon a time and how his father could still seem able to be taken in by it.

"Well, now that I've met you—er—may I call you Jane? No, I certainly can't blame Hugh for deserting me," Mr Wishart told the young wife of his late Private Secretary, and as he took Jane's hand he glowed in the refreshing sensation of being able to say for a change what he really did feel.

The subject of Little Todday was not broached at supper. Indeed, it was postponed until the following morning, when Hugh drove Mr Wishart to Edinburgh.

"I wish you could persuade the Reverend Mr Macalister, Hugh, that his defiant attitude can achieve nothing. Those Protection people are still looking for an excuse to evacuate both islands. We have been opposing such a scheme at the Scottish Office, but now they have been concentrating on Little Todday, and the kind of thing that happened last week has played right into their hands."

"There was no violence, sir."

"No, but there was a threat of violence. Our people from St Andrew's House were quite clear about that."

"It was hardly a threat of violence. Father Macalister merely told the Sheriff that, if the police took any forcible steps to evict the crofters who have received notice to quit, the whole party, police included, would be put on board the contractor's tug and sent back to Snorvig."

"If they'd done that, it would have been violence."

"It would only have become violent if the official party had resisted deportation," Hugh argued.

"Deportation, yes, that's another thing. The Ministry of Protection is pressing for the deportation of the Reverend Mr Macalister," Mr Wishart said gloomily.

"They could hardly do that in peace-time, sir."

"They might accuse Mr Macalister of seditious behaviour. That would involve his arrest and prosecution. And then they could make the two Toddays a protected area, which would mean he would never be given a permit to land there again."

"I should have thought after the ignominious position in

which the Government have put themselves over Archbishop Makarios they would hesitate to put themselves into an equally ignominious position over another reverend gentleman. The next thing they'll be doing is to discover a diary kept by some member of the I.R.A. proving that Father Macalister is responsible for blowing up police-stations in Tyrone."

"That's very extravagant talk, Hugh. I wish you would realize the Government is convinced that the whole future safety of the country depends on the successful outcome of this new strategic conception. It is fairly obvious that the Russians have been taken aback by our determination to have our own H-bombs and our own rockets. That explains Bulganin's anxiety, which was most apparent in that letter he sent to the Prime Minister."

"Well, sir, can you give me any instance in the whole history of mankind when war was stopped because both sides were afraid of destroying one another? And how can this island of ours with its crowded industrial life hope to shoot it out with a land mass like Russia without being completely destroyed in the process?"

"Rather a pusillanimous attitude, Hugh," Mr Wishart observed.

"Yes, I daresay it is. A lot of people thought it was pusillanimous when the British Raj abdicated in India, but where should we be to-day without the pusillanimity of that Labour Government?"

"I'm not prepared to argue about India, Hugh. For better or worse the Government has decided what is the best way to defend our country, and having made that decision it can't be expected to have its plans held up by one minute island with a total population of well under a thousand. The kindest thing you can do for your friends on Little Todday is to persuade them to accept the inevitable. We have made arrangements to settle the crofters in various parts of the West Highlands. I may tell you that it was never our intention to ask them to leave their homes until the spring.

We were merely anxious to impress upon them that there was nothing they could do to change the Department's mind. Now thanks to this display of force . . ."

"There was no display of force."

"Threat of force."

"There was no threat of force, sir."

"I don't know what else you can call an announcement that a sheriff, various officials of the Department of Agriculture and four members of the police force will be deported unless they deport themselves. Anyway, it has played right into the hands of the Protection people, and it is only thanks to the patience and calmness of Sir Duncan Forbes that the evacuation of the whole population of Little Todday has not been placed before the Cabinet as a matter of urgency in the interest of national security."

"Am I at liberty to tell that to Father Macalister?" Hugh asked.

Mr Wishart hesitated.

"No, I can't authorize you to do that," he replied at last. "You can of course hint when you are persuading Mr Macalister—I'm afraid I can't bring myself to call him Father Macalister—yes, you can hint that a repetition of what took place last week might have grave consequences not only for himself but also for his parishioners. Meanwhile, the Department will send one of its Land Officers to notify the crofters that they will not be called upon to evacuate their houses until April because the Ministry of Protection does not propose to begin work on the aerodrome until then. However, a good deal of equipment of various kinds will start being unloaded now that the new pier is so well advanced, and probably the task of levelling portions of the ground will begin next month."

"The rocketeers will find the people of Little Todday much more of a problem than those of the other islands."

"We realize that."

"But from what we heard last week," Hugh said, "the people of Great Todday are beginning to wonder whether the proposals for their future were as attractive as they seemed at first. That runaway rocket shook them badly."

"Yes, we all thought that guided missile warning over the wireless a great mistake. And now here we are coming into Edinburgh. Do try, Hugh, to dissuade your friend Mr Macalister from making himself too prominent."

"I don't think any argument I can use will dissuade him. I'm glad I'm not still your P.S., sir."

"You don't regret giving up the idea of a political career, Hugh?" his late chief asked a little wistfully.

"No, sir. I can't say how grateful I am that Jane was on the *Island Queen* that May morning."

Mr Andrew Wishart sighed.

Chapter 14

THE MISGUIDED MISSILE

IN the middle of February two bulldozers were landed on the new pier at Kiltod. Exactly what happened to them during their first night on Little Todday remained a mystery, but in the words of Father Macalister, writing to Hugh MacInnes, the bulldozers became oxdozers no longer capable of any kind of ferocious behaviour.

At 5 Whitehall Circus, Air Chief Marshal Sir William Windermere, General Sir Hubert Cutwater, the Chairman of the Protection Research Policy Committee, Major-General H. E. Kortright, the Director of Ballistic Warfare, Sir Grimsby Wilberforce, the Permanent Secretary of the Ministry of Protection, Sir Duncan Forbes, the Permanent Under-Secretary of State for Scotland, and Mr Andrew Wishart, a Parliamentary Under-Secretary of State for Scotland, were gathered in a panelled room overlooking the river Thames to reach agreement on the necessary steps to be taken to prevent Little Todday's throwing any more spanners into the great work that the Ministry of Protection believed it was doing to safeguard the country's future.

"I think the position is well summed up in a report which Mr Bickers, the Minister of Protection . . ."

Sir Grimsby Wilberforce broke in to whisper something to Sir William Windermere.

"I apologize, gentlemen," said Sir William, "I should have said Mr Truefitt, the Minister of Protection; I'd forgotten for the moment that Mr Bickers was no longer Minister of Protection. After all, Mr Truefitt is the seventh Minister we have had in the last four years. One loses count sometimes, what?"

Everybody made a discreet sound of having been amused,

everybody, that is, except Sir Grimsby Wilberforce, whose position as a permanent official demanded a charitable attitude towards impermanent ministers.

"I should mention that Group Captain Oakenbotham was instructed by me to send his report direct to Mr Bickers just before Mr Bickers was succeeded as Minister of Protection by Mr Truefitt, and so although Group Captain Oakenbotham's letter is addressed to the Right Honourable Richard Bickers it was received and passed on to me by the Right Honourable Leonard Longley Truefitt to discuss appropriate action. I hope I have clarified the position?"

There was a murmur of agreement.

"Group Captain Oakenbotham's letter is dated February 28th and was dispatched from Snorvig, Great Todday, on the same date:

"Sir,

I have the honour in accordance with instructions received from Air Chief Marshal Sir William Windermere, G.C.B., to send you my report on the state of affairs now existing on the island of Little Todday in the Western Isles of Scotland. I might mention that Outer Isles, Outer Hebrides, and Long Island are also in common use as geographical descriptions for the Western Isles . . ."

"I'm glad Group Captain Oakenbotham has made that point clear," said Sir Hubert Cutwater. "There has been some confusion about those different names, and it is important to know exactly where we are."

An irreverent onlooker might have fancied an expression of something like contemptuous amusement in the eyes of Sir Duncan Forbes as Sir William Windermere resumed his reading of the Group Captain's report.

"I regret to report that the attitude of the natives . . ."

"I rather take exception to that use of the word 'natives'," said Mr Wishart. "I know of course it doesn't mean South Sea cannibals, but I remember once when I was doing an overseas broadcast for the B.B.C. that I was asked not to use the word. Apparently it's in bad odour everywhere, and the inhabitants of the Western Isles might resent it."

"I think you're right, Mr Under-Secretary," said Sir William. "I'll have the Group Captain warned about that." He turned back to the report:

"The attitude of the—er—inhabitants is definitely unco-operative, and indeed may even be called positively hostile. The men who have been working on the new pier at Kiltod inform me that if a tool is left about it invariably disappears, presumably in the sea. The surveyors have now had their measurements changed five times and removed altogether four times. Last autumn a bulldozer which had been landed with some difficulty owing to the incomplete state of the new pier was run into by the only lorry on the island, and in reporting the incident Police-Sergeant MacGillivray expressed his firm opinion that the lorry had been deliberately set at the bulldozer. Ten days ago two more bulldozers were landed and driven up to do some of the preliminary levelling for the proposed aerodrome, part of which will involve the cementing over of a good many acres of grazing ground immediately, and in April it is hoped to start demolishing some of the houses of the crofters. Nobody has been able to ascertain how the two bulldozers were deprived of their vital parts on the night of February 19th, and although these parts can probably be replaced, much time will have been wasted, and until the island is put in charge of a military guard I do not think that they can be considered secure against sabotage.

"I have ascertained that Lt.-Colonel W. C. Bullingham, commanding the 1st Ballistic Regiment now being trained in Mid Uist, could provide a platoon for that purpose, but he is unwilling to expose his men to the hardship of sleeping under canvas at this time of year and I was unable to guarantee him billets, because unfortunately not being at war we cannot compulsorily billet military personnel on civilians.

"It may seem, Sir, that the bulldozer incident lacks

importance, but we shall soon require to land valuable and highly secret material in connection with the proposed rocket range on Little Todday and sabotage might have very serious consequences for the progress and security of our work.

"I regret to inform you that the leader of the malcontents is the Reverend James Macalister, the Roman Catholic priest on the island, who wields great influence. Indeed, it is no exaggeration to say that the . . ." Sir William hesitated for a moment, "the inhabitants," he continued "do all he tells them to do. I called on the Reverend Macalister to remonstrate with him about the treatment of the bull-dozers, but he received my strong protest with absolute levity by calling them oxdozers. My personal belief is that there is no possibility of proceeding with our own work on Little Todday until the Reverend Macalister is no longer in charge of the Roman Catholic congregation there. Air Commodore Watchorn informed me that at first there was a certain amount of opposition from the Roman Catholic priest at Balmuir in West Uist but that everything had been amicably settled, that the people of all three of the Uist islands were working hard and that he had never seen more enthusiastic navvies anywhere. Indeed, they are so enthusiastic that the manager of the sea-weed company is trying to recruit labour from the island of Harris because so many of those who were working on the sea-weed have gone in for navvying instead."

"That's very encouraging," Major-General Kortright commented.

"I do not myself believe," Sir William read on, "that the people of Little Todday will make good navvies even if the Reverend Macalister is no longer on the island, but we might be able to find accommodation at first for a platoon of the 1st Ballistic Regiment in some of the houses vacated by the crofters. I do not know what powers you have, Sir, to remove the Reverend Macalister from Little Todday, but if you have such powers I venture to submit that the exercise of such powers would do a great deal to ameliorate the situation on Little Todday where a rapid development of the work is adumbrated from May onwards.

I have the honour to be, sir,
Your obedient Servant
Henry P. Oakenbotham
Group Captain, R.A.F.

The Rt. Hon. Richard Bickers, M.C., M.P.
H.M. Minister of Protection
5 Whitehall Circus, S.W. 1"

The Air Chief Marshal put the report down.

"As I told you, that letter was passed on to me by the new Minister of Protection, Mr Truefitt, for appropriate action," he said.

"Obviously the appropriate action is to get rid of this turbulent priest," Sir Hubert Cutwater guffawed.

"Yes, but Mr Truefitt has noted in the margin that he has no powers to deal with this R.C. padre," said the Air Chief Marshal. "And he's rather a formidable proposition. I met him when we undertook that exploratory mission to Little Todday. What do you say, Mr Under-Secretary? You met him, didn't you?"

"I didn't actually meet him," Mr Wishart replied. "But I heard him speak at Nobost and I can well imagine what a disturbing influence he might have on these simple islanders."

"Simple islanders," Sir Duncan Forbes murmured to himself.

"If that 18B order was still in force," said Major-General Kortright, "we could put the fellow in jug without telling him or anybody else why we had."

"Yes, but we've gone back to Habeas Corpus now," Mr Wishart reminded the General. "Do you see any way of removing Mr Macalister without offending against Scots law, Sir Duncan?"

Sir Duncan Forbes shook his head.

"We can't say he's a Communist if he's an R.C., can we?" Sir Hubert Cutwater asked.

"It would offend Roman Catholic opinion," said Mr Wishart quickly. There was quite a strong Roman Catholic vote in his constituency, and he did not wish to lose it.

"Couldn't we ask his bishop to give him a living on the mainland?" Sir Hubert suggested. "We could say it was advisable for the sake of peace. Bishops are always anxious to avoid trouble."

"If it could be proved he had incited this peculiar operation on the two bulldozers," said Sir Duncan, "we might have grounds for proceeding against him by law, but we shall never get such proof. And unless we have it, the repercussions that would arise from deporting him would be serious. The Ministry of Protection must bear in mind that many people in Scotland, and in England too, view this rocket scheme with considerable perturbation. I tell you I was thankful when the people at Balmuir gave in so meekly. If they had made a stand it might have precipitated a political crisis. You agree with me, don't you, Mr Under-Secretary?"

"I do indeed," the Under-Secretary replied fervidly. "We must not allow this business to become a sectarian battle. We must emphasize its prime importance as a measure of national security and economy."

"Do you still think that our project last year to evacuate the whole population of Great and Little Todday is impracticable?" Sir William asked.

"Absolutely," Mr Wishart declared firmly. "The Secretary of State will not consider it."

"We have given the matter long and anxious consideration here," said Sir William, "and we have now decided not to press for the evacuation of Great Todday, but the experimental projects we have in mind for Little Todday are so vitally important that we feel it may become imperative to secure a base where we can work with absolute secrecy. Frankly, we feel that as we have been able to persuade the Scottish Department of Agriculture to take over twenty-two crofts there is no valid reason to prevent them from taking over the whole island in the public interest."

"I cannot agree with you, Sir William, and I am sure the Secretary of State will find himself unable to accept such a proposal," said Mr Wishart. "Sir Duncan Forbes can tell you what difficulties we have had to contend with in dealing with the future of the twenty-two crofters who are now under notice to give up their houses and land. The problem of resettling nearly a thousand people is more than we can possibly contemplate."

"It certainly is," Sir Duncan insisted.

"I wonder if you'd care to hear what Dr Hamburger has to say about the scope of our proposed experiments on Little Todday?" Sir William asked.

The Parliamentary Under-Secretary and the Permanent Under-Secretary emitted a simultaneous negative.

Feeling that he may have sounded too brusque, Mr Wishart added that he was not scientific enough to follow any nuclear exposition with sufficient grasp of the subject to make his opinion of the slightest value.

At this moment a Wing Commander came into the room and handed Major-General Kortright a note.

"Good Lord!" he exclaimed in consternation, when he had read it. "One of our Thunderbuzzards has gone astray."

"That's another rocket, I suppose?" Mr Wishart asked.

"It is indeed," Major-General Kortright replied. "This is going to be rather a blow for poor Dr Hamburger. He had set his heart on blowing up Rockall with a Thunderbuzzard. It has a range of two hundred and fifty miles with controlled hovering."

"Do you mean this ghastly affair may have blown up part of my constituency?" Mr Wishart exclaimed, his vision of succeeding Walter Douglass as Secretary of State for Scotland fading like a morning dream.

"No, no, no," the Director of Ballistic Warfare assured him. "It won't be carrying a nuclear warhead."

"But, damn it, if it fell in a crowded street it could kill quite a lot of people," Mr Wishart protested, "and if it has a range of two hundred and fifty miles it could easily reach Lennox."

"That's true," Major-General Kortright agreed. "But it's highly unlikely the Thunderbuzzard will have turned east. It has probably come down in the sea like that British Borzoi last October."

"I think the Secretary of State should be informed at once," said Sir Duncan. "If it has come down somewhere on the mainland, he will have to stand the rocket . . . racket I mean."

For Sir Duncan Forbes to slip over a word showed that he was in a state of almost emotional apprehension not at all like him.

Presently the Permanent Under-Secretary was talking to the Secretary of State at the Scottish Office.

"Mr Douglass hopes that the Ministry of Protection will not issue another of those guided missile warnings," he turned to say to Sir William Windermere, softening down what the Secretary of State had actually said.

"Look here, Duncan, I hope these damned Protection fellows aren't going to broadcast the misbehaviour of one of their infernal toys."

"No, Sir Duncan," said the Air Chief Marshal. "After very careful consideration the Ministry has decided that in future if a rocket should go astray it will be a top secret. The aircraft manufacturers, who are hoping to establish an export trade for our guided missiles rising to many millions of pounds annually, think it inadvisable to advertise minor mishaps that must occur during the—er—teething troubles of an industry that we believe is still only in its infancy."

The Wing Commander came in again with a signal from Balmuir which he handed to Major-General Kortright.

"Thunderbuzzard has just passed over Balmuir travelling

due south after failure to respond to control. We estimate Thunderbuzzard may come down in the sea somewhere south of Barra Head."

"I hope it doesn't carry on and land in Northern Ireland," said Sir Duncan. "They're nervous enough there already about explosives."

"There is no explosive in the Thunderbuzzard. This is an experimental flight," said Sir Hubert Cutwater a little irritably.

The Wing Commander came back a third time.

"Could you take a call from Group Captain Oakenbotham, sir?" he asked Major-general Kortright. "He is on the line now in the Ballistic Planning Room. He is speaking from Great Todday, and he says it is urgent."

The Director of Ballistic Warfare hurried out of the room.

"I hope the people on Little Todday haven't blown up the new pier, Andrew," Sir Duncan murmured to the Under-Secretary.

"Don't suggest such a thing even in joke, Duncan," Mr Wishart whispered back earnestly.

Presently Major-general Kortright returned. He was looking grave.

"The Thunderbuzzard has been located," he announced. "It has come down on Little Todday. It passed over the low-lying ground in Great Todday on the west of the island and went on to descend on Little Todday. Apparently there was rather a nasty panic on Great Todday."

"What about Little Todday?" everybody asked.

"That's the trouble. They won't let Oakenbotham go ashore to find out what has happened. He has sent a signal to Bullingham in Mid Uist asking for a sergeant and a dozen men from the Ballistic Regiment to be sent down immediately to place a guard on the Thunderbuzzard, but he says there is no possibility of their reaching Great Todday for some hours even if a westerly gale which has sprung up allows them to cross the Sound of Todday from Nobost, and he has reason to suppose that the people on Little Todday intend to smash up the Thunderbuzzard. He asks me to authorize him to use armed force if necessary to effect a landing and prevent such an occurrence."

"Armed force?" the Air Chief Marshal repeated. "What sort of armed force has he got?"

"Apparently he can count on the police-sergeant in Snorvig and on a certain Mr Waggett, who owns Snorvig House and is the shooting tenant of the Department of Agriculture. The only snag is that two rifles were missing when the Home Guard was disbanded in 1945, and this chap Waggett, who commanded the Todday company, thinks they may still be hidden on Little Todday."

"I strongly advise no action being taken by Group Captain Oakenbotham on his own," Mr Wishart urged. "You must realize what would be made in Scotland of any shooting incident. I'm sure Sir Duncan agrees with me."

"I certainly do," said the Permanent Under-Secretary.

"But we can't have a lot of wild rebels against authority destroying one of our Thunderbuzzards," said Sir Hubert Cutwater. "Do you realize the amount of research that has gone into this entirely new system of guidance? It is the success of the Thunderbuzzard which will enable us to sell our obsolete Bloodrushers to the other members of N.A.T.O."

"But have these Thunderbuzzards been such a success?" Mr Wishart asked.

"Of course they have," the Director of Ballistic Warfare exclaimed eagerly. "This one took a wrong direction, granted. But the point is that it hovered over Little Todday before it came down. Not even the Yanks have got a rocket which hovers before it pounces. Oakenbotham, who saw it all, was staggered by the gentle accuracy with which it came down. There it is lying on this damned island and we have to sit here and let these mad islanders smash it up merely because you politicians are afraid of the effect a little judicious force will have on your votes. I don't know what the country is coming to."

"We only have Group Captain Oakenbotham's opinion that they may damage this rocket," Mr Wishart pointed out. "He may be misjudging the reaction. Probably they were annoyed at first when this rocket came down on them. And I can't help feeling some sympathy with their point of view. Suppose it had landed on one of the chain-stores in Princes Street, you couldn't have blamed the people of Edinburgh for smashing it up."

"You Scotch people—Scottish I mean—you Scottish people really are rather extraordinary, if I may say so," the Air Chief Marshal put in. "You always seem to think that it's much more important to the rest of the world if something goes wrong in Scotland. We poor English blokes are always ready to admit we have made a mistake. However, we're getting away from the subject. What we have to decide is whether we shall authorize Group Captain Oakenbotham to do whatever he thinks is best to save this Thunderbuzzard from being damaged. What do you feel about it, Sir Grimsby?"

The Permanent Secretary of the Ministry of Protection put a finger to his forehead to suggest profound thought.

"My own feeling is that we should not authorize Group Captain Oakenbotham to use armed force," he replied at last. "If the local situation convinces him of the necessity to use armed force, we should leave ourselves in a position to be able to repudiate his action if it seems advisable or on the other hand to commend his action if it seems advisable. I never believe in tying down the man on the spot with positive instructions. We must allow scope for discretion."

"Did Oakenbotham give you the impression, Kortright, that he and this fellow Wagger felt sure of being able to intimidate these islanders?" Sir Hubert Cutwater asked.

"No, I think he thought it was a forlorn hope," said Major-general Kortright. "I think I had better get through to him on the telephone and tell him to warn the islanders that if they lay a finger on the Thunderbuzzard—the consequences—the very grave consequences will be upon their own heads."

"I expect that's what they felt about the Thunderbuzzard," Sir Duncan whispered to Andrew Wishart.

"If my suggestion is approved, I'll try to establish contact with Group Captain Oakenbotham immediately."

There was a murmur of agreement and Major-general Kortright went back to the Ballistic Planning Room to establish contact with the Group Captain, whom he had warned to stand by for a call from London. It reached him just as one of the girls in the post-office at Snorvig had decided to let a lorry-driver who had broken down near Garryboo telephone to another lorry-driver in Snorvig to bring some spare part along with him. And it was the end of this conversation in Gaelic which reached Major-general Kortright's ears as he picked up the receiver. He did not lose his presence of mind.

"Be careful what you say, Group Captain. It's possible that they are trying to tap our line from that place off High Street, Kensington."

"High Street, Kensington, sir?" exclaimed Group Captain Oakenbotham who, supersonic ace though he had been at getting his aircraft to fly faster than sound, was always a little behind sound with his own brain.

"Yes, R.E. Headquarters," the General snapped.

"The Sappers, sir?" asked a now completely bewildered Oakenbotham.

"No, no, no. I overheard a conversation in what I think was Russian," the General hissed.

There was a moment or two of silence as the Group Captain's mind gathered speed.

"Oh, I think what you heard, sir, must have been conversation in Gaelic."

"Good god," the General muttered, "I can't say I like the idea of our top secret stuff being handled where a couple of Russkis could easily pass themselves off on our people as Gaelese, Gallickers, or whatever you call them.

Well that can be discussed later. What is the situation now?"

"I was waiting for your authorization to use armed force if necessary. Mr Waggett has a Mauser pistol which he snatched from the hands of a Hun who was aiming at him in the Kaiser's war."

"Group Captain, please don't ever use that word again. We cannot afford to upset our German allies at this moment. There are no Huns to-day even in Eastern Germany. We have given anxious consideration to the situation in Little Todday brought about by the unfortunate behaviour of the Thunderbuzzard and we do not feel we are in a position to authorize you to employ armed force. We feel we must rely on the judgment of the man on the spot. The only steps we can authorize you to take are to warn the people of Little Todday that any sabotage committed by them will involve them in the gravest consequences."

"I have already done that. But I will do it again. Oh, please hold the line, sir. Sergeant MacGillivray has just come in."

There was a pause.

"I'm afraid it's too late, sir," the Group Captain said. "Sergeant MacGillivray reports that a thick column of smoke is going up on the middle of Little Todday, and he's afraid the people there are trying to burn the rocket. I shall go over at once, and as soon as I've found out the situation I will call you again."

"Approved," the General snapped, and hung up. Back in the conference room at the Ministry of Protection he reported the news from Group Captain Oakenbotham.

"Well, if they really have destroyed the Thunderbuzzard," said Sir William Windermere, "that will make it a good deal easier for us to put our original plan into operation."

"You don't mean that plan to evacuate the islands of Great and Little Todday?" Mr Wishart asked nervously.

"I don't think that for the present at any rate it will be necessary to do anything about the larger island," Sir

William replied. "But obviously it is impossible for our Protection plans to prevent war with some of the super-deterrents we are devising if work of the most secret nature has to be carried out in an island whose inhabitants have shown themselves incapable of grasping the most elementary principles of patriotic behaviour. We will wait for a full report from Group Captain Oakenbotham, of course, but I fear it will not be satisfactory. I shall ask Mr Bickers . . . Mr Truefitt I mean . . . to put our recommendations forward at top level, and I have no doubt they will be accepted as imperative for the success of the new strategic plan."

"I am speaking without having been able to consult the Secretary of State for Scotland," Mr Wishart said. "But I urge you not to take for granted his acquiescence in your plan."

"I suggest we should instruct Group Captain Oakenbotham to proceed at once to London," said Major-general Kortright. "If he can reach Mid Uist to-night he could be flown south to-morrow morning and report to us to-morrow afternoon."

"Yes, and if it transpires that these islanders really have destroyed the Thunderbuzzard," said Sir Hubert Cutwater, "I cannot believe that Mr Walter Douglass will still oppose evacuation."

The wind which by evening was blowing with hurricane force prevented Group Captain Oakenbotham from reaching Nobost that night, and on instructions from Major-general Kortright he dictated his report to the most reliably secretive stenographer in the Ministry of Protection that evening. Some of the edge was taken off the secrecy by the telephone operator in Snorvig listening in until she got bored after a quarter of an hour.

"*A Thighearna,*" Katie MacRurie commented, "this Ministry of Protection will have a terrible big bill for their telephone."

The Director of Ballistic Warfare went back to the

Ministry after dinner to wait for Group Captain Oakenbotham's report to come in.

"And yet that fellow in the *Sunday Excess* says we don't really do any work in Government offices," he said to the Wing Commander who had fed him with signals from Balmuir that afternoon, at which the Wing Commander smiled the sad smile of one of the unappreciated workers of the world. Here is the report taken down that evening:

"*From* Group Captain Henry P. Oakenbotham, O.B.E., A.F.C., R.A.F.

"*To* Major-general H. E. Kortright, C.B., C.B.E., D.S.O.

"After receiving an urgent call from Air Commodore Watchorn to keep a look out for a Thunderbuzzard rocket which had been launched on an experimental flight over Rockall and had failed to return to Balmuir rocket-launching station I perceived what I immediately recognized as the Thunderbuzzard passing above the low land south of Garryboo in the north-west portion of Great Todday at a comparatively low speed in the direction of Snorvig. Suddenly it swerved to the west and after hovering over Little Todday it made a perfect landing in what will be approximately the centre of the proposed aerodrome.

"There was an angry demonstration by a crowd of Great Todday people when I reached the pier at Snorvig preparatory to crossing over the Coolish, as the stretch of water between Great and Little Todday is called. I attributed this demonstration to the panic which the apparent approach of the Thunderbuzzard had caused to the people of Snorvig. There was a good deal of jeering as I boarded the tug which Messrs Knowall, the contractors for the work on the new pier at Kiltod, have with invariable courtesy always put at my service when requested. I then proceeded across the Coolish to Kiltod, where a number of the inhabitants of Little Todday were gathered. I regret to say that when I attempted to land I was informed by the Reverend James Macalister, the Roman Catholic priest on the island, that he would be unable to prevent his parishioners from taking violent steps to prevent my landing. I pointed out that it was my duty to make an immediate report on the condition of the rocket which had descended on Little Todday, to which the Reverend Macalister replied that the rocket would soon be in no condition at all.

"I warned the Reverend Macalister that any interference with the rocket by the islanders would be regarded as a subversive action the consequences of which could not fail to be extremely serious for their future. Furthermore I warned the Reverend Macalister that I should not hesitate to employ force if necessary to effect a landing and inspect the rocket. I then returned to Snorvig, where Police Sergeant MacGillivray at once agreed to accompany me back to Kiltod. Mr Paul Waggett, whose conduct deserves the highest commendation throughout, volunteered to accompany Sergeant MacGillivray and myself armed with a Mauser pistol which was a relic of his service in World War 1914-1918. I told Mr Waggett that he must only threaten the people of Little Todday and under no circumstances fire at them. This he promised but added that if we should be fired at by rifles he supposed he could reply to the fire. He informed me that when the Home Guard was disbanded in 1945 two rifles were missing from the ceiling of his company and that he had always suspected the Little Todday platoon of having concealed them in order to kill the grey seals which are legally protected. I was standing by to await telephonic approval of my action from the Ministry of Protection when Sergeant MacGillivray directed my attention to a column of smoke rising from Little Todday. The wind was increasing from the west and therefore the fumes were reaching Snorvig.

"I was instructed by telephone to proceed at once to Nobost in Mid Uist so that I might be flown down to London by the R.A.F. Unfortunately the force of the wind increased so rapidly that a crossing of the Sound of Todday to Nobost that night was not feasible. However, the Coolish being protected from the west by Little Todday I was able to cross to Kiltod accompanied by Sergeant MacGillivray and Mr Waggett. My landing was not opposed on this occasion, and Sergeant MacGillivray, Mr Waggett and myself proceeded as quickly as possible to the place where the Thunderbuzzard had descended about two miles from Kiltod.

"I regret to inform you that when we reached the Thunderbuzzard the smoking remains were surrounded by a disorderly mob who were smashing them with axes and other weapons. At the same time two bagpipers were playing reels to which those who were not engaged in attacking what was left of the Thunderbuzzard were dancing wildly. Although I was unable to follow what the Reverend Macalister was saying in Gaelic it was obvious that he was encouraging the islanders in their deplorable behaviour, and this was confirmed by Sergeant MacGillivray, who speaks the language. I asked Sergeant MacGillivray if it would be advisable to arrest the Reverend Macalister, but he said that if we tried to arrest him we should all be thrown into the sea, and I did not feel justified in exposing a member of H.M. Police Forces to such a contingency. I therefore returned to Snorvig and after writing this report I telephoned it to the Ministry of Protection. I shall await instructions as to what further action is adumbrated. Meanwhile, I have forbidden the two local correspondents of the Press in Snorvig to communicate any news of the Thunderbuzzard until an official communiqué has been issued."

Chapter 15

THE BRIGHT IDEA

WHETHER or not the Cabinet would have given way to the Ministry of Protection's pressure upon them to agree to the evacuation of the people of Little Todday if the people of Little Todday had not maltreated that Thunderbuzzard must remain a Cabinet secret. The Government merely announced that it had been found necessary to arrange for the resettlement of the population of Little Todday in West Sutherlandshire in order to provide the most favourable conditions for the development of the new strategic plan to ensure that a nuclear attack upon Great Britain would involve the aggressor in nuclear reprisals. Not a word was said about that misguided missile. However, the fate of the Thunderbuzzard could not be kept secret, and although the announcement of the evacuation was made without any mention of it the incident was generally believed to be responsible for the Government's action, and there was a repetition of the protests about the three Uists. The Government, sensitive about Cyprus and still suffering from the hangover from Suez, did not want to be accused of bullying any more islanders. So Mr Oliver Slimmon, one of the members of the Cabinet who was supposed to be a popular attraction, appeared on television, a crocodile's tear glistening in a corner of his eye and his mouth full of soft fruit, to assure viewers that the resettlement of the population of Little Todday hurt the Government more than it hurt the people about to be resettled.

"We don't *want* to upset a way of life. We wouldn't do it if we didn't know it was necessary for the future safety of our country that it should be done. I can't tell you why the Minister of Protection had felt bound to advise the Government that the island of Little Todday . . . what a jolly name, isn't it? . . . must be vacated for the sake of national security. I can't tell you because I don't know. But it's no use having military advisers unless you take their advice, is it? We trust them and I'm asking you to trust us."

The fruity voice stopped: the crocodile's tear ceased to glisten in that humbugging eye. Mr Slimmon tried to sustain an expression of intense sincerity until he was faded from the screen. Then a pretty girl with a charming smile took his place to tell viewers that they were being taken to Vienna with the cooperation of Eurovision to see the finals of the Central European table tennis championships.

In view of the fact that every croft would be vacant by September 30th, by which time it was estimated that the prefabricated houses required for the resettled population in Wester Sutherland would be ready, it was decided to leave where they were the twenty-two crofters already under notice to quit, and to hold up all work on Little Todday until it could be handed over to the ballistic planners as a solitude.

The Government's proposed murder of a small island in the interest of scientific destruction continued to rouse great indignation, but it was indignation expressed in words and not in deeds.

The correspondence columns of *The Caledonian* seethed with denunciations, but nobody did anything. Members of the various Home Rule associations wrote to point out that this was a fresh violation of the Treaty of Union, but none of them did anything. Several religious people wrote to protest against the Government's un-Christian behaviour, but they were immediately answered by other religious people who were able to discern in the Government's action an evangelical example. One correspondent wrote to ask, in view of the discovery that the winkles on the coast of Caithness near Dounreay had become radio-active, what steps the Government were taking to prevent the lobsters of the Western Isles from being similarly affected. The public anxiety about the effects of radiation became sufficiently vocal to make it seem opportune to call upon Dr Emil Hamburger to explain in a broadcast what nonsense it all was.

"A woman would have to eat at least twenty thousand radio-active lobsters before she became sterile," Dr Hamburger declared. "And a man would have to eat at least thirty thousand."

With lobsters at the price they were nobody felt he was likely to be able to eat two lobsters a day for the next forty years. The anxiety of the marriage bed was lulled.

To the credit of Mr Thomas Macaulay, considering that the transfer of the population from Little Todday to another constituency would not deprive him of a single vote, he did his best to rouse Parliament to a sense of its moral responsibility, and in this he was most warmly supported by the Labour M.P.'s for Scottish constituencies who were not themselves Scotsmen.

As we know, behind the political scene the Scottish Office had done its best to dissuade the Government from seizing Little Todday for the new look in national defence, but once the Government had decided to disregard the opinion of the Scottish Office the Scottish Office toed the line as meekly as any mushroom ministry spawned to find an excuse for further Government expenditure.

And what was the reaction to the proposed murder in Great and Little Todday? It is comforting to record that the larger island repented of its inclination to imitate the children of Israel once upon a time by bowing down before the Golden Calf. The lorry-drivers refused to take a hire from anybody connected with the proposed camp for ballistic trainees. The girls refused to rock and roll with the Teddy-boys. The children screamed derisive epithets in Gaelic at the contractors' workmen who offered them sweets. Big Roderick, who had been barely distinguishable from an enormous jelly after the approach of the Thunder-buzzard, was now adamantine in the rigour with which he treated mainland customers in the Snorvig bar. Simon

MacRurie was almost tremulously subservient to the Reverend Angus Morrison who preached every Sabbath sermons that Archbishop Makarios might have listened to with admiration. Those like Dr Maclaren, George Campbell the headmaster of Snorvig school, the Biffer and others who had condemned the rocket scheme from the first were accorded as much respect as Chinese sages in the days of the Ming dynasty.

The coldness with which he was treated preyed so deeply on the mind of Sergeant MacGillivray that he wrote to Colonel Lindsay-Wolseley of Tummie, the convener of the police committee of the Inverness-shire County Council, begging him to do all in his power to persuade the Chief Constable to transfer him to the mainland.

"That beetroot-headed MacGillivray coming back to Kenspeckle?" Donald MacDonald of Ben Nevis bellowed. The Chieftain was now over eighty but nobody would have suspected it from his voice.

"He's anxious to leave Great Todday," Colonel Lindsay-Wolseley said. "He feels very upset about Little Todday being taken over for this rocket range."

"So he should," the Chieftain declared. "I don't know what this infernal Government is thinking about. I'm resigning as Chairman of the West Inverness-shire Primrose League."

"You're not going to join the Labour Party surely?"

"Of course I'm not going to join those Bolshies. But I'm never again going to sit on a Conservative platform," Ben Nevis proclaimed majestically.

Sergeant MacGillivray did not obtain his transfer for some time and he had what was for him by now the disagreeable job of trying to find those who had been responsible for breaking most of the windows in Snorvig House one night.

"I'm afraid it proves that at heart the people here are completely lawless," Paul Waggett said to the Sergeant when next morning he was showing him the damage that had been done. One doesn't expect gratitude in this world, but when one thinks of all I've done for both islands in the last twenty years or more it does make one wonder why one ever did try to do so much."

"Ah, well, Mr Waggett, they have been a bit upset lately. That rocket was a big shock to them."

"*I* didn't panic. *You* didn't panic, Sergeant. Why should *they* panic?"

"They've been worried about the future ever since the Clach Mhôr fell that night you talked to them in the hall about these atoms."

"Superstition is no justification for breaking the windows of Snorvig House."

"No, no, Mr Waggett. I'm not after saying that it is. But they didn't like it here when you took that pistol of yours over to Kiltod. It really put their backs up, as you might say."

"I was merely doing my duty just as you were, Sergeant."

"Well, I'll be frank with you, Mr Waggett, and say right out that the people here have never been the same with me since you and me and Captain Oakenbotham . . ."

"Group Captain. You want to be careful to get the correct rank," Waggett put in.

"You and me and Group Captain Oakenbotham went over to Little Todday that day and nearly got ourselves pushed off the pier. And after all, Mr Waggett, you can understand their feelings. If the Government is going to clear everybody off Little Todday the people here naturally ask themselves what's to stop the Government clearing them off if it suits the Government."

"Oh, I realise they don't grasp the larger issues that are involved in our new defence policy," Paul Waggett said loftily. "All the same, defiance of the Government is defiance of the Government and you can't expect the Government to give way to threats; it wouldn't be a Government if it did. I know that Group Captain Oakenbotham is worried about the attitude of the people here and I expect he will strongly recommend drastic steps being taken to show them the folly of trying to oppose the Government. That's why he has gone down to London."

"Just as well," Sergeant MacGillivray muttered. "I wouldn't have liked to have the job of trying to find out who it was pushed him off the pier on top of your broken windows."

Paul Waggett sighed. "I might have felt a pang at going away from Great Todday for good," he murmured in a voice of gentle melancholy. "As it is, when Mrs Waggett and I leave Snorvig next week we shall leave it without the slightest regret."

"You're not coming back, Mr Waggett?"

"No, I feel fairly sure the Ministry of Protection will pay me the price I am asking for Snorvig House, and we are going to look for a house somewhere in the Green Belt."

"In the Green Belt?" Sergeant MacGillivray repeated in mystification. "Where at all would that be, Mr Waggett?"

"A protected piece of unspoilt country all round London," Paul Waggett replied dreamily.

Sherwood or Arden would have looked like suburban parks beside that Green Belt which stretched like a limitless savanna before Paul Waggett in his vision of the future.

"Jane," Hugh exclaimed at breakfast, "something *must* be done about this damnable business." He passed her the letter he had been reading from Father James:

Uisdein a charaid,

You'd better be coming here with Seonaid for our last Easter. We haven't yet decided whether we will make the Barbarians put every one of us off the island by force in September but things are moving in that direction. Our friends in Great Todday are behaving like bricks. God forgive me, I didn't know they had it in them. We had considered whether we would send a petition to the Queen but we thought it wouldn't be fair to spoil the memory of that visit to the Outer Isles, the most welcome royal visitor since Tearlach came to

Eriskay. We must try to keep our good manners even if the Government cannot behave itself.

Try to come with Seonaid. My heart is very heavy and she will lighten it with her singing. My blessing on her.

Do charaid dhileas,

Seumas MacAlasdair

"Something must be done," Hugh repeated. "And Easter will be here in less than a fortnight."

That morning down at the MacInnes manufactory in Selwick Hugh was looking with approval at some wool which had just come back from the dyers. Suddenly he clasped a hand to his head and exclaimed:

"By G—, we'll try it!"

One of the staff hurried across. "Is anything the matter, Mr Hugh?" he asked anxiously.

"No, no, just an idea that struck me. This is a jolly shade of rose, Mr Lauder."

"Yes, we like it very much, Mr Hugh."

"Who are the dyers?"

When Mr Lauder told him Hugh asked to be put through to them on the telephone.

"This is Hugh MacInnes of MacInnes Woolwear. I wonder if your Mr Benson could spare me a few minutes of his time this afternoon . . . no, no, nothing wrong at all with the shade. We're delighted with it . . . thanks very much. I'll be with you at half-past three."

When Hugh was seated in Mr Benson's office at the dye-works he asked first if the interview could be considered completely confidential.

"Certainly, Mr MacInnes," he was assured.

"I want to know if it's possible to use a dye of that shade of rose on birds," Hugh said.

"On birds?" Mr Benson echoed in amazement.

"Yes, it's an experiment I want to make. But if you supply me with such a dye, have I your solemn promise, Mr Benson, not to let anybody know that you have done so?"

"I will not say a word, Mr MacInnes. You can rely on that. And I think I know the dye you want. Soudan Red S. This must be dissolved either in olive oil or liquid paraffin and applied with a brush."

"I should think olive oil would be better. What would be the effect of sea-water?"

"Soudan Red S would stand up to sea-water, not for an indefinite time perhaps, but certainly for a very long time."

"And it would have no ill effect on the birds painted with it?"

"None at all," Mr Benson said.

"Then could you let me have enough of the dye with instructions how to mix it?"

"We could mix it for you, Mr MacInnes, and put it into a carboy. How many birds are you proposing to paint?"

"About a couple of dozen I should think," Hugh said.

"May I ask if the birds are geese? I understand that in California they paint geese various colours for decorative purposes."

"No, these birds would not be geese."

"I don't think you'll need a carboy," Mr Benson said with a smile. "We'll give you the dye in a gallon tin and let you have some more of it in powder in case you need it. And be careful not to dye yourself. It's potent stuff. Better use gloves."

"Will you be able to let me have the dye within a week?" Hugh asked.

"You shall have it the day after to-morrow in a sealed tin."

"And the bill?"

"And the bill," Mr Benson chuckled. "Will I send them both to MacInnes Woolwear?"

"No, please send them to me at The Cottage, Greystones, Langley. Or no, better not; I'll call for the dye myself."

That evening Hugh wrote to Norman Macleod:

Dear Norman,

I've had an idea. You know how pink the gulls on Pillay can look in the sunset. If we could make that pink permanent I believe we could stir up bird-fans all over the country to protest against these unique visitants to our coasts being driven away by rockets. And as you know the Government would probably be much more worried by the indignation of bird-fans over upsetting birds than they would be over upsetting people. It's no good resenting that. We must take advantage of it, and see if Operation Hoax comes off. Jane and I will be in Little Todday next week, and I'll bring the pink dye with me. Meanwhile, will you and Duncan Macroon and anybody else who you think would be absolutely dumb get across to Pillay and somehow trap all the gulls you can. Not black-backs. Herring-gulls will be best. I leave you to work out how to trap them. We'll want about a couple of dozen. Till next week.

Yours ever,
Hugh

Norman Macleod met Hugh and Jane when the *Island Queen* arrived at Snorvig a week later.

"We've got over thirty of them wired in on Pillay like hens in a hen-run," he told Hugh. "Duncan and I took Hugh Macroon and Alan Macdonald into the secret and of course Kenny Macroon because we wanted the *Morning Star*. They'll all be as dumb as death. But listen, Hugh, we ought to get the job done as soon as possible while this fine weather lasts. We don't want to be cut off on Pillay for a month or more."

"We'd better get over to-night," Hugh said. "We can start operations at dawn."

"No, no, the weather looks good for another two days. We'll start by six o'clock to-morrow from Kiltod in the *Morning Star*."

"What will the people think we're going to Pillay for?" Hugh asked.

"That's the beauty of it. Father James is sending us over

to put the statue of St Tod in that cave above Fearvig to keep away the Barbarians. Everybody is delighted and feels sure that the good man will knock sparks out of the Government."

So six o'clock on the morrow saw Hugh MacInnes, Norman Macleod, Duncan Bàn, Hugh Macroon, Alan Macdonald and St Tod himself aboard the *Morning Star*. Father James came down to the pier to wish them success.

"I'll offer Mass for your intention, boys," he told them, "and ask Almighty God's blessing upon the operation. See that the holy man is comfortable. If he keeps the Barbarians off we'll bring him back in triumph to his own church."

The island of Pillay extended to something over three hundred acres. It rose up from the sea along its western face in a series of rocky terraces at first and then by steep grassy braes to the summit, which consisted of a level plateau of rough herbage and heather dotted with numerous small lochans. On the east the cliff fell sheer to the sea from about three hundred feet in a magnificent sweep of black basaltic columns whitened by the droppings of innumerable sea-birds. The southward side was equally sheer but not so high, and along the southern end the shore was strewn with huge fragments of basalt from which it was an arduous task to reach the braes above. The only landing-place was below a small hook-shaped headland running north-west from the coast of the island below which a ledge of rock provided a rough quay. Fearvig, the little bay formed by the headland, faced due west and only after a spell of calm weather did the heavy ground swell allow a boat to get alongside the rocky ledge. The grazing was good, but the difficulty of performing the various operations that sheep require through the year, coupled with the heavy losses over the cliffs, made the island unsuitable for sheep. However, Pillay offered an ideal breeding-place for the grey Atlantic seals which were never persecuted by the Macroons who claimed a legendary descent from a seal woman. So much for Paul Waggett's tale that the Little Todday platoon had hidden two of their rifles in order to shoot seals. There were no missing rifles: it was a fantasy like his own capture of the Mauser pistol, which he had bought in 1922 from one of the clerks in the London offices of Messrs Blundell, Blundell, Pickthorn, Blundell and Waggett.

After the statue of St Tod had been firmly fixed in the small cave above Fearvig the party proceeded to carry out the task which had brought them to Pillay, and a pretty formidable task it was. Hugh had taken the precaution to provide the dyers with gloves, but even with that protection their hands were all very sore from the pecks inflicted on them by the infuriated herring-gulls. It was high noon before the last rose-dyed captive was released to fly screaming away and join the throng of birds on the eastern side of the small island.

That night the glass dropped rapidly and by morning an equinoctial gale of Force 8 was raging in sea area Hebrides.

"It'll be a long time before anybody can cross the *sruth* to Pillay," Norman Macleod said.

"Just as well, Martin Leslie will be here for Easter," Hugh said. "And I don't want him to start looking for nests of the rarity in case he finds pink birds and white birds married to one another."

Martin Leslie was a Fettes contemporary of Hugh's who having already won much popularity for himself as a broadcaster about birds had become last year a star performer on television in a fortnightly series called *You May Find This Rarity* in which viewers were taken on a conducted tour by him, Wilfred Cobbett and Claude Mayhew all over Great Britain in search of rare birds and rare flowers and rare butterflies. Hugh had told Martin Leslie of persistent reports from Little Todday that what appeared to be some kind of a pink gull had been seen flying between Little Todday and Pillay.

"There's no such thing as a pink gull," Martin Leslie had replied firmly. "There are one or two pinkish gulls of course but not on our coasts. There's Ross's gull, Rhodostethia rosea, up in the Arctic. But it's a terrific rarity and we know very little about it."

"There you are, Martin."

"What do you mean, 'There you are'?"

"Mightn't this bird with a long name have decided to come south?" Hugh asked.

"Why should a Rhodostethia rosea suddenly decide to come south?"

"I should have thought it was the kind of move any creature living in the Arctic might make. Don't you remember that walrus which came to Little Todday, when we were still at school? You and I were terrifically keen to go and look for it. However, these pink gulls on Little Todday may be an illusion. I've seen them look as pink as flamingoes in the sunset."

"Exactly," said Martin Leslie scornfully.

"I once saw a bunch of them sitting on the Gobha—that's the rock on which the whisky ship was wrecked. And until they suddenly turned white when the sun went down I could have sworn they really were pink."

"Well, if it was anything like that film *Whisky Galore* I don't wonder they looked pink," Martin Leslie said.

"All the same," Hugh insisted, "pink gulls or no pink gulls, it would be fun if you came to Little Todday for a few days at Easter. The birds on Pillay are a marvellous sight."

"As a matter of fact I had intended to go there and try to get some pictures for *You May Find This Rarity* before these confounded rocket-busters ruin everything."

So it was arranged that Martin Leslie should arrive in Little Todday on Easter Monday and be put up at Bow Bells with Mrs Odd.

Chapter 16

THE GLORIOUS RESTORATION

"THERE'S one!" cried Hugh.

Martin Leslie and he were sitting above Tràigh nan Eun on the morning of Easter Tuesday. The wind had dropped, but a thunderous ground swell was breaking against the cliffs of Pillay; a landing there was impossible and likely to remain impossible for some time, the weather forecast being heavy with depressions all over the Atlantic. Martin Leslie put up his binoculars.

"Can't get it," he said, and just as he spoke a pink bird alighted on the sand below them.

"I say, this is absolutely fantastic," Martin Leslie gasped. "It's a gull. That's certain. It's not Ross's Gull—Rhodostethia rosea," he decided. "Too large for one thing, this bird is as big as a herring-gull. Indeed, except for the colour it might be a herring-gull. No, it certainly isn't Rhodostethia rosea. The tail is wrong. That's not a wedge tail. Extraordinary! I can't identify it with any gull we know."

"It may be a hitherto undiscovered species," Hugh suggested.

The reflection of a shining dream flickered in the eyes of Martin Leslie. *Larus sanguineus usually known as Leslie's Gull was discovered by the brilliant young ornithologist Martin Leslie in the Outer Hebrides of Scotland; it must be considered the most notable addition ever made to the avifauna of Great Britain.* Ross's Gull is pinkish, but this is definitely pink," he emerged from the dream to observe.

"Definitely," Hugh agreed. "You scoffed at me, Martin, when I told you about the reports of this pink gull, and I did wonder myself if it might have been an optical illusion caused by a rosy sunset. But there's no doubt about it, is there?"

"Here comes either its mate or more probably another cock-bird. They're quarrelling over something that's been washed up on the beach," Martin Leslie exclaimed. "Oh lord, I wish I could get across to Pillay," he groaned.

"No chance of that," said Hugh. "Aren't you satisfied by what you've seen already?"

"I'm satisfied that a gull unknown even to Howard Saunders is presumably nesting on Pillay. But I want to see the nest. I want to see the eggs. And later on I shall want to see the young birds. What's so interesting about the gull family is that some develop a black or darker upper plumage with maturity and others have this darker upper plumage when immature and lose it afterwards. I think the upper plumage on the back of those two is slightly darker. I wish I could be sure, but I'm afraid to shoot one."

"I should think so," Hugh said firmly. "You'd be lynched by the National Association of Bird-watchers if you did. And I wouldn't be too sure that either James Fisher or Peter Scott or James Robertson Justice wouldn't shoot *you*."

"It's a good job Larus sanguineus—that's only a provisional name—wasn't seen first by Jimmy Justice."

"Why?"

"Nobody would have believed him. They'd have said that Technicolor had gone to his head. But I think you're right, Hugh. It *would* be a mistake to shoot one."

"It would be fatal because it would spoil the campaign you've got to launch."

"What campaign?"

"A campaign to stop these rocketeers from taking over Little Todday. You make the most remarkable ornithological discovery in years, and are you going to stand by and let it be nullified? If Rhodo and the rest of it is known as Ross's Gull, why shouldn't this chap be known as Leslie's Gull?"

"It might be, of course," Martin Leslie admitted

modestly, returning for an instant to that shining dream of his.

"It jolly well will be," Hugh declared emphatically. "That is if you don't shoot one of them. When is your next television half-hour?"

"We're starting our new series of *You May Find This Rarity* the week after next. Wilfred Cobbett has some wonderful shots of Anemone pulsatilla—the Pasque anemone—taken on the Berkshire Downs."

"Couldn't you show some pictures of the new gull? Look, Martin, I've got a plan of campaign. You must write letters at once to *The Times*, *The Caledonian*, *The Manchester Guardian*, *The Spectator* and *The New Statesman*, announcing your discovery and pleading with bird-lovers to do all they can to dissuade the Government from frightening away these birds with rockets. You could say that a possible explanation for their leaving the Arctic is the increase of air-traffic over the Arctic. Blame the Russians for that of course. And then when you've started the ball rolling you let 'em have it on television."

"I'm able to take some coloured film pictures of them," said Martin Leslie. "I brought my camera."

"And you didn't bring it along with you this morning," said Hugh reproachfully, "because you didn't believe in the existence of these pink gulls."

"No, I didn't. I wouldn't believe in their existence now if I hadn't seen them with my own eyes. I do wish, though, that I could get over to Pillay."

"That's out of the question at present, but later on when the young birds are hatched the sea will probably be kinder. Then you can do another television half-hour. The public can't resist young birds gaping at them, whatever colour they are. I suppose you'd expect to find the young ones pinkish, or would you expect no sign of pink in their first few weeks?"

"I really don't know," Martin Leslie replied. "But I think I should expect indications of pink."

And Hugh made up his mind that with the help of Norman Macleod and Duncan Bàn his friend should find later on that his expectations had been fulfilled.

"Yes, we might do a visit to the nests in the same programme as a wonderful set of shots Claude Mayhew got last year of Arion's caterpillar meeting the wood-ants and being taken down to feed on the ant-grubs. You can see the tempting liquor being exuded by the caterpillar and the ants lapping it up. I wouldn't be surprised if one of the temperance societies wrote to ask us if they could use the film to illustrate the evil results of strong drink."

"But who is Arion?"

"The Large Blue butterfly. Yes, that would make a wonderful double," Martin Leslie said.

"Pink and blue," Hugh commented. "What a pity glorious technicolor hasn't reached television."

And this was the letter that Martin Leslie sent to various editors, all of whom printed it:

Sir,

In the course of searching for rarities in the flora and fauna of Great Britain for a television series put out by the B.B.C. I visited the small island of Little Todday whose future has recently been under discussion following upon the Government's decision to move the population to the mainland next September in order to provide a rocket range where experimental work on guided nuclear deterrents can be carried on in absolute secrecy.

Just north of Little Todday and separated from it by a tidal race which makes landing except in the calmest weather impossible is the small basaltic island of Pillay, one of the most renowned breeding-places for marine birds in Scotland. Last Monday I reached Little Todday in the hope of visiting Pillay and securing some pictures. Unfortunately the heavy sea running made a landing impossible, but to my amazement I saw through my binoculars what seemed to be a pink gull in flight. I should have believed that I was suffering from an optical illusion if a few minutes later one of these pink gulls had not alighted on the sandy beach of a small cove on Little Todday above which I was sitting. The birds were barely a hundred yards from me and I was able to watch their movements for some time and confirm my belief that they are a species of gull hitherto unrecorded.

On successive days I was able to observe as many as half a dozen of these pink gulls, the under plumage of which was of a clear rose colour and the upper plumage of a very slightly darker shade. The birds were of great beauty and when seen flying in the mixed company of fulmar petrels, razor-bills, guillemots, puffins, kittiwakes, lesser black-back, greater black-back and herring gulls provided a truly remarkable effect.

It may seem too early to put forward any theory about the provenance of these gulls, but I may perhaps be allowed to hazard a guess that they are of Arctic origin. Ornithologists will recall that Ross's Gull (*Rhodostethia rosea*) is of a pale rose colour and that its extreme rarity has not yet allowed us to learn anything about its habitat beyond the fact that it is an Arctic bird, I can state positively that the birds seen by me on Little Todday were not *Rhodostethia rosea*. This new gull lacks the dove's bill and wedge-tail of Ross's Gull.

Several of the inhabitants of Little Todday informed me that during the last two springs they had occasionally seen a pink gull, but that having been laughed at by one or two visiting bird-watchers they had not mentioned the subject again. I think it is safe to presume that this is the first spring in which more than perhaps a single pair has reached Pillay.

The arrival of this hitherto unknown and extremely beautiful bird to breed upon the minute island of Pillay has unfortunately coincided with the Government's recent announcement that Little Todday is to be turned into a secret rocket range. If, as may be suggested, this gull has left the Arctic to search for new nesting quarters on account of the great increase of air-traffic over the Arctic during recent years it can hardly be supposed that it will tolerate the noise of rockets.

Is it too much for bird-lovers to hope that the Government, which has been at such pains to protect the St Kilda wren, will reconsider its decision to transfer Little Todday into a secret rocket range? The Nature Conservancy might be prevailed upon to accept a secret rocket range on the island of Rum, a desert island from which it is proposing to exclude the public. After Dr Emil Hamburger's convincing denial of any danger from radiation surely nobody will be worried about the effect of 'fall out' on the large population of red deer on Rum.

Yours obediently,

MARTIN LESLIE

Hugh and Jane were back at Greystones when this letter was published.

"I thought you were trying an April-fool joke on young Leslie when you told me about these pink birds," Sir Robert said to his son.

"I know you don't believe me, but there's no doubt about these pink birds," said Hugh. "You'll be able to see them for yourself next week on television."

That afternoon Hugh went to call on Mr Gibson.

"I know what you've come about, Mr MacInnes. I read that letter in *The Caledonian* this morning," said the dyer. "Don't worry. Nobody except you and me knows anything about Soudan Red S, and nobody ever will know. It seems to have been a success."

"It was a terrific success, Mr Gibson."

"I'm glad. Ah, I don't like the way we're starting to make these H-bombs and rockets. I think we're plain daft. But I doubt if these pink gulls of yours will frighten that Government of ours off their rocket range."

Mr Gibson had not realised the power of television when he said that.

A few days later Martin Leslie, Wilfred Cobbett and

Claude Mayhew appeared on the screen. They had long ago lost the self-consciousness that afflicts most members of a selected group of talkers when they have to talk in public for the first time under the lights. They no longer seemed uncertain whether to talk naturally to one another or to remember that they were talking to an audience whom it was their duty to face from time to time with a self-conscious smile.

"Are you going to be able to show us any rare or local butterflies this evening, Claude?" Wilfred Cobbett growled amiably, leaning back at ease in his armchair and lighting up a large pipe as he asked this question.

"'Fraid not, Wilfred," Claude Mayhew replied in a lighter voice but with equal aimiability. "It's a bit early in the season for butterflies. I mean to say it's no use my taking you along to show you a few Orange-tips."

His companions laughed as naturally as they could under the handicap of remembering that Orange-tips had been decided upon in the preliminary run-through as the cue for a laugh.

"Talking of Orange-tips reminds me that once when I was a kid at prep-school I caught a female Orange-tip and thought it was a Bath White."

This came from Martin Leslie and was the cue for a second laugh.

"Well, we mustn't waste time talking about butterflies that Martin Leslie didn't catch once upon a time. So I'm taking you to the Berkshire Downs right away," Wilfred Cobbett growled, with a smile at Martin Leslie to show he did not mean to bite his companion.

The picture changed to a view of the three rarity seekers tramping along over a stretch of short turf that might have been anywhere on the Berkshire Downs or on any other downs for that matter. Rightly the series never gave a clue to where the rare flowers were to be found. There would not have been an orchis left in Great Britain if they had. The Pasque anemone was then shown nestling close to the turf, but alas, its violet glow could not be appreciated. Nor could the delicate hue and fragrance of the wild English tulip growing in an Oxfordshire wood display more than a shadow of *Tulipa sylvestris*.

When the team was back in the studio Martin Leslie addressed his companions almost solemnly. "And now," he said, "I'm going to show you both something neither of you has ever seen before. Such a rarity that nobody has ever seen it before."

"This sounds exciting, Martin. Where are you taking us?" Claude Mayhew asked.

In a series of shots the three rarity-seekers were shown for a moment at Euston, then at Obaig, then going on board the *Island Queen*, then landing at Snorvig, then crossing the Coolish to Kiltod, then walking over the machair of Little Todday, and finally sitting above Tràigh nan Eun with Pillay in the distance. This journey had been accompanied by a running commentary from Martin Leslie. And then came the view of about twenty gulls tearing into some offal on Tràigh nan Eun, the new rose-red birds being easily distinguished by viewers in spite of the lack of colour.

"You will never find such a rarity as this again," the voice of Martin Leslie was heard saying. "And the terrible thing is that unless you find it for yourselves within the next few weeks you will never find it because Little Todday is going to be turned into a rocket range after next September. And then these lovely newcomers from the Far North will have to seek elsewhere a sanctuary from the air activity which has probably driven them from the Arctic. Claude Mayhew, Wilfred Cobbett and I believe that even now the Government might be persuaded to give up the idea of a rocket range on Little Todday if all of you bird-watchers will help to avert what without exaggeration can be called a mortal blow to British bird-life. If you do feel strongly about this threat make your indignation heard and save these beautiful refugees from being driven away from our shores to seek a home elsewhere, perhaps in Siberia."

In moments of the wildest optimism Hugh had never dared to hope for such a response as that television broadcast evoked. He had known that the name of bird-watchers in Great Britain was legion, but he had not realized the size of legion. The majority of that vast audience which followed *You May Find This Rarity* from fortnight to fortnight went to bed that night resolved to prevent the Government from violating the sanctuary of what was popularly known as the Pink Gull.

Letters poured in to the Press. M.P.'s hoping to secure a rise in their pay fairly soon sank exhausted beneath the weight of mailbags crammed with correspondence from constituents threatening to oppose that rise unless their M.P.'s came to the rescue of the Pink Gull. Palace Yard was choked with deputations waiting to present petitions to various Ministers. Boy Scouts, Girl Guides, Wolf Cubs and Brownies were marching about all over the country carrying pink banners inscribed SAVE OUR PINK GULL. There was a monster procession from Hyde Park which marched by way of Constitution Hill, the Mall, and Whitehall to demonstrate in Downing Street and outside the Houses of Parliament by whistling 'Lilliburlero' in unison, after which the procession gathered for a mass demonstration in Trafalgar Square at which various speakers backed by the slogan BIRD-WATCHERS OF THE WORLD UNITE round Nelson's column nearly put the microphones out of action with their furious eloquence. A rumour in the crowd that the President of the South Midland Bird-watchers' Association was Lord Alanbrooke secured for him such an ovation that when he returned home that night he told his wife that he was seriously considering standing for Parliament at the next General Election.

Meanwhile, what of Great and Little Todday? The *Island Queen* was packed from bow to stern with people on their way to see the Pink Gull with their own eyes and the MacPayne directors called Captain MacKechnie out of retirement on the Isle of Skye to command the *Puffin*, an elderly craft which was to have been broken up this very summer, in order to relieve the strain upon the accommodation of the *Island Queen*.

"Och, well, I don't mind so much about these Pink Culls," Captain MacKechnie said. "But I'll do my pest to save the old *Puffin* for another summer."

Paul Waggett had already left to seek his Elysium in the Green Belt and therefore he was no longer on the pier to warn visitors that shooting and fishing were strictly prohibited. His place was taken by vigilant volunteers from Great and Little Todday who relieved anybody carrying a shotgun of his weapon, to be returned to him when he left the islands. It was decided that until Snorvig House was sold to the Government, bird-watching hikers should be allowed to use it as a hostel, for there were so many of these bird-watchers on Great Todday that the contractors' Teddy-boys were hardly noticeable.

This was the beginning of the end. The Government did not acquire Snorvig House and it would be bought very cheaply by Big Roderick in order to be turned into an annexe of the hotel.

Joseph Macroon managed to secure another boat which was named the *Pink Gull* and he was believed to be making more than £200 a day by ferrying bird-watchers between Snorvig and Kiltod. He would have bought a couple of lorries as well had not public opinion in Little Todday been against him over that.

"If rockets are likely to frighten our beautiful and peculiar birds, Joseph," Father Macalister warned him, "lorries will be just as bad for them, and we don't want to have our last few months of peace interrupted by lorries."

Joseph knew when it was prudent to yield, and he did not import the lorries.

The boat owners of the two islands made an agreement with one another not to land any of the bird-watchers on Pillay even when the sea made landing possible. This act of self-denial was given prominence in the Press, and many who had heard with indifference of the proposed fate of the island at the hands of the Government when only the future of human beings was involved were deeply moved when they heard of the islanders' determination to protect the Pink Gull, and swelled the agitation to preserve Little Todday from being turned into a rocket range.

By the middle of May the Gallup poll showed that the Government was steadily losing votes. The Opposition had not considered the transference of the population of Little Todday to Wester Sutherland as brutal a violation of human rights as the power given by the Rent Act for landlords to raise the rent of a cottage from five shillings to as much as ten shillings a week, but now with political advantage in view they lost no opportunity of putting down embarrassing questions about the future of Little Todday.

The Government made one last effort. Mr Oliver Slimmon, that supposedly popular Minister, appeared on television to see if he could allay with his unction the nation's anxiety about the future of the Pink Gull.

The crocodile's tear was dry, but the soft fruit in his mouth was still juicy.

"We've all been hearing quite a lot about the Pink Gull lately, haven't we? Has it occurred to any of you that if this pink bird has left the Arctic it may be an omen? These fellows on the other side of the House who are trying to stir up trouble for us naturally welcome this pink bird. Birds of a feather flock together, eh?" This was breathed out with an oleaginous chuckle. "I'm sure you've all of you heard that saying, haven't you? Now, don't think I'm against everything pink. I'm not. I'll tell you this, if a Member of the Opposition were to offer me a pink gin in the smoke-room of the House of Commons, I wouldn't refuse it because it was pink. I'd refuse it because it was gin. Some people think we're against this pink bird because it is pink. In fact we're not against this bird at all. But we do realise that what we are doing in the Hebrides to provide a deterrent from war may have alarmed our friends in Russia—yes, our friends—I'm not ashamed to go back to those wonderful days when you and I were making tanks for Russia and could call them our friends. But friends do sometimes fall out, and just now our Russian friends have got into their heads the ridiculous idea that we are planning to attack them with our deterrent. I'd prefer to use another word, which doctors use. I'd prefer to call our nuclear rockets a prophylactic against war. Our splendid boys in Burma used to take mepacrine to ward off malaria. They didn't mind walking about looking like lemons, because they knew that it was their patriotic duty not to get malaria. And that's what we all have to do when we think about these prophylactic nuclear missiles to develop which the Government after long and anxious consultations with our expert advisers chose the Outer Hebrides as the most suitable location. Yes, what we have to do is to take these rockets as our boys took mepacrine. I'm proud to tell you that's the way the people of West and Mid and East Uist are taking them. They're revelling in the prospect of the benefits they're going to receive from our great strategic plan. Oh, I know, those lovely islands won't be as quiet as they used to be, but the people there have made up their minds to put up with a little noise from jet planes for the sake of peace. There has been a great agitation all over the country to stop the Government from frightening away these pink birds with rockets, but I'm told the only noise a rocket makes is 'whoosh'. I'm talking to you bird-watchers now, and mind you I'm a bird-watcher myself. Only this morning down in my constituency in Surrey I was watching a pair of lovely little tom-tits feeding their babies, and I don't mind telling you I had quite a lump in my throat. Oh, I do wish you bird-watchers could realise what an encouragement it is to Communists all over the world when they hear of you getting all worked up like this about some pink birds. Think over it again, won't you? No wonder Colonel Nasser believes he can turn the Suez Canal on and off like a bathroom tap when he hears of this fuss you're making about the arrival of a few pink birds. Do think over what I've been saying to you to-night."

The fruity voice was silent: the oily smile trickled away: the screen was blank.

Yet in spite of Mr Slimmon's vocal ointment public opinion remained acutely inflamed, and the Gallup poll revealed a further fall of the Government in popular estimation.

On May 29th the Government surrendered. In the six o'clock news the announcer read the following communiqué issued from the Ministry of Protection:

"After a careful review of the suitability of the islands of Great and Little Todday in the Western Isles as a training ground for ballistic deterrents it has been decided to abandon the scheme to resettle the inhabitants of Little Todday in West Sutherlandshire and to transform Great Todday into a training-ground for the 2nd Ballistic Regiment and the Electronic Corps."

And for the rest of the evening the Chief Information Officers, the Principal Information Officers and the Senior Information Officers of the Ministry of Protection had a laborious time trying to convince representatives of the Press that the decision to leave Great and Little Todday alone had been due to consideration for shipping not for birds. The mouthpieces of bureaucracy did not suppose for a moment that consideration for the human element was worth mention.

During those weeks before this Glorious Restoration Day Hugh had listened anxiously every evening to the news on the wireless in case the mystery of the pink birds should be solved by some enterprising ornithologist. And now his mind was at rest. By announcing the unsuitability of Little Todday the Government had committed themselves. They could not announce its suitability in the future even if

Leslie's Gull (*Larus sanguineus*) should be unmasked as the familiar herring-gull.

"Jane, darling darling Jane, Little Todday is safe," Hugh cried and caught her in his arms.

He asked his father if MacInnes Woolwear could spare him for a week so that he and Jane could visit the island which was no longer for burning.

"I expect you're pretty pleased, aren't you, my boy?" Sir Robert asked.

"Pleased is a feeble word for it," Hugh told his father.

The weather, which had been gusty and wet during the second half of May, had cleared by the time Hugh and Jane reached Little Todday, and on a flawless morning the Dot took the *St Tod* over to Pillay to bring back the statue of the saint from the cave where he had been standing on guard to his own island. Pipers led the procession from Tràigh nan Eun across the machair, the buttercups a sheen of gold, the daisies all open-eyed in the sun. St Tod was carried by eight crofters on a kind of portable platform and the children scattered flowers before him.

"*A Dhia*," Duncan Bàn murmured to Hugh. "I would almost be swearing the holy man winked at us."

St Tod was replaced upon his pedestal in the towerless church of Our Lady Star of the Sea and St Tod, and at a Mass of thanksgiving Father Macalister went up into the pulpit to preach a very brief sermon, first in Gaelic and then in English to a crowded congregation.

"Brethren, by the grace of Almighty God we have been spared from a fearful calamity. Let us show for the rest of our lives in our behaviour and in our thoughts our gratitude to God. Let us pray that the behaviour of our own Government in this business may be a sign that a new spirit is abroad on the air of the world. It may be that history will one day record as the first sign that common sense was returning to humanity the decision not to turn our little island into a site of destruction. Rockets are the dangerous toys of children. Peace will never come securely because people try to secure it by frightening one another. Peace can only come when the world turns back its face to Almighty God."

The Reverend Angus Morrison was waiting in the chapel house when Father Macalister came in after Mass.

"I should have dearly liked to share in your service, Father Macalister, but . . ."

"I know, I know."

"But I want to say how much we in Great Todday rejoice with you on this day of rejoicing."

The priest was obviously much moved by the minister's visit.

"You'll have a sensation, *a Mhaighstir Aonghais*?"

"I will indeed, *a Mhaighstir Sheumais*."

The priest and the minister raised their glasses.

That afternoon Hugh and Jane drove Mrs Odd over to Tràigh nan Eun. Half a dozen of the saviour birds were wheeling about over the sea between Pillay and Little Todday.

"And they're still in the best of pink, bless their hearts," said Mrs Odd.

GLOSSARY

('ach' and 'ich' as in German)

Chapter 1

19. *a Thighearna* (a heearna), O Lord
19. *a bhalaich* (a valich), O boy.

Chapter 2

36. *glé mhath* (glay vah), very good.

Chapter 3

41. *Am bheil Gáidhlig agaibh* ('m vail gahlic agav), Have you Gaelic?
43. *clàrsach* (clarsach), stringed musical instrument.
45. *sgeulachdan* (skaylachkan), tales.
45. *bean Iosaibh* (ben yosav), Joseph's wife.
52. *taing do Dhia* (tyng do yeea), thanks to God.
53. *Ruairidh Mór* (rooary mor), Big Roderick.

Chapter 4

56. *Peigi Ealasaid* (paygi yalasetch), Peggy Elizabeth.
57. *deoch an doruis* (joch an dorish), drink of the door.
58. *Uisdean Mac Aonghais* (Oosh-chan Mac Anooish).
58. *céilidh* (cayley), literally visit, but used for entertainment.
59. *a Chruitheir* (a crooyer), O Creator.
59. *Uidhistich* (ooyistich), Uistmen.
59. *cailleachan* (calychan), old women.
60. *bodach* (botach), old man.
60. *gu leoir* (goolyor), in plenty (galore).
62. *ma tà* (ma tah), then.
63. *beannachd leibh* (byanacht leev), good-bye.
65. *a bhobh bhobh* (a voav voav), exclamation of dismay.
66. *oidhche mhath agus cadal mhath* (oyche vah agus catal vah), good-night and sleep well.

Chapter 5

68. *Tigh a' Bhàird* (ty a vard), the Bard's house.
68. *Éisd* (ayshch), listen.
68. *A Dhia* (a yeea), O God.
70. *briagh briagh* (briya briya), lovely, lovely.
76. *A dhuine a dhuine* (yunye yunye), man, man.
77. *m'eudail* (m aytal), darling.

Chapter 6

81. *Mic an diabhuil* (mic an jeeoil), sons of the devil.
81. *Pàbanaich* (pahpanich), Catholics.

Chapter 8

123. *A Dhia nan Gràs* (a yeea nan grahs), God of Grace.

Chapter 10

150. *Thig a stigh* (hig a sty), come in.

Chapter 11

161. *a Shimidh* (a heemy), O Simon.
164. *seadh, seadh* (shudha), exclamation of agreement.
169. *ah cachd!* (cachk), literally 'O dirt', exclamation of derision.
173. *Suas Todaidh Beag* (sooas todiy bayg), up Little Todday.

Chapter 13

192. *Suas an t-Siorram* (sooas an tchooram), up the Sheriff.

Chapter 15

222. *a charaid* (a charetch), friend.
223. *do charaid dhileas Seumas Mac Alasdair* (do charetch yeelus Shamus), your faithful friend, James MacAlister.
227. *sruth* (srooh), stream.